P.S. I LOVE YOU

JO NOELLE

LITTLE BOX PRESS LLC

P.S. I LOVE YOU: A TWICKENHAM TIME TRAVEL ROMANCE

Visit Jo's site at http://JoNoelle.com or connect with us on Facebook @JoNoelle.

P.S. I LOVE YOU

Cora Rey wanted a fresh start in life, but being thrown back in time to 1850 isn't how she expected to do that. She discovers that Victorian England isn't the pleasant social whirl Jane Austen led her to believe, but when in Rome—or in this case Twickenham . . . She's determined to have the vacation of a lifetime, especially in the company of a certain duke.

Simon Tuttle never expected to become the duke of Hertfordshire, never wanted it, but now he is, and eligible women seeking a title consider him the next trophy to be taken in the marriage mart. A union of convenience is the most he hopes for due to the shame-filled secret he bears—until he meets Cora. Now, he imagines that a love match could be possible after all. Hiding his secret from society has been easy—hiding it from Cora proves impossible. Can Cora love a man like him despite learning the truth?

CHAPTER 1

Maybe it was the fringed battlements lining the top of the walls and guarded with gargoyles that made Cora's skin tingle as they approached Twickenham Manor. The sky outside was the same bluish-gray it had often been in London, but it wasn't oppressive here. It was mysterious.

Cora felt like Cinderella arriving at the ball. She gaped out the window as their driver pulled up in front of a white Gothic castle. The homepage had said it was a manor house, but the size rivaled a royal address. Getting out of the car put her right beside a large, open gate to the side yard. She walked through and pulled out her camera to record the turrets, paths, and gardens. Stone-carved lions, dragons, and lizards hid among the bushes and sat atop the stone walls used as handrails on the sides of the exterior stairs. This was the highlight of their vacation in England—a full week living like Jane Austen.

The early morning dew must not have burned off yet because, to Cora, it looked like the entire lawn, all the way to the Thames, and the garden were flocked with glitter. Every plant and flower sparkled magically with tiny rainbows. Her finger ran over the petal of a rose climbing around the tunnel that led to the doorway, and the dew from it clung to her, shining as if with its own light.

Her heart skipped a beat. She could feel it. This was the new beginning she desperately needed in her life. She nearly hadn't come. Her roommates Reese and Kaitlyn had invited her. Kaitlyn's brother and his best friend had come, too. The others had deep roots of friendship and history between them, and from what she'd seen from the glances the men threw toward the women, sparks of romance as well. But because she'd only known the girls a couple of months, she felt like she was butting in on their vacation. It was natural for them to pair up, and it was natural for Cora to avoid crowds. She laughed at herself—same old Cora. But standing in this place, feeling the magic of it from centuries past, made her glad she'd come.

The group gathered at the desk just inside the ancient-looking front door to check in for their immersive Regency experience.

"Cora Rey?" the man at the desk called.

Cora stepped up and signed the paperwork.

"We have all in ready for you," the butler said. "Your chamber will be the lilac room, Miss Rey." He handed the key to a woman who came to stand next to him. "This is Miller. She will be your lady's maid during your stay and will be at your call whenever needed."

The young woman curtsied to Cora. "This way, miss." She led Cora through the house, past the grand salon with its walls decorated with spears arranged in sunburst patterns, past a library with bookcases pointed like cathedral windows, and up the curving marble staircase. "The manor is huge, and it can be a bit tricky to find your way around until you get used to it. There's a map in your room to help."

Cora had studied the map that was sent with the orientation materials. One thing stood out as unusual, though. The map she'd received showed three levels, but this home had four. Why hadn't that floor plan been included? What was the secret?

"This is it, miss." Miller twisted the key in the lock and opened the door. "Your things have been delivered there," she said, pointing to the large walk-in closet beside the en suite. "Would you like help unpacking?"

Several dresses already hung in the closet. The Regency costumes had been part of the package she'd chosen for her experience. It was surprising how new they looked, and they appeared to be the exact size she would need.

"No, thank you."

"Then I'll be back at six to help you dress for dinner." The young woman set the key on the side table. "Aunt Nellie will be around to greet you before then."

Cora made short work of putting away her clothes, then pulled out her bio for a quick review—she was a wealthy American heiress, looking to marry advantageously.

Several minutes later, someone knocked on Cora's door. When she opened it, a beautiful woman walked into the room. Cora tried to decide her age, but she couldn't settle on it. She could have as easily been thirty as fifty. Was her hair really gray or dyed to look like it? The woman was ageless.

She stared at the woman's eyes. They were the same silver-blue color as the eyes of everyone who worked there that she'd met so far. The color was mesmerizing. Perhaps they were all related.

"Welcome to Twickenham Manor. I'm Aunt Nellie. I'm no one's aunt, really, but that doesn't seem to matter so much," the woman said, then put her arm around Cora's shoulders and led her to the stuffed chairs by the large windows. "Have you settled in yet?"

Cora liked her voice. It was soothing and friendly—very grandmotherly. "Yes. I was just looking over the orientation materials."

"Don't worry too much about those. You'll have plenty of time to get it all down. In fact, you'll be able to do even more than is listed in the agenda, should you choose to." The woman laughed as if she'd just made a joke. "You'll have more time than you can even imagine." She waved her hand around a bit. She stood. "Do you have any questions?"

"Not yet. I'm just excited to be here."

"It will be a grand week. Now, I'm off to meet the others." When she got to the door, she paused and turned back. "This is a new beginning for you, Cora Rey. I'm so happy you've come."

Cora was, too. The woman didn't know how much that meant to her—a new beginning. Aboard the train in London, the message board and automated voice had warned riders to "mind the gap" between the train and the platform as they entered or exited at each stop. The phrase had caught her attention and resonated with her.

Mind the gap. That's where she was in her life. Her mother had died before she was out of elementary school. Then Cora had graduated with a special education degree a year before her father was diagnosed with cancer. She taught for a couple of years, then returned to college soon after her father succumbed. Now, with her master's degree and another graduation behind her, she had a gap. There was no family to go back to. Various roommates had filled that gap over the past two and a half years, but now what?

This seemed like just the thing she needed—to be completely diverted into a new life starting today.

Each day of the immersion experience was like living in a BBC movie. Her time was filled with walks in the gardens, lessons with the dance master, amazing food, painting, needlework, and lavish dinners with the twenty-some guests enjoying the immersion experience, too. Late at night, Cora would sneak into the music room and play pieces that would have been heard in that period. This truly had been the most amazing vacation imaginable.

An hour before the ball on the last day, Cora's maid arrived. "I have your gown, miss. Are you ready to dress?"

"I am. Aunt Nellie has provided amazing clothes." The dress was an apricot-colored fabric overlaid with off-white sprig netting. The applique along the netting resembled small feathers near the waist of the dress and grew into a more rich design of peacocks and trees at the bottom. "I can hardly wait to wear that."

Cora freshened up, and Miller helped her dress in the beautiful gown. She wanted to twirl like a toddler and feel a rush of joy just to be dressed in the poofy costume. She gave in and threw her arms wide, laughing as the ceiling circled above her in a dizzying dance. "This is perfect," she said when she stopped. "Thank you, Miller, for everything this week."

"Oh, miss, you're lovely. What a night this will be for you." Miller clasped her hands over her chest. "Magical in every way."

The Full Moon Ball was everything Cora expected in a true Regency event. Women in colorful silk gowns swirled around the dance floor, guided by men dressed in the finest attire the Regency had to offer. Cora was a little sad when the midnight dinner was called—half the evening was over. She slipped her phone out of her bra and took a few more pictures. She would have hundreds to remember this trip.

Reece found Cora. "Come on. We're going exploring."

Cora tucked her phone away and followed Reece and Kaitlyn up the staircase to the top floor. The door at the top of the stairs stood open. Cora peeked inside. It was huge and completely lined with racks of clothing. They looked like costumes from every era in history. She wondered what they used them for.

"So, this is the secret level?" Cora called to her friends. "It just makes you want to open every door, doesn't it?" She followed the group to the left.

At the end of the hallway, Kaitlyn and Cyrus stood one on each side of an open door. "We found this earlier and thought you'd all like to see it." Kaitlyn swept her hand in front of her to gesture them to enter.

Cora loved the dark red wallpaper lining the gallery walls. The white and gold of the fanlike flourishes of molding that webbed across the ceiling of the long narrow room added more elegance. Every room she'd seen in Twickenham Manor had stained glass windows, and this one had them nearly from floor to vaulted ceiling. She imagined the warmth of the light that would fill this room in the day. Portraits covered the walls, and Cora looked closely at the ones near her.

"Cora, come look at this one." Cyrus was pointing toward a full-sized mural at the far end.

"No way," she whispered to herself, surprised at what she was seeing. Their whole group was depicted there. She walked across the room never taking her eyes off herself in the mural. She and her roommates were wearing much fuller dresses, Victorian instead of Regency, but it was them. The paint seemed to flow with pinpricks of light. The hairs at the back of her neck tingled. "How ... ?" She didn't even know what to ask.

"It's a little freaky, isn't it?" Jem asked.

"More than a little," Reese mumbled.

"I've got to have a picture of this." Cora turned her back to the wall and positioned herself and her other-self in the screen, taking several selfies. "Everyone. We need a picture of this. Stand by your ... selves in the mural." Not everyone fit in the viewer. "Squash up a bit." She held her phone up again. *Yes.*

The group was too large to get in the photo frame in a single shot. She angled it toward the far end. Lightning flashed, and she blinked hard to clear the little dark dots floating in her vision. When she held the phone up again, her friends were ... gone. How did they ... ?"

"Not funny," she called. She turned to the left and right. Did they just bring her up here for a practical joke? If they did, she had to admit that it was an impressive one. "Where are you?" The room beyond the mural was dark. The paint where her friends had been standing looked like dull, normal paint, but her picture was still illuminated, pulsing with the strange light.

She leaned closer and felt a magnetic tug, drawing her toward the wall. Tiny lasers of light shot into her, stinging like piercing hooks and yanked her toward the portrait. The rhythmic pull increased, and her hands shot out to brace against the wall and stop her fall. Blood roared in her ears, and heat flashed through her. The wall fell away, and rays blasted like lightning. Cora fell headfirst through her portrait, tumbling and spinning. She felt stretched and then compressed. Numb. When the blinding light burned out, Cora was sitting on the floor, her head dizzy, feeling as if she might hurl.

CHAPTER 2

The fuzzy outline of the room began to clear.

"Oh," screeched a woman with her gray hair styled in an intricate bun. "And who are you?" Although the woman had been initially surprised, a smile overtook her face, and her eyes sparkled with warmth.

Cora looked up at her. "Aunt Nellie?" The woman didn't answer, but seemed not to remember her. "Cora Rey. I'm one of the Americans." Cora tried to push up to stand, but her legs were weak.

Several other people with Nellie stood as if they were frozen. Cora glanced from Nellie to the wall and to the woman again. She was glad to be sitting on the floor because she was sure that she was dizzy enough to fall if she weren't. The room was possibly the same one, but it was different, too. It had fewer portraits. She checked behind her—no mural. *What in the—?*

"You've arrived! You're friends came hours ago. Not that you're late, but here you are." Aunt Nellie's voice sounded excited. "That makes five of you—all in a day. And all Americans." She turned to a man entering the room. "That's a record, isn't it? Have we had so many at a time?"

"As you say, ma'am."

Back to Cora, she said, "Stay right here. I'll be back with you." Then she chuckled. "Of course you will. You have nowhere to go, really."

Cora looked at the windows. Dull evening light radiated through the heavy curtains that covered them. "But it was midnight ... I was at the ball." Her pulse increased, and a little fear bubbled through her stomach. With some effort to untangle her skirt from around her legs, she stood, though a bit wobbly.

Aunt Nellie pointed to each of the people with her, giving them assignments. "Ring Cook for the cream puffs, macarons, fruit tarts, and those pretty little tea cakes she made today. Oh, and my special blend of tea. We're going to need plenty of that."

A beautiful woman sat on a velvet settee at the far end of the room. From the style and fineness of her dress, she seemed more regal than anyone Cora had seen at the immersion experience yet. "Aunt Nellie, I'll wait for my daughter in the next room while you take care of your new guest."

"Nonsense. You'll join us, won't you?"

The woman inclined her head and walked over.

"Let's have tea here." Aunt Nellie chose a table near the door. Soon, a maid arrived with a tea tray.

Cora could see why the other woman's bio had included a title of nobility. She could carry that part well.

"Lady Cottrell, may I make known to you Cora Rey? Cora, this is Lady Bethany Cottrell."

"My pleasure," both women said.

Lady Cottrell added, "Welcome." Then to Aunt Nellie, she said, "Now that I see you have a guest, I'll plan some events."

"Oh, yes. Miss Rey seems just the age to get on with your Lady May. They'll have a time of it, won't they?"

"I think so, too." Lady Cottrell turned a bright smile to Cora. "Our family is closely associated with Aunt Nellie. I'd like you to meet my daughter. In fact, I was here waiting for her. She should be back soon. When is it you're from?"

Cora opened her mouth to ask if she meant "where," but Nellie interrupted. "My other guests will start arriving in half an hour for the ball. We'll have to get you ready quickly."

"I'm not sure what ... " Cora felt ... off. This wasn't making sense.

"This is very disorienting, isn't it?" Nellie patted Cora's hand. "I understand. Really, I do. This is not my first trip to Piccadilly Circus." Lady Cottrell giggled at that, but Nellie continued. "Oh, I almost forgot—the tea. The aroma helps you a bit, but when you drink it, well, that's when it's special." She began to arrange the little desserts on plates. "I imagine you have a few questions. What's the last thing you remember before the flash of light?"

"My friends. Where are they? Are they—"

"Fine. Fine. Your friends arrived about an hour or two ago. The magic isn't very predictable, but you all arrived safe and sound. Well, bewildered is more the truth of it, but that's temporary."

"They're here too?" They had stood near the mural together, but now they were all separated. She shook her head. Was she dreaming?

"Well, not here here. They're either getting dressed or resting up for tonight. Oh, you must be so excited for the ball. Aren't you?"

"I was already at the ball, then we went upstairs, and stood ... " Cora looked back at the wall. Her head felt thick and slow.

Aunt Nellie said, "It's faerie magic. That's what causes this lovely little mess you and your friends got caught in."

"Magic?" Cora looked at Lady Cottrell, who smiled at her in return. Cora wondered if she was playing along with the script, and they expected Cora to as well. "Mess?"

"This home is built on ancient ley lines. The fissures burp out magic during the full moon. In ancient lore, that magic was the way the fae took care of the earth, to renew the world. Now it's just a nuisance. We've built this monstrosity of a house to cover it up, but it jerks people into other time periods willy-nilly."

Nope, she wasn't buying the story. Cora looked at Lady

Cottrell, who nodded in agreement with Aunt Nellie. "True. True. But for some of us, we've found what we never could have otherwise." She turned a kind smile toward Nellie. "Thank you for that."

Nellie patted the woman's hand and continued telling Cora her story. "The mural you stood beside was used to send you back to your own time strand—oh, more than a century ago. The magic in the paint worked like a lightning rod, which is fascinating, really. If you'd been standing anywhere else when the magic belched, you probably wouldn't be here now." Her eyes lit with excitement, and her smile dimpled warmly at Cora.

"The mural was made in the past, and I stood by it in the future. Are you saying that I've been to the past before?" Cora asked. The confusion was grating on her. She wanted to leave—go somewhere that made sense again.

"No. You just got here." Aunt Nellie began to pour out the tea. "It was painted in the past that was then in your future, so you could go back to the future from your future past."

Cora stared at Aunt Nellie, trying to understand what any of that meant. She wondered if they were still playing a part—if their Regency experience had veered into fantasy. The women seemed too sincere to be acting. "That's circular reasoning. Something didn't happen before it can happen," Cora said. She pressed her palms against her temples.

"Oh? I suppose this all makes sense to you?" Nellie gestured her arms wide around her. "No? Then perhaps I'm right. Time isn't circular or linear, dear. Time is a fuzzball. Things happen out of order all the time precisely to keep things *in* order."

"Then send me back," Cora said.

"Yes, I will. But I can't. At least, not now." Nellie bit the inside of her cheek. "You'll have to stay as my guest." Her voice rang with kindness, but the words sounded final. She picked up some tongs and a cup of sugar cubes. "Do you take sugar or cream, Cora?"

"Both, please." Cora needed something to calm her nerves. Maybe if she humored the crazy lady, she'd get some information to help figure this out.

Lady Cottrell leaned toward her and whispered, "It's all going to make sense very soon. She'll send you back as soon as she can, but that's on the next full moon. You needn't worry. In fact, I'm sure you're going to have an amazing time for the next few weeks."

As Nellie completed the service, Cora decided to play along until they had a reasonable explanation. "What happened? You were in the future, too. That was you, right, Aunt Nellie?"

"Yes. I suppose I'm in a lot of futures and pasts." Her voice turned melancholy. "That's the way of faerie folk. I don't like to dwell on it." Then she brightened her smile and added, "Drink up."

Cora looked around the room. No electricity. No central heating vents. The house was the same, but different. She felt stunned. What if Nellie's explanation was true?

Aunt Nellie lifted her teacup again and raised her eyebrows at Cora, who tipped her cup also. The first touch of tea on her tongue was like Pop Rocks to her mouth, but the sweet taste invigorated her mind and calmed her heart rate. After the second sip, warmth spread throughout her body, radiating ... calming. Cora loved it here. She loved Nellie. She loved her friends. She loved Lady Cottrell. She loved ... *wait!* She pinned Nellie with a stare. "Is this some type of magical faerie roofie?"

"Yes, of course. Drink up. It will help you accept all of this and move on, and it will save me a lot of time. It's a big change for you, after all."

"I'd forgotten how lovely this special tea blend of yours is," Lady Cottrell said after she drained her cup. "Might I have a bit more? The pot refills itself, right?"

Nellie poured for her.

Lady Cottrell giggled. "It makes me feel a little like that time in college when I ... well, never mind that." She took a sip, then asked, "What made you come to England in the first place, Cora?"

Cora found the truth spilling out of her lips with ease. "I wanted to live in a dream for a few days. I felt compelled to come —that there was something here I couldn't live without."

"It was that way for me. too," Lady Cottrell whispered. "I'll introduce you to my daughter tonight at the ball. I hope you'll want to visit with us while you're here."

"I'd like that very much. Thank you." Although Cora expected that it was the magic talking, she told herself she should finish the tea. Complete, though maybe temporary, happiness and acceptance about her situation were better than confusion.

In a few moments, Cora, feeling quite mellow, was escorted to her room. Her head felt much clearer as she lay at the end of an enormous feather-topped bed, putting the pieces together. The effects of the roofie were wearing off, but she retained her understanding—minimal though it was—of her situation. Aunt Nellie was a faerie, who guarded a magical Twilight Zone. Cora was in 1850 England. And she'd be there until she wasn't.

A month ago, Cora had earned a Master of Education degree in special education from The Ohio State University. A week ago, she traveled to England with her college roommates for a celebratory vacation in honor of their combined graduate status. An hour ago, she was sucked backward through time and ejected into Victorian England, with a crazy lady as her guide and no idea what exactly made that happen.

A tap on her door brought her attention to a black-haired young woman who curtsied and looked suspiciously like Miller. "May I help you dress for the ball, miss?"

Whoa. Déjà vu. "That's you, isn't it, Miller?"

The woman bobbed another curtsey, "Yes, ma'am."

Cora felt several surprises pass through her mind. "Is everyone here always here? I mean, are you fae like Aunt Nellie?"

"Yes, ma'am. May I help you dress?" Miller raised her hand when Cora opened her mouth to ask another question. "Aunt Nellie is the person to get answers from. I'm here as your lady's maid in this time and place."

"I'm ... I'm ready." *For whatever comes.* Her grandfather had been a true-blue-through-and-through Texas cowboy, and he had a saying. "When life gives you cow pies, burn them for heat." She always thought that might have been the grossest thing imaginable, but she'd learned the gist. Make the best of everything. Honestly, getting stuck in Victorian England for a while seemed like a win.

Cora sat up. She'd wanted the vacation of a lifetime. Well, you couldn't get better than a little time travel thrown in. *When in Rome —go native.*

Properly dressed and coiffed, Cora joined a packed ballroom of guests. Her dream was coming true. A crowded ballroom. Elegant dresses. An orchestra and a dance card tied around her wrist.

Her friends were at the ball before she arrived. They met on the side and repeated everything that had happened—lightning, Nellie, fuzzball, and the special tea.

"I'm going with this. It will be great," Cora told them before they drifted apart to join in the dance. She certainly hadn't planned a real trip into the past because that would be crazy, but it had happened just the same.

A couple of hours later, the dream had officially ended. The only bright spot had been meeting Miss May Cottrell, the daughter of the woman she met at tea earlier. They planned to meet up the next day to get acquainted. As for the rest of the night, the dance card had become like an albatross. No one had sought her out for a dance. No eyes had turned jealously toward her, and she knew that the debutantes were glad they weren't her. How long would she be stuck here? She had no way of knowing. Frustration built.

Two things were guaranteed to ease Cora's mind—creating music and hand-to-hand combat. Although she was itching for the second, it was improbable in the nineteenth-century ball gown she was wearing. Music would have to do for tonight.

Images of Cinderella escaping only to lose her shoe flitted through her thoughts as Cora Rey deserted the ballroom completely unnoticed half an hour before the midnight chimes would ring from the large clock in the hall. Her dancing slippers whispered against the marble floor as she charged toward the south end of the manor house, taking very unladylike steps.

Incredibly, she was living *part* of that old fairy tale—no cars, no phones, and no immediate way back to her own century.

Fewer sconces dotted the hallway before her, and the smell of paraffin candles burning became less pronounced. No one would be in the morning room since the party was in the exact opposite corner of the sprawling mansion.

Tonight, she had made a huge error by telling one of Aunt Nellie's friends her age. At twenty-seven, she was irrevocably stamped an old maid. Ineligible. Undesirable. The news spread faster than Twitter, and she was left to sit in the shadowy corners or to retrieve drinks for the caustic matrons seated nearby. She did that gladly to avoid hearing them cluck their tongues and say, "It's a pity you didn't come to England earlier. You might have had a small chance to marry," or, "Someone will find use of you. You've a pretty face."

Trolls on Facebook have nothing on these old biddies.

Yes, she wanted a husband and children. *Someday.* She just didn't think she was past an imaginary time limit. She hadn't noticed so much as one tock or tick of her biological clock.

In her real life, one hundred sixty some years in the future, she was a teacher—and loved it. Maybe her students filled that place in her heart reserved for her own children, and she never thought to hurry that part of her life.

Her hand swept out and snatched a lit taper from a hall table, and she continued on her way. *I'm supposed to be an heiress. For all they know, I'm as rich as the queen of Spain. I'll be leaving here soon, anyway.* A twinge of panic pinched at her heart, but she didn't explore it—she *would* go back. She was sure of it.

When she reached the end of the hallway, she eased a door open and peeked inside. The room was dark. *Perfect.*

The morning room was on the far east side of the home. A long bank of floor-to-ceiling windows welcomed the morning rays that rose above the lake and woods beyond. But tonight, she came here for the pianoforte. As Cora set the candle on the music shelf, she pushed her breath out.

She shoved her disappointment away, instead imagining notes carving out a familiar reality from her memories, one where she sat in the study, her father at work at his desk, the smell of lilacs thick on the breeze through the window. She was grateful for the solitude—thankful that no one would hear her play. No judgment would be made. Sometimes the mere look at an instrument caused gut-tightening performance anxiety. She reminded herself that there was no audience. She sat on the bench. This would just be for her. Cora's shoulders relaxed, and she closed her eyes to choose a piece to fit her mood. As her fingers hovered above the keys, the tips lightly brushing the ivories, the door she'd just entered rattled.

Cora quickly licked her fingers and thumb and snuffed out the flame, then eased behind the heavy damask curtains over the window.

The thick walls of the home left a space at least three feet deep in the window alcoves. Thank goodness since her dress filled the space. In fact, she was fairly certain that her dress wouldn't even make a little pregnant-looking lump in the drapery.

She could hear the door creak open and someone enter, then close the door with a quiet snick. The sound of boots on the tile hinted to her that it was a man. Cora squeezed back into the corner as far as possible. The silvery moonlight might still give her hiding place away if her shadow fell on the curtain. She hoped the light was too pale and the curtain too thick.

The sound of the boots stopped, and the sofa creaked.

Someone came here to sit in the dark? Now?

She strained her ears for the slightest movement. The handle on the door rattled again. *For the love! Does everyone come to the morning room in the middle of the night? It's obviously a misnomer.*

She didn't have to strain to hear the couch creak again and boots walking quickly to where she was hiding. Suddenly, the curtain drew away from the window, and a man slid in beside her. He was tall, maybe a foot above her five feet two inches.

His eyes opened as wide as she felt her own. They both

drew their fingers up to their lips, silently shushing each other—as if either of them *wanted* to be overheard.

The door opened and closed another time, slamming. Then she heard the tumbler fall as it was locked. Cora threw her shoulders and palms up in an exaggerated shrug. He just smiled widely. This time, she recognized the sound of dance slippers and boots moving across the room.

A single candle brightened the room a bit. A woman's breathless voice said, "My mother won't miss me until the midnight supper is served."

Oh, no! Cora so did not want to hear this.

The man beside her turned as if to leave their hiding spot, but she grabbed him by the sleeve and shook her head emphatically.

"That only gives us ten minutes." The new man's voice was followed closely by the obvious sounds of panic-induced kissing, moaning, and sighing.

On second thought, Cora wished she had let the man beside her interrupt the tryst. This could get embarrassing fast.

The handle rattled another time. Repeated knocking pounded on the door, and a man shouted, "Lucy, are you in there? Open this door."

Cora was startled, and the man beside her jerked to attention. She shook her head toward him again. Wouldn't it be just as bad to find them together behind a curtain as to have the couple get a few minutes alone? She pulled him down to sit on the floor as a second man dove behind the curtain and landed literally in the first man's lap.

"Lucy, do you hear me? I'll get the key if I have to. Open. Now." The pounding on the door took on a new intensity.

Cora considered her options. Stay hidden and wait for everything to blow over. Reveal herself and bring the whole thing to an end with a little embarrassment. Or create an alibi. A midnight make-out session was probably a capital offence even for consenting adults and embarrassing for the woman to be caught by her father in that position. An alibi might work.

"Stay!" Cora commanded the two men. Then she jerked her dress from under her legs and crawled from behind the curtain, shaking her dress out to stand. The woman in the room gasped in surprise.

"It's okay. I'm your alibi. I came here to play the piano. You came to listen." Cora moved the new candle to the music deck and pointed the woman toward the sofa. "Sit. I'll get the door. My name is Cora Rey, by the way."

The young woman curtsied. "Lucy Radnor," then sat.

Cora turned toward the door and called out, "Coming." Perhaps she should have felt more nervous than she did. She planned to tell the truth—she had come here to play the pianoforte. She just hadn't expected or wanted an audience.

When she opened the door, a man with a thick mustache, twisted at the ends, and bushy sideburns stomped into the room. His equally bushy eyebrows pressed toward the center of his face as he looked at Cora.

"Are you a piano lover, too?" Cora asked, her voice calm and inviting. "I was just going to play a new piece for Lucy. Would you care to listen?"

The man huffed and pivoted, surveying the room. "You ... she was ... where is ... ?"

Cora waited while he spun this way and that. When he stood before them, blowing a frustrated breath through his nose, Cora said, "I only have time for one more song. Would you like to stay or not? We really want to get back to the midnight dinner."

The older man looked around again, his eyes squinting into the dark corners. Cora felt a little uneasy as he paused, looking toward the sofa and window beyond. Why should she care if the men were discovered? But she did. She had a soft spot for the first man she thought might have tried to escape the ball the same way she had, and for the other, whose escape looked a lot more fun than the first two.

"Lucy." The man held out a hand to her, which the woman took. They walked to the door where they paused. He asked Cora, "May we accompany you back?"

"No, thank you. I won't be along for a minute or two." She turned away and walked toward the piano, dismissing them both. After a long moment, Cora heard their steps retreating down the hall. When she returned and closed the door, both men surged out from behind the curtain, laughing. The second man grabbed a candlestick from the piano's music deck and touched the flame to the oil lamp overhead. Soft, buttery light brightened the room.

The men slung their arms around each other's shoulders. The man who had been hiding beside her had light hair and dark blue eyes. Cora was mesmerized as his smile transformed his face, making him look more youthful than she had first guessed. She couldn't help it—she thought he looked like a Ken doll. Tall and broad-shouldered, perfectly sculpted nose and jaw, thick, wavy sandy-blond hair, right down to the full-lipped smile and dimples.

The man beside him with curly white-blond hair was of a slighter frame and height, though still much taller than her. He turned toward his friend. "And why might you be hiding in the curtains, Simon? And with a woman I don't think I've met." He bowed at the waist toward Cora. "Miss, I am delighted to serve as a witness in your claim against him, or *for* him, as it were." His face was alight with mischief. "You've been caught in the parson's mousetrap, Simon." Then he addressed Cora again, giving a deep bow. "Well done, miss. You've won my sincere admiration and a fine husband."

Simon's face flushed, and his eyes darted toward Cora with a look of fear just before he bowed as well, but his throat bobbed once deeply with obvious worry.

Cora couldn't help but let the pause extend. *Make them sweat.* She knew the rule of this day—caught alone, save her honor, marriage required. She walked back to the pianoforte, considering how she might turn this situation on its ear, and ran her finger slowly around the edge of the case.

She smiled and rolled her eyes, then addressed the shorter man. "I was hiding there first." She turned then to Simon. "*You* were the trespasser. Marriage isn't required—I didn't compromise you. I can't imagine marrying a man when I don't even know his full name." In this century, getting caught kissing would be grounds for a marriage offer. Kissing him might be fun. Definitely worth a try. Marriage—no.

He stared, his mouth dropping open, but he only said, "Thank you. But only *you* can be compromised—I cannot."

His friend barked a loud laugh. "It seems I am in need of an introduction."

"I'm Cora Rey." She noticed the taller man didn't offer his name, so she extended her hand. "Since we're certainly familiar enough to hide together in the dark ..." She paused and smiled at Simon. "Or have *you* lay on my lap." She looked at the shorter man. "I'll give my own introduction, thank you very much."

Simon stepped forward and took her hand, not in a clasp but gently by the fingers and lifted as he again bowed. Before his indigo eyes left hers, he said, "I'm Simon Tuttle. My friends call me Albans." He completed his bow, bringing Cora's fingers to his lips.

Time seemed to stop for Cora—maybe even her breathing—as his lips lingered and his hand beneath hers slid across her palm, his fingers caressing her wrist. Her stomach tumbled and fizzed as she watched him slowly rise to his full height again, towering above her. *Oh, my!* Now she realized who he looked like. Her nine-year-old self had fallen in love with John Smith in Disney's *Pocahontas*, and the man standing before her was the flesh-and-blood version.

He inclined his head to the left and said, "And this rake here is Mr. Everett Hawley, who will one day be leg-shackled for the price of a single kiss."

Everett bowed. "Miss Rey. You're one of the Americans."

"Please call me Cora."

Then Everett replied to his friend, "That was the closest Lucy and I have come yet to getting caught out. Her father is rightfully suspicious." But then his face and voice softened. "I believe she's bound my heart. I would much rather offer for her than for her to think I'm forced."

Cora caught the look on both Everett's and Simon's faces —Everett appeared sincere and Simon sad though he nodded as if with understanding. She sensed that there was something left unsaid between them but fully comprehended by both.

Simon cleared his throat. "May I escort you to dinner?" he asked Cora as he winged his right arm toward her.

"Do we have to go back?" Cora asked, causing Everett to laugh again, but she continued. "I hate playing the games that are going on in the ballroom."

Simon winked at her. "Then change the rules, or the game, to please yourself."

The three walked the long hallways back. Everett strode ahead of them as if he were a lookout. Maybe he was. Simon paused when Everett stopped at a corner, then turned to Simon and nodded. He and Cora continued on, reaching the same corner to see the room emptying through doors at the other end.

"I'll go ahead. I'd like to find a spot near Lucy. Pleased to make your acquaintance, Cora."

"And yours, Everett. It's a delight."

He left through the doors, and Cora took a step away as well. Simon's hand covered hers at the crook of his arm. "I would be pleased to share your company. If you so choose."

It wasn't a question, but Cora heard the uncertainty in his voice. "Yes, thank you." She could not think of a better way to end this dreadful evening than to sit with a new friend.

Simon led them to a table in the corner of the room and seated them in a position to watch the throng of guests filling the massive hall. She looked around and saw her friends at different tables. Shortly, a dinner of venison was served. Honestly, Cora had never understood people's aversion to the gamey taste of wild meat. Her appreciation of all things hunted began early in life—and this meal was heavenly. Someone sure knew what they were doing in the kitchen.

Each time a couple passed their table and caught Simon's eye, the man and lady bowed their heads and said, "Your Grace." Simon appeared to take it all in stride, but Cora was in awe at the respect Simon received by the simple greeting.

"What interests do you have?" Simon asked, spearing a white carrot.

Cora quickly popped a small bite of meat into her mouth to buy a little time, considering which of her interests to choose that might be reasonable for this time period. Teaching children—no, not with her current status as an heiress. Krav Maga—definitely not martial arts. "I enjoy music." *Yikes! Now I have to remember who was popular at this time.*

"Do you have a favorite composer?"

Called it. "I don't think so. Currently, I like Mendelssohn's violin concerto, but Schumann's piano concerto is wonderful as well. I would love to see Wagner's *Tannhauser*. There's so much incredible music right now."

"I agree." He was slow to continue. "I haven't ... " He swallowed hard. "I haven't had as much enjoyment in recent days." He took a breath as if to continue, but his lips pressed together like he was damming up the words.

Finally he asked, "Do you also play an instrument?"

My answer for this question could make me a rock star in this century, but I don't think I want to go into all the instruments I play. "Yes."

His eyebrows lifted in expectation of her continuing.

"Yes, *Your Grace*," Cora said, emphasizing his title, hoping to pull off the snarky comment, but she couldn't hold back a giggle. He joined with her, and the sound of it shot through Cora, straight to her heart.

She pondered how she had always read about companionable silence, but she never understood it until now. This man was comfortable to her. He just felt right. When they finished their meals, Simon escorted her back to the ballroom.

"They're Grace-ing you again," Cora whispered, somewhat

closer to his ear than she had intended to, then raised a fan to conceal a sly smile.

"You can't throw a cat without hitting someone or another called 'Grace' or 'Lord' at this or any other society party," he answered.

Cora nearly snorted. "I didn't expect you to say that."

"My mother's family is Scottish. They have a colorful way of saying things."

"Sorry. Your comment gave me a very vivid picture of a mangy cat landing on some man and then scrambling from table to table in a fright-filled panic."

A low laugh rumbled in Simon's throat. His eyes twinkled. Cora found her hand pressed to her stomach, chills erupting across her skin. How she loved that sound. For the way he was dressed and the deference he obviously received from the gathered crowd, Simon was a man of respect, yet he was genuine.

When they were back in the ballroom, they stood where the other guests were gathering. Music greeted Cora's ears. Not a song but instruments tuning—violin, cello, French horn, flute, and more. She listened, picking out the different instruments that were readying to play. It signaled the recommencement of the ball, causing an ache in her gut. She would not resume her duties babysitting the matrons in the corner.

At the same moment that Cora said, "I suppose I'll leave the party now," Simon asked, "May I have this dance?"

She found she couldn't say no. Her imagination leaped into action, envisioning his warm hand on her back. In fact, it was hard to speak at all, but a broad smile broke across her face, and her chest filled with excitement when she nodded her assent. "One dance before I leave."

He led her to one end of the ballroom and positioned them near the orchestra. Soon, couples filled the room. The first strains of the waltz don't just require that they assume dance position, but given their difference in height, she reached up for him, and he leaned nearer to her. She understood why the waltz had been frowned upon earlier in that century. There was immediate intimacy in the dance position, and her chest filled with tingly expectation.

With the rest of the instruments silent, the light, quick touch of the piano keys began the first notes of Chopin's "Grande Valse Brilliante." She knew there was a special difficulty with this piece —the small string section and woodwinds played the melody, lilting in two-four time, while the background bass viol and oboe carried the typical three-four time needed to dance the waltz. Unless the dancers were confident they could follow the right instruments, they might choose to sit this one out. She had believed the piece was written for concert performance for the piano and not for dancing, but here they were.

Simon's grasp at her waist tightened as he led her backward into the first step. It was warm and comforting to be held by him, and her hand fit perfectly in his. They rose and swayed together in the close hug. With the room circling far beyond them, they stepped through dizzying turns and slow or quick steps as the varying tempo demanded.

Cora marveled at his strength and grace and gave herself up to his arms. She would still leave after this dance, but for now she felt like Cinderella, swooped up in a dream dance with Prince Charming.

CHAPTER 3

Simon

Simon Tuttle, Duke of Hertfordshire, Earl of St. Albans. During his introduction to Cora, he had said, "I'm Simon Tuttle. My friends call me Albans." *Though technically true, they should now call me Hertfordshire.* He cringed inwardly at the misfit of that name. He had grown up as Lord Simon and wished he could hear his own familiar name more often, especially from her.

He'd failed to mention "duke" or "earl." Oh, and he knew why. Since the death of his father and both older brothers, the universe had singled him out to be the trophy that would be taken in the marriage mart come spring—only the women on the hunt weren't waiting for April. They had gotten it into their bonnets to contrive to become Simon's duchess as soon as possible.

Every event he'd attended since returning three weeks ago from his rustication with his mother's family in Scotland had turned into a troupe of actors with each woman more daring than the last. Thank heavens for Everett's reconnaissance, or Simon was sure he would have been trapped within mere days of stepping onto England's soil. He was grateful he'd missed the Season. Now he had just short of a year to steel himself for the onslaught.

It came down to this—he hid. He had attended several events, if one accepts *attending* to mean walking through the door. Last night, he was determined to spend a quiet evening apart from well-meaning family and friends who would introduce him to not-so-well-meaning misses and their mammas.

At the Lambeth's dinner party on Friday last, two out of the three young ladies invited suddenly became ill and requested that he escort them home. Thankfully, they made miraculous recoveries when it was learned that he would, of course, make his carriage available to both of them, and he would ride atop with his driver to aid the comfort of the women.

If he was supposed to be hiding last night, as he'd been determined to do, why did he walk Cora to dinner? Why did he relish the delicate touch of her hand pressed on the sleeve of his coat? He longed to feel that warmth again. And why did he study the color of her eyes to learn they were not blue as he first assumed but the color of violets? Her dress, a shade or two lighter, exaggerated their color.

He'd spent a restless night considering the curl of her hair, the tinkling sound of her laughter, the unladylike snort, and the pleasing curves of her gown. It wasn't just that she was attractive to look at, but she was also bold, intervening to protect Lucy or Everett. Simon thought on how he'd nearly blurted his secret to her not an hour after they first met.

Somehow Cora was different, and he wanted to satisfy his curiosity by getting to know her. He hoped it would take a very long time.

While just a day ago, he had shunned female attention, he hoped Cora was attracted to him. That thought brought him right back to where all this musing had started. He didn't fully introduce himself because he wanted her to be attracted to *him*, the man, not the titles.

Simon had never thought to gain the titles, and he felt they hung on him like a wet coat as if he were a child who wore his father's jacket out in a storm. But he believed in the responsibility the titles bequeathed. He was now responsible for the security and welfare of his mother and two younger sisters, the survival of hundreds of working families, and the husbandry of thousands of acres.

Everything was entailed to the estates. It made him a very wealthy man, but only him. Had he succumbed to death prior to his sisters, they and his mother would now be poor relations who must live on some cousin's kindness or, worse yet, take positions of employment.

Simon launched from bed, leaving his daydreams behind, and dressed for the day. He was determined to make small fortunes for the women in his family should he die. Each of his sisters had generous dowries set aside, and his mother would have a widow's portion, but neither of those gave them independence should they need it.

Attending the Full Moon Ball last night with Everett had been fortunate for meeting the lovely Cora, but his real reason for visiting Everett was altogether different. As Simon entered the dining room for breakfast, Everett finished filling his plate at the sideboard. Simon likewise selected eggs, scones, and pork, then sat beside him. "When do we meet with your man of business?"

"Soon." Everett put his fork down. Simon steeled himself, recognizing something serious was coming. "So, that woman last night ... " Everett's eyebrows wiggled. "Are you going to marry her?"

"I only met her last night." Simon thought that would end the conversation and shoved sausage in his mouth, but Everett stared at him and shrugged.

"You are, you know. Time doesn't matter."

"We only danced once."

"A waltz, and that's more than you've done since you were twenty. Oh, except Lady—ouch!" Everett glared at Simon and rubbed the spot on his arm where Simon had hit him. Everett laughed again. "You are."

CHAPTER 4

Cora Rey

Cora glanced around. No one. She stepped into the shadows of the tree line around the mansion's back park, but the ground became increasingly soggy and uneven as she neared the Thames. She backtracked to the outer edge and stood between sparse trees, where she would still have enough privacy from curious eyes for a workout and not throw out her ankles.

At the disastrous ball a week ago—though she admitted meeting Simon wasn't a disaster—Lady Cottrell had introduced her to her daughter, May, and invited her to spend the next few days with her in London. It wasn't the same town Cora had just visited. The London Eye was conspicuously missing, and there were no modern buildings. However, Big Ben still stood, holding court with the neighboring palace and cathedral. And the whole city stunk. She had returned late last night to Twickenham Manor to attend a picnic Aunt Nellie had planned.

It was peaceful here. After her workout, she would enjoy a few moments wandering through the woods before returning to the manor house. She pulled the earbuds from where her phone was stashed in her bra and selected a mix. What would she do when the battery ran out? She'd have to conserve.

She stared down at the hopeless dress she wore, wishing for leggings and a sports bra or anything Spandex. When she kicked one foot in front of her, her toe caught in the material, nearly tipping her.

She studied the skirt, yards and yards of blue material folding over itself and hanging to her ankles. For a moment, she considering taking the whole thing off and wearing the shift underneath. Way too risqué for this time period—even for Americans. Cora pulled the hemline up on both sides, pushed them backward between her legs, then pulled the ends to the front and tied them. It was ugly but functional as it drooped near her knees. It would allow her more freedom of movement.

Music pulsed as her body moved through warm-ups and into a kickboxing routine. But today, even the movement and the decibels directed into her ears couldn't dampen her memories. Her father's last day, last hours, were fresh behind her eyes. If she were back in her time, today would mark three years since he died.

He was lying in the library where she'd had the daybed removed and a hospital bed rolled into place. That was his favorite room, and because of him, it was hers too. A lifetime of his reading of ancient cultures and world history was shelved there, and several bookcases held her own collections. Her memory scanned the shelves. She'd read his books, and he'd read hers. Reading and discussing literature and the world was their special bond.

All the instruments had been removed weeks before to make room for the medical monitors and equipment—all of them except the harp. Her father claimed he had a right to hear harp music as he stepped ever closer to heaven.

But that day, her father wasn't talking about the economics of ancient Greece, the causes of World War I, or the early trade routes across Africa. He wasn't regaling her with stories about antics in his college years or his relationship with her mother. He spoke sparingly when pain etched his face between increasing doses of medication. "I love you." Later he was able to say, "I know your mother would be proud of you." Right before midnight, he died.

Cora intensified her Krav Maga workout. Roundhouse kick. Pummeling. Closed fist. Open fist. Sweeping someone's legs. She imagined herself being grabbed, choked, and bear-hugged and executed releases from each. Sweat trickled down the sides of her face and the middle of her back. The breeze had picked up and cooled her as much as possible through layers of fabric.

She would end with relaxing yoga positions—standing ones. But not yet. She extended her workout.

All my days are precious gifts. Her dad's favorite saying bounced through her thoughts. She wondered how a man being consumed by cancer considered each day worth living, but he maintained his optimism to the end. Cora's left arm hooked through the air, her right hand fisted and ready near her chin. Then she stepped forward and kicked her foot swiftly to chest height.

What if I'm stuck here? In this time and in this place? This would become my life. Frustration bubbled up. There were no paved roads. She couldn't shop online. And the debate on women's rights was new and unpopular. The music in her ears reminded her to start her cooldown, but she hit repeat and started the exercise over. *What kind of a life could I possibly have here?* Every cliché she'd read haunted her—needlework, afternoon teas, balls, and musicales. Well, the last two were all right but probably not frequent enough. Her arms and legs moved through the motions of protecting herself and attacking with little thought taken.

Her father would have loved the opportunity to be pulled into the past and crawl through history with his own experiences and senses. He would have made the best of it. Although believing Nellie when she said she could send her back, Cora needed to have some kind of plan should she have to stay.

She could teach. It settled her to know that even here were children who would need her, who might be less understood or tolerated in this world than even the one she left. The history of anyone with differences that society saw as a disability wasn't good. They were abandoned to orphanages, hidden in cellars, or killed for the inconvenience of being born. Her outrage at the barbaric conditions those children must live in steamed into her workout.

Refocusing on her exercise, Cora imagined someone grasping her neck and shoving her against a tree. Feeling the bark along her spine, she dropped one shoulder lower and swung both arms up the center of her body, and then pushed them out as if to bend the elbows of an attacker. Her fist rammed toward the soft tissue between the jaw and neck. At the same moment, she advanced, kicking her knee repeatedly toward his invisible groin.

Her music switched to a slow instrumental piece again, signaling the stretching set. She'd been a little too aggressive with the defensive moves, but her tension had diminished. A thick cloud of dust blew past her. She turned to see the cause as Simon dismounted his horse and hit the ground on a run toward her. Thankfully, she knew him. Still, her muscles tightened, and her heartbeat quickened.

He stopped not far from her and whipped his head around, looking into the forest. His chest heaved, and his eyes were still wary when he turned toward her. "Are you all right? Were you attacked?" His words were gentle but earnest.

"I'm fine. There's no one here but me. And now you." He had seen something suspicious and come to her aid. She felt deep gratitude. "I was only taking in some exercise."

Although he quickly shifted his eyes away, Cora caught him staring at her legs. Knowing she was going to work out this morning, she had opted not to wear stockings and the dozen underskirts this fashion demanded.

He focused on her face. "Exercise? It looked like you fought for your life."

Cora fumbled with the knotted material at her waist. She had embarrassed him. She shook herself inwardly and pushed a smile onto her face. "That's why I chose to exercise here. Can you imagine if I did that in the parlor or the garden?" The skirt unraveled and dropped down.

When Cora looked up, Simon walked closer and held out a handkerchief. She took it and wiped her face and neck. "Why are *you* here?"

"I went out for a ride and saw you doing—the only word that comes to mind is 'combat.'"

"That sounds about right. It gets my heart pumping." Cora reached down and fluffed her skirt. "I should get back to the manor," she said, then pointed toward the manor house.

"No, I don't live there," Simon replied.

It took Cora a moment to decide what question he thought she'd asked to give that response, and she tried to keep the confusion from showing on her face. "I'll see you at noon for the picnic, then."

He mounted his horse and rode away. Cora hurried back to her room to clean up and change. The morning passed quickly, and soon Cora and her friends were walking to the field for the picnic. Other houseguests ventured out past the formal gardens, too.

"Aunt Nellie doesn't do anything in a less-than-grand style," Kaitlyn said as the women moved away from the carriages bringing guests.

Tables topped with white linens and piled high with food dotted the rear lawn, and a legion of servants stood ready to assist with the guests, or with the food, horses, and games. There seemed to be more people working than enjoying, but there were plenty of those, too. Carriages and gigs continued in a long procession, delivering their occupants until the road finally cleared.

Cora scanned the area. She wasn't looking for Simon per se. She was just looking for ... anyone she knew, and it so happened that she knew him.

Aunt Nellie joined the women. "What a morning it's been. I always have something new going on—new goals and such. It helps the decades pass. Now I'm trying to learn how to send something through time that didn't appear as a result of the ley lines." She leaned in, and the women huddled closer. "It isn't going well. I painted a lovely still life on my bedroom wall, so I could try to send back a vase of roses. I tipped the vase against its image, and —" Nellie's hands formed a ball, then blasted apart. Her eyes widened as she made an explosive sound. "You'd think a red feather pillow blew up in my room. The vase melted into a heap on the carpet."

Cora wondered if sending their group back was as certain as Nellie had made it sound a few days ago. Blowing apart wasn't on her bucket list.

"Well, make merry." Aunt Nellie waved to them as she scampered off to greet some guests.

Cora had witnessed some of Aunt Nellie's other attempts. She had painted a spoon, a shoe, and a candle. The paint sparkled like the mural Cora had fallen through. The likeness of the objects was very detailed. Still, they were all failures. They twisted, caught fire, and turned to water, respectively. This attempt might be the most spectacular one yet. It seemed to her that each effort was getting farther from the desired result instead of closer.

Cora's voice shook a little when she said, "Human trials are out of the question. She *can* send us back, right? She's done it before? She said she has."

The other women were silent. The expression on Kaitlyn's face said she might be as nervous as Cora felt while Reece's eyes held barely concealed fury.

Cora silently considered a future in this time period, which sounded better than ending up as a lump on the carpet. It was unacceptable. They *would* return to their time. She would resume teaching. Her life would go on as planned. She just needed to keep a positive outlook and do something to take her mind off the time-travel business.

"Well, it's a beautiful day, no rain for once, and I intend to enjoy the afternoon," Cora said.

"Oh, don't you worry. It will rain," Kaitlyn replied.

Cora's attention flitted from one group of party-goers to another. The women were dressed in their best with tightly cinched waists and bell-shaped skirts. The men seemed well turned out, too, in as many pastel colors as the ladies. She recognized introductions being made and flirtations taking place. There was one thing all had in common. They were here to make a match.

It was the same game played in the ballroom at the Full Moon Ball. It was a game she was bound to lose by the rules of this century. But what if she did as Simon suggested that first night and changed the game? She'd have to think about how to do that.

Across the lawn, Cora recognized Simon's powerful form standing in a small group.

"Have a wonderful picnic, ladies," she said to her roommates as she hurried off. She only felt the slightest twinge of guilt for not spending more time with them. Throughout the whole week of the immersive experience, she'd seen the smitten looks Cyrus had been sending Kaitlyn—the same ones Jem had for Reese. Cora was a fifth wheel. And more than that, she wanted them to have this time together.

She recognized a few other people she'd been introduced to as well—Everett and Lucy and May. She'd spent several days with May and Lady Cottrell in London, and liked them very much. May had none of the pretense so many others displayed around Simon. A handful of other men and women rounded out the group. When someone approached, Everett seemed to protect Simon from the arrival of the newcomer.

Let's see how good you are at this tactical game, Everett. Everett always seemed to hover near Simon and run interference for him. Cora angled herself to approach from Simon's flank. She opened a parasol and held it close to her head, so little of her face would be seen. She decided to walk a straight line as if she were going to the fountain by the pond. As long as she didn't walk toward them, they shouldn't take notice.

When she was firmly behind Everett's back, where only Simon would notice her, she flipped her parasol to the other shoulder, turned and faced him directly, tipping her head toward the pond, giving him a genuine, inviting smile, then turned back and continued walking.

She stood along the water's pebbled edge, gazing over the surface to the rolling hills beyond when she felt his presence behind her left shoulder. She didn't think she had heard him or even seen his shadow since it fell the other way, but something about Simon was like gravity that gently tugged her toward him.

"Do you fish, Mr. Duke?" Cora asked without facing him.

Everett snorted a laugh. "'Mr. Duke!' That's an American —making one of the highest-ranking members of the peer common." He raised his voice. "So, Mr. Duke, do you fish?"

Cora looked to see if she'd offended Simon since Everett had repeated the question to him but caught Simon shoulder-bumping Everett good-naturedly. "I suppose I need a lesson in titles and such," she added. "Perhaps even a tutor."

"Yes, I fish." Simon stayed on her left but angled to look into Cora's face.

"I do too," she replied. "Only fishing—not catching. It's a perfectly good way to spend an afternoon pretending to be productive."

"Perhaps I can arrange for you to visit my estate and take in some fishing."

Cora handed her little purse to Simon and then leaned down and chose two smooth rocks from near her shoe. "Perhaps." She skimmed the first pebble across the surface of the pond. "Hmm, two skips. I can do better." She paused, moving the second rock between her thumb and finger. When she found the surface she wanted, she flung the pebble, side-armed, across the surface. "Three skips. Better."

Simon piped up from behind her. "Was that three skims?"

That's what she'd just said. Cora checked Simon's expression. He looked serious. Then she saw Everett, smirking, holding back a laugh at some joke. He chucked a rock at Simon's knee and received the quick reaction of Simon lobbing one near Everett in return.

"How about a contest?" Everett asked, gesturing to the pond. "To determine the champion stone skimmer?"

"Though your little purse looks quite fetching with my morning suit ..." Simon held his hand up and swung the purse around his wrist. "I must return it to you to if I'm to win the game." He handed it back.

Cora set it aside and removed her gloves, earning raised eyebrows from both men. "This is a serious competition, one I intend to win." She handed the gloves to Simon. "Get over it. And please put them in your pocket."

The men removed their gloves as well while she began the search for acceptable rocks.

"Best of five pitches," she yelled back over her shoulder.

During the selection, the small group drifted apart in search of the perfect stones. When Cora rejoined the men, Everett was telling Simon he could only have five, and Simon was dropping the rejects to the ground. She stepped into their little line on the shore with Everett to her left and Simon on her right, but the men quickly shuffled, ending with Simon on her left and Everett to his left.

Each took a turn flinging their arms in wide arcs and throwing the stones across the tense surface of the water.

Simon counted aloud as his rock skiffed the top of the pond. "Two, three, four!" His smile turned full-force on Cora. His eyes were bright with excitement before he bent slightly at the waist and said, "I've bested your three. Sorry to nudge you out of the lead."

Cora caught her breath. She completely understood why women went out of their way to try to meet him.

At the end of five rounds, Everett was declared the winner for six jumps by one of his pebbles.

The diversion had given her a chance to determine her course while on this little vacation. *I'll join their game and turn it on its ear.* Her father would tell her to embrace life, to live this one as fully as she did the other one.

Simon was the runner-up at four skips.

As each replaced their gloves, Cora said, "I don't have family here and only Aunt Nellie to help me make connections. I wondered if you two would help." It was his idea. Perhaps he'll help her.

"Of course," Everett replied.

"Who would you like to meet?" Simon asked as he pulled on his second glove.

"Eligible bachelors." She looked between the two of them. "Ten to twelve would do."

The seam that attached the thumb of Simon's glove ripped across his palm. His stare met Cora's gaze.

She wondered how big of a faux pas she had made, but the men didn't seem critical of her plan. Cora reminded them, "I'm here, of course, to marry. Without family history or reputation or relations to make introductions, I'm at a disadvantage. It would be an enormous service for you to weed through the men who would not make good husbands."

Simon's finger lifted into the air, and his mouth dropped open, but no words came out during a long pause. Finally he said, "Everett, may I ask you a question?" He turned to Cora. "Excuse me—us, Miss Rey. I'll—we'll return in a moment." He pulled Everett by the shoulder and took two steps, but turned back. "Wait here." He spun away, then toward her again. "Please."

Everett and Simon moved off a few paces and began what looked like an impassioned conversation. Occasionally, Simon gestured toward Cora while Everett laughed often.

From the looks of it, she doubted they wanted to help, but she continued to watch. *Well, that would make the game a bit harder. Not impossible, though. I came on this trip for an immersive experience and got an authentic one instead. We may have taken Aunt Nellie's little detour down a rabbit hole, but the principle is the same. Soak it all in.*

When the men returned, Simon replied, "We're considering who we might introduce you to. It could be a while before we can."

"That's fine, and thank you."

As they walked back to the central lawn area to watch the children's games, Cora wondered what pieces of Simon she was still missing to understand him. *Probably quite a lot since we only met a few days ago.* Still, there was something familiar that she couldn't put her finger on.

During the rough-and-tumble of the children's games, Simon introduced her to the people who were near them. At the end, he walked Cora back to Twickenham Manor. "Your company was a pleasure." He bowed slightly.

"I had a wonderful afternoon as well." Before she reentered the house, she remarked, "There's something about you. I don't know what, but something."

Although his eyes widened momentarily, his smile overcame any hesitancy Cora thought she'd detected a second earlier. Long, shallow dimples sculpted his face.

The next morning, a letter was delivered with her breakfast tray and sat beside a plate of eggs and ham. The plain linen paper, folded and sealed, the wax stamped with a rearing stag, had only her name on the front. She slipped her finger under the seal, then unfolded the pages to read.

Miss Cora Rey,

It would be my pleasure to escort you in the evening two days hence and provide you with the introductions you desire if you are available for the event. We will attend a dinner at the home of Lord and Lady Stafford at their residence, Mount Lebanon, at nine in the evening to be followed by a pageant on the River Thames. Mr. Everett Hawley, Miss Lucy Radnor, Lady Radnor, and our mutual acquaintance, Miss May Cottrell, will accompany us for the events. Your acceptance is eagerly awaited.

Your servant,

Mr. Duke

Cora smiled at the nickname that not only concealed his identity to anyone who might see the letter but affirmed his friendship with her. She quickly dressed and went in search of paper and a pen for a written response. A maid directed Cora to a secretarial desk in the library. The wooden desktop was cleared. "Is there paper I could use?" Before the maid left the room, she added, "And a pen?"

"Yes, miss." The woman touched the top of the cabinet, lowering a dropdown table onto an arm that swung out from below. Inside were trays of paper and bottles of ink. Beside the ink were pens, sort of. The tools resembled the ones used by calligraphers.

Oh, no. "Thank you." Cora hoped her tone conveyed more confidence than she felt, but she sat down and slowly began selecting paper to place on the desk. The door whispered closed, and she let out a breath. *Is nothing easy in this century?*

Over several minutes, she struggled with the ink and pen through several attempts only to have unreadable words on ink-splotched paper. She hit on the problem and swirled the tip of the pen around on the ruined papers to remove the excess ink, wiped it with the paper, which she threw on the fire grate, then sat again. This time dipping only the end in the ink, she was able to write two legible words at a time. With much effort, she had a passable letter.

CHAPTER 5

Simon

SIMON RETIRED TO HIS ROOM BEFORE OPENING THE LETTER. HE chuckled deep in his chest at the salutation as he dropped into a thickly padded green-striped chair.

Dear Mr. Albans Duke Grace Tuttle,

Thank you for the invitation. I accept. Your servitude is greatly appreciated. I expect to have this business tied up within the month, so you won't have to worry about a long commitment to me.

Cheers,

Cora

P.S. How did I do on your name? I thought if I threw a few titles up there, I might hit on the right combination. About that tutoring position—it would be great to know who is a "Sir" or "My Lord" or "Your Grace" or a "Mister." It seems to matter a great deal here, as I was informed by the many guests who visited Aunt Nellie's parlor this morning with hope of hearing news of you.

I would like to understand this business of titles and wondered if you would provide me with a little insight. Maybe that isn't something you've thought about since it's always been part of your life.

What was it like to be a little dukelet? Did you get to wear long pants? Did you play outside with friends, or did you stay inside and learn to be proper and stern? What do you do when you aren't duke-ing about? Do you have hobbies? Or a favorite color? Do you travel? Have you been to London to visit the queen? What did you do there?

Simon found himself laughing at the "dukelet" and "duke-ing about" comments. He was amused at how irreverent Cora was about the prestige of the peerage. It fit her and her relaxed manner. It was warm and enchanting.

Simon felt a spike of interest at the prospect of seeing Cora join the party. It surprised him that she admitted to not wanting a long commitment from him. That was certainly contrary to every other female of his acquaintance. But *she* was contrary to every other woman—even in the way she moved. His mind ran through memories of watching her dance and fight. She was intriguing.

He planned his route, so she would be the last to enter the carriage. If he first picked up Lady and Miss Radnor followed by Everett, the ladies would sit opposite him, and Everett would be beside him. When Miss May joined them, she would also sit on the bench with the ladies. That's all who would fit. When Cora arrived, she would have to take the only remaining seat, between him and Everett.

A smile grew across his lips at the thought of the rustle of her skirts as the carriage swayed. He fondly anticipated that when the carriage made a strong left turn, Cora might be just off balance enough to sway against his shoulder and arm. The pleasant ride would lead to a pleasant evening as well.

He imagined her walking on his arm, sitting across the table or near him, and stealing glances at each other through the evening. He wondered what the sparkling pageant lights shooting from the boats would look like reflected in Cora's eyes. Would he have a moment with her to himself?

When he considered his role of matchmaker, the excitement appreciably darkened, something he didn't chose to examine very closely after Everett's unlikely prediction. He knew all too well the expectations held for his marriage and bride, someone with an impeccable family history and social standing nearly equal to his own.

Which standing was that? Of being a younger son who was elevated as a result of extreme grief? He was a younger son still in his heart, one who would do his duty to family but considered how to remain true to himself along the way.

Although more prospective brides attended London events, they were often treated with suspect by titled gentlemen who knew they were looking to purchase a title.

But wasn't that exactly what the heiresses from America were doing? In exchange for their large dowries, they became a lady or baroness or duchess. What was Cora's story? Why was she looking for a title when they appeared to be of little value to her and of less esteem? She seemed a paradox—an enchanting, beautiful paradox.

Picking up the paper again, Simon walked to the window and reread the letter. He looked at the careful writing with thick lines where the pen had moved slowly. He studied the unique shape of some letters and the unusual spellings. He read it again and again until he imagined he could hear her voice and laughter as she teased him from the page.

Cora had said she thought he was different. Shame burned deep in his gut. Did she know his secret? If so, she was out of his reach. If society should find out as well, he would be saddled with a wife of convenience and in name only. Maybe he shouldn't want Cora to be with a man like him. She would find his fault eventually. Would she think him less? And even if she didn't already know, she'd asked him to help her with introductions, clearly not considering him a prize.

For a fleeting second, he wanted to twist the paper into a wad and toss it in the fireplace. But he couldn't. It would be his consolation prize should she leave. Instead, he folded it and placed it in a drawer.

That evening, Simon's almost-full carriage made its way slowly over the roads, stopping in front of Twickenham Manor. Simon's pulse raced with anticipation as the footman lowered the stairs. He stepped down to assist Cora.

"You're very lovely tonight, Cora." Although her hair had been pinned on top of her head, several tendrils hung about her shoulders. Simon wondered if the curls were natural. It seemed an inconsequential thing, making him even more curious.

"Thank you. I'm looking forward to this. I've never been to a pageant on a river before."

Before she lifted her foot to the second step, the carriage jostled back and forth, then settled again. Cora disappeared inside, her skirts trailing her. When it was apparent they were arranged, Simon stepped inside as well.

Lady Radnor had obviously jumped into the seat where Simon had expected Cora, and Cora sat in the middle of the seat opposite him between May and Lucy.

Disappointed, Simon took his seat but not before he noticed Everett's stiff expression, which clearly said that he didn't like the idea of rubbing thighs with his possible future mother-in-law.

To Simon's surprise, he very much liked having Cora sit opposite him in the coach where he could watch her expressions. The conversation had turned toward the monarchy, and Cora seemed alive with the exchange.

"Well, it's been a hundred years or so, hasn't it, since there was a queen on the throne? It's exciting—it doesn't happen often that a woman leads a powerful nation. We haven't managed it in America."

Lady Radnor and her daughter seemed interested in their gloves or the seams of their dresses, not joining in at all. Now and again, Lucy glanced up as if she would interject something, but each time her eyes slid toward her mother, and she cast them down again. May seemed to listen with interest and an amused expression on her face.

Simon noticed that Lady Radnor's lips looked unusually thin and pressed together. He wondered how long she would endure Cora's fascination with talking about politics.

"Female rulers are a bit more likely under our system than yours," Everett commented.

"Yeah, I suppose when you leave God in charge of political succession, he slips in women more often than voters would—who are also all men."

Lady Radnor's jaw dropped open with her mouth forming an O. She didn't say anything. Simon wondered what could be said —the reasoning was sound. America must educate women better on world matters than England did.

"The queen's quite progressive," Cora continued.

"What evidence will you present for that claim?" Simon asked. He had a hunch that she would relish expressing her views and not shy away from the opportunity.

"For one, she knew her own mind, resisting familial and political pressures early on as queen. More evidence can be seen when she supported the removal of slavery from all the territories of Britain. That can't have been popular, but I applaud her."

Simon knew Cora had more to say when she took a breath, but Lady Radnor threw herself into the conversation. "She wore a lovely white gown at her wedding."

Cora seemed stunned, maybe trying to fathom some connection between the dress and slavery.

"Oh, yes. I'll be married in white, too," Lucy said.

For one quick moment, Simon saw a dainty ridge form between Cora's eyes. Would she take back the conversation or join the inane frivolity? What was next—the weather?

Sitting on Cora's left, Lucy nodded enthusiastically. "And I'll wear flowers in my hair just as she did." Her eyes flicked to Everett's and dashed away just as quickly, reminding Simon that he had an obligation to free Everett from his duty as Simon's nursemaid.

Cora looked at Simon. When her mouth dropped open and snapped back shut, he wondered at the resolve it might take for her to acquiesce the topic of discussion. He wondered at this confident, intelligent woman who could discuss skipping rocks and political analyses with equal comfort. He determined to find a time and a place where he would reopen the dam of thoughts behind her now-pressed lips.

Simon watched as Cora rearranged the fit of her gloves and smoothed her dress. He saw a small smile cross her lips with no real enjoyment or life behind it, her eyes and cheeks completely unaffected. So, she didn't care to talk of fashion—a very positive trait.

The coach trembled to a stop. Simon assisted Lady Radnor out followed by Miss May Cottrell. The ladies made their way to the home's entrance. Cora was the third woman to exit, and although Simon's hand was raised to help her, she stood crouched in the doorway, looking around with interest for quite some time. Between the hinge and the door, Simon saw Everett's face very near Lucy's.

Ah, that's twice she's played at Cupid for the couple.

Cora finally alighted, and Simon reluctantly released her to assist Lucy.

The double doors to the grand dining room swung open, and his party was introduced. "His Grace the Duke of Hertfordshire, Earl of St. Albans." All eyes turned their way, and the introduction continued. "Lady May Cottrell, Lady Radnor, Miss Lucy Radnor, Mr. Everett Hawley, and Miss Cora Rey of the Americas."

A few guests gathered as Simon's group mingled with the rest. The women drifted off with Lady Radnor introducing the young women here and there.

At the slap on his left shoulder, Simon clamped down on a startle then turned to see a friend from Eaton. "Wetheridge." He couldn't say that he was glad to see him. He wasn't.

"Though you've been a duke for nearly three years, you've successfully avoided the parson's mousetrap, have you?"

Everett shook hands with the man and answered for Simon. "Deucedly hard to get married since he's been hiding out in the wilds of Scotland all that time. What about you?"

Before Wetheridge could answer, Simon said, "One doesn't have to hide out in Lifton, but the effect is the same by just being there. What brings you up from the south—sheep or cattle?"

A jab at Wetheridge's county's industry usually brought a stunning retort, but this time, there was no answer. Simon noticed an appreciative look in the man's eye directed over Simon's shoulder at Cora, who along with May and Lucy was set to join the men.

Simon debated how to withhold an introduction.

Just then, he heard Everett say, "Lord Wetheridge, may I introduce Lady May Cottrell, Miss Lucy Radnor, and Miss Cora Rey."

The first two women dipped a curtsy, and Cora tipped her head in acknowledgement. Then Simon addressed the ladies to complete the introduction. "May I present Lord Wetheridge. His family seat is a barony in Devon."

When Lord Wetheridge stood from bowing to the women, he extended his arm to Cora and asked, "May I engage you for watching the pageant with me?"

"Sorry, chap. You're too late for that." Simon stepped up and presented her his arm as well and was pleased when she laid her hand on it. A small victory, but a satisfying one.

Wetheridge's eyes barely glanced toward Simon and quickly returned to Cora. "No worry. Since I am merely a baron, I should like to escort you to dinner."

Simon's mouth opened but snapped shut. He wanted to deflect that offer as well, but knew Wetheridge was likely correct. Simon would go through the doorway long before Cora was seated.

"I would like that very much." Cora smiled. "You'll have to tell me all about Devon. I have never visited there."

The way she leaned a bit toward Wetheridge in answering him looked to Simon as if she really meant it.

"How are you three men acquainted?" Cora asked.

"Cousins," Wetheridge and Everett answered at the same time Simon replied, "School."

She nodded.

Although a short time passed, the room filled with people and noise, thick with conversations, but much of that was lost to Simon. Before the panic he felt in his chest rose, he maneuvered the group to the side of the room, his back toward a wall with only the corner to his left, effectively controlling the size of group surrounding him.

How would he manage dinner? He had strategically avoided this type of social gathering. He would have sent regrets, but it was the only invitation this evening, and it appeared to his dismay that he would accept even *this* challenge to be in Cora's company again.

Just as Wetheridge predicted, Simon escorted a lovely, though elderly, woman to dinner. His seating assignment placed him between two gray-haired women dripping in diamonds. As the courses were served, the conversation partners paired, and he turned, thankfully, to the right.

"We've had unseasonably mild weather. Have we not?" Simon asked.

"I can't hear you. I'm sure you were saying something proper. What was it about—the weather or the furnishings?' Her voice cracked with some effort to be heard.

"The weather." Simon found himself leaning much closer.

"Yes. The leather is quite becoming on the seats. It's new since the last time I was here."

As the conversation, of sorts, continued, Simon found his chest tightening. He had passible hearing in one ear, but the other was of little help to him. He felt as if he were staring into his gloomy future.

Just before the conversation partners turned, Simon's first partner said, "You'll have little luck with Anabelle. She's earless as a beetle."

Even as a child, he knew the descriptions of those without hearing were flung about without kindness: stone deaf, out of hearing, deaf as an adder.

The other woman smiled at Simon, but her eyes slid away quickly to attend to her soup course. He spent a rather silent dinner, volleying between the two women, leaving him plenty of time to watch Cora.

Though he could only see her profile when she spoke with Wetheridge, he noticed the many times they laughed, and he found himself cursing the social demands of his own titles. He imagined the ringing sound of her voice and her eyes glowing with mirth at the bounder who was enjoying her company instead of him.

Cora sat near the middle of a long table, as far away from his as could be, at the fourth and final table to be seated. Simon noticed those seating assignments all seemed to be debutantes and eligible young men, many of whom hadn't come into their inheritances yet and only claimed honorary titles with surnames as he had expected to for the rest of his life. He also noticed the lax nature of dinner etiquette around her with conversations obviously being directed across the table. From his count, Cora would meet at least four of the men around her without any effort.

At the end of the meal, the groups set out to gather in the ballroom, seeking their parties before being led toward the back lawn abutting the Thames. Lady Radnor could not be found until the masses had already departed, and not until then could their group move forward.

Lucy took her mother by the arm, and Everett quickened to follow. "I'm ready to burst with excitement." May clasped her hands and quickened her pace, excitement apparently driving her to catch up with the crowd who went before them. As their group outpaced them, Cora and Simon slowed their progress a bit.

"You're not terribly good at the matchmaker business, but don't worry. After you've practiced on me, you'll be ready for whatever your younger sisters throw at you," Cora remarked in the teasing tone Simon was beginning to recognize.

"You doubt me? I've introduced you to many eligible men." Simon cringed at who was on that list.

At that, Cora raised her eyebrows, seeming to challenge his statement. She stopped walking, and Simon had to turn back a step to stay beside her.

"At least several," he amended. "And 'eligible' is a relative term. Granted they are not married, but nor should they be."

Cora began walking down the hallway again. "Oh, yes, you said Lord Bellion was a cad. You introduced the Hon. Michael Wyndham as a puppy. Mr. Echols, you called a rapscallion. Oh, and you refused to introduce me to the duke of Norshire, saying he was a rake."

"His Grace, the Duke of Norshire." Cora waved off the correction of how to say the formal title as Simon continued as if punctuating each word. "He eminently is. And you're welcome."

Cora folded her arms in front of her. "Oh, thank you. But you know, you can tell a lot about a man by the friends he keeps."

"Oh, no." Simon wagged his finger. "They are not my *friends*."

Less than a week here, and Simon knew she had more than a handful of interested parties. Every event they would attend would be ankle- to knee-deep in eligible, and occasionally desperate, men. Simon considered—not for the first time—why he had agreed to this matchmaking scheme. The more time he spent in Cora's company, the less likely he felt to make an introduction to anyone of quality.

"Tonight, I've met Lord Saalfeld," Cora added.

"N'er do well," Simon said with a chuckle. He cringed inside, knowing that the man had his affection engaged elsewhere to no avail.

"A Mr. McElroy. You cannot say that he is less than upstanding."

"A boor."

"And the Hon, Vernon Shelby, who seemed immediately taken with me."

"Fop."

Cora pretended not to listen to him. "And Everett introduced me to Wetheridge." Simon opened his mouth to make another comment, but Cora stepped in front of him and placed her finger over his lips. "Don't say a word," she commanded quietly. "We had a lovely dinner conversation."

Simon closed his eyes as her hand lingered. A forceful desire tempted him to kiss that lovely pointer. He would not allow the indiscretion or the scandal it might cause for her should someone see. He knew if he opened his eyes, she was close enough to kiss properly.

No.

Can I trust myself? He nodded once and felt Cora's finger move, then opened his eyes and added with a smile, "Wetheridge is an interloper."

Cora laughed lightly at that. "If he hadn't escorted me, someone else would have. Are you determined to disparage every man I meet?"

"Yes, and without guilt or shame in doing so. As your dearest substitute relative, I must use discretion to make only proper introductions for your own welfare. And when I don't, to warn you off."

"But is he a good man?" Cora asked.

He wouldn't lie to her. "Wetheridge is a fine-enough fellow." He paused only momentarily, then added, "And if you can stand manure on the lawns around your great house, he could turn out to be a worthy husband—in a few years."

"Well, I think that's as close as you're going to get to complimenting any of them. That puts seven men on my list, leaving off the rake. I'll just have to spend a little more time with each to narrow it down."

Simon led her through the doors into the ballroom. "Nearly all of the people you've met have pockets to let. Except for

Ti. His wealth runs deeper than many small nations on the continent. We should be careful that the men you meet are interested in more than your fortune."

"If you don't like the options I have, you might suggest some of your own. I'm just saying you could give a little more effort."

Simon thought about the effort he'd like to give. Perhaps it shone in his eyes, for Cora became still and silent. Her eyes locked with his, and her lips parted ever so slightly. A blush rose across her cheeks.

Oh, what she does to me. He cleared his throat and led her out to the lawn. The gathering was large, and their group became stretched out as they proceeded. "I'll redouble my efforts." He glanced about outside with a little zip of energy still dashing through him. He tried for a tone of boredom. "Anyone in particular you'd like to meet?"

CHAPTER 6

Cora Rey

Cora looked around the lawn and the river just beyond that. It was a beautiful setting for whatever this pageant was. The sun was low in the sky behind them, though it wouldn't be dark for nearly an hour more. Who did she want to meet? "I haven't any idea who is married and who isn't." People milled about or sat in chairs. Some of the men reclined on blankets where women sat. Everyone faced the river. "I'll have to rely on your recommendations for possible suitors."

"I'll do my best," Simon answered, but his voice was dull. Cora saw the slightest flinch to his face, and his body tensed for a second, then he relaxed and pointed to their friends on the left side close to where they were now, hurrying to join them.

She was caught off guard, tongue-tied. *Does he think I completely friend-zoned him? I guess it could look that way.* It's just that he had recommended that she change the game, so she requested his help. But it was obvious by everyone's attention to him that he should have been beyond wanting the attention of a mere American. *Maybe I'm reading too much into this.*

Cora glanced over his shoulder and again noticed a young woman in a light pink dress she'd seen inside. The dress and hair had reminded her of her favorite book of nursery rhymes she had when she was little. The young woman looked like Bo Peep with a flaring skirt and golden ringlets framing her childlike face. Cora was sure the girl and her mother had been close to where their group gathered inside and now stood just a few steps behind them again. The older woman whispered furiously in Bo Peep's ear and ticked her head toward Simon.

Whatever the mother advised, the daughter seemed reluctant to perform, but with a push, she was propelled toward Simon's left. The girl looked back, and the mother waved her forward until she walked stiffly just two steps behind Simon. If Simon moved to his left without looking, he'd trip over the girl.

The mother extended her arms as if to shove her daughter. Cora pulled Simon in front of her and out of Bo Peep's way. As a result, Cora collided with the girl. Both women sprawled on the grass, Cora landing under the debutante, whose mother gave a defeated shriek.

Cora laughed, realizing it must look quite absurd to have tumbled together. "I suppose one of us will have to propose. Mustn't we marry now?" she teased the young woman.

In a second, the young women's mother was upon them, surveying the situation with squinting eyes.

Cora rolled out from under the girl. "No harm done."

Another man reached to help Bo Peep stand as Simon did for Cora.

"Perhaps you should watch what you are doing." The mother's voice had an accusing note to it. "The bottom of Annie's dress is ripped."

Cora shook out her skirt, then patted Annie's arm and casually replied, "Better to have a little rip than a big scandal."

The mother's eyes popped wide open as a harrumph belched from her. "For whom?" She spun on her heels, hooked arms with her daughter, and marched her back toward the house.

Simon and Everett laughed, not quite under their breaths but certainly straining to hold it in as they watched the women leave.

"You were very nearly trapped," Everett commented.

"Yes, no thanks to you," Simon replied but without any real accusation behind the words.

"You've some dirt on your dress." Lucy pointed near the hem of Cora's skirt, but her eyes flicked around the gathered groups of guests nearby pretending poorly not to gawk. "Maybe we should go back home."

Cora picked up her hem and swatted the dust away. "There. Hardly noticeable. Let's stay." She and Simon joined their party just as their host and hostess stood.

Some men dressed in ancient-looking clothing climbed aboard small boats that bobbed along the riverbank and rowed them away from shore. Lord and Lady Stafford called attention to the gathering. Lady Stafford recited her lineage, eighteen generations from William the Conqueror to herself.

Lord Stafford proceeded with a retelling of the Norman invasion. The men in boats landed on shore, fought with English forces, then retreated and led the English to their deaths at the hands of hidden reinforcements.

At the end of the pageant, Cora was awed at the incredible opportunity that was hers to sit in history and feel it firsthand. This wasn't a dry college text but the story of real families. She thought of her father, grateful for his appreciation of history and instilling that love in her.

The group talked excitedly about the pageant as they drove home. She wished Simon a heart-felt thanks and good night.

The next morning, Cora sat in bed with a breakfast tray. She wasn't completely used to what passed for breakfast yet—bacon, baked beans, tomatoes, mushrooms, sausage, scrambled eggs, and toast with bitter chocolate to wash it all down. None of that held her interest this morning. Instead, she lifted a letter from the tray.

On the front of the envelope, beneath her name, the words, "I spied a little mouse under her chair," were penned. Cora didn't need a return address to know the letter was from Simon. Excitement sparkled through her—he was willing to play her game when she'd asked if he'd visited the queen. He could have mentioned the contents of her letter last night before the dinner or pageant, so why didn't he? Perhaps he hoped she would relish a surprise. That was true.

Dear Miss Rey,

Since you have put me to work finding you suitors as if I were your next of kin, I shall collect you at six this evening for more introductions. We are expected at a small gathering for dinner. There will be music provided afterward, and dancing was implied as well. We will be part of the same entourage as last night.

Regards,

Mr. Duke

P.S. No doubt we had a passable evening if you are still willing to read these words. Between the time I read your questions and when I whisked you off to the dinner party, I thought to answer your interrogation, resulting in this letter.

At the risk of disillusioning you, I was never a little duke-let. That might imply my status in the family was that of an eagle. My childhood bore a closer resemblance to being a duke-ling. Perhaps you know the classic tale of the ugly duke-ling—that metaphor suites me better.

My mother has assured me that, unlike Athena, I was once an infant and thereby must have worn a muslin gown for some time. As a boy, my pants were forever in need of repair because of the next question I will answer.

Proper and stern are still outside of my grasp, perhaps because I spent as much time as possible climbing trees and attempting to sneak up on the trout in the stream that created the north boundary of the estate. I might have accurately been called a hooligan. More than once. Confessions on that later.

My favorite color? Until recently, I would have said blue, but I'm leaning more toward violet.

The last question—hobbies? Though my interests have changed, I can yet claim hunting and fishing.

That's it—I'm dull and much more interested in what you would tell me about America and about growing up there. I imagined a rustic, uncultured populace, but since meeting you, I find that concept won't stick. What is your town and home like? And your family? What interests do you have? Why did you come to England? Would you share a story of you as a child?

I suppose that since I've asked you to divulge potentially incriminating details, I should be the one to lead the way.

We have established that I was not the dukelet, but I was also not the spare heir, either. This afforded me more leisure and less expectation than was perhaps prudent for a seven-year-old boy.

Once, I fancied some tiny and rather ugly grey fish I saw in the marsh. Wanting to keep the lumpy little beasts, I gathered them with a cup pilfered from the kitchen into a water basin I retrieved from my room. I scooped dozens into the bowl and went home only to notice they were so thick in that shallow water that they hardly had room to move. Thankfully, my mother, only a month prior, had a small decorative pond installed in the back lawn, and I deposited them inside.

I visited them often and observed them grow more grotesque daily. Soon, as is the way with young boys, my attention turned to some other interest, and I forgot about my charges.

My parents organized a party for the official dukelet's birthday, robbing the schoolrooms of neighboring estates to populate our back lawn. Servants readied the party early that morning, and by noon, we greeted our guests in the ballroom before leading them to tables near the flower gardens.

No sooner were we seated than hordes of greenish-brown frogs hippidy-hopped across the lawn. Girls screamed and boys dropped to their knees, scooping up the amphibians. Mayhem ensued, and more than one frog was launched airborne toward the young girls, landing on tables, dresses, and bonnets.

There it is. I'm a calculating social menace, who had an early start.

I look forward to your reply.

Cora laid the letter on her lap, still laughing at his humor and savoring the friendship evident in it. Though he spoke sparingly in large groups, he shared freely in writing or when they were walking alone. He was a puzzle. But those pieces were coming together for her, and tonight, she would test out her theory. She penned a reply and then went about the day.

As the assembly gathered before dinner, Simon escorted Cora toward several groups of women, introducing her not only to mothers and daughters but also to the men gathered around the edges of the groups.

Again, she wasn't seated anywhere near Simon. She wished she could have more of his company. She noticed, however, that the woman seated on his right must be very engaging, since she monopolized him the entire time.

Although there were dozens of guests at dinner, many of the men evidently took off for cards immediately afterward, leaving Simon and Everett and several other gentlemen in the room busy leading women out for dances. While Everett traveled around the room, seeking his partners, Simon only danced near the music ensemble. Cora also noticed that he always positioned himself to the woman's left to ask her for a dance, then extended his right arm to her when she arose.

Everett at least fulfilled his side of the bargain by introducing her to many men. Each time, though, she found that she compared the men unfavorably to Simon—shorter, older, grouchier, paler. The list went on.

After some time, Simon returned to Cora. "May I have this dance?"

Cora considered how she might uncover his secret, then asked, "I would love to, but it seems so stuffy—may we dance near the doors open to the terrace?"

Simon looked toward the other side of the room and back at the musicians. "Of course."

He led her around the outside perimeter. Although it wasn't a crush, Simon walked as slowly as if it were. Twice, he stopped to make introductions.

So now he's serious about my request? Right now? Suspicious.

By the time they reached the other side of the room, the sets had already formed, and the octet began to play.

"I'm afraid we are too late to join. May I interest you in some punch?"

"Yes. Thank you." While he was gone, Cora positioned herself next to a large potted bush on her left. She squeezed up close enough so the only reasonable places to stand would be directly in front of her, which she had never seen him do, or with her to his left. If she was correct, he wouldn't want to do that, either.

A woman's voice drifted from the other side of the plant. "Yes, His Grace, the Duke of Hertfordshire. I'll be his duchess one day. I just know he is smitten with me. We talked all through dinner."

"Talking doesn't mean he is smitten," another woman answered.

Cora bent back a little to look through some thinner branches and saw the woman who had been seated on Simon's right at dinner.

"I tell you—he is." The woman's voice lowered, and Cora strained to eavesdrop. "He kept looking at my mouth. He seemed quite enamored with my lips. It may seem scandalous except that I'm sure he intends to marry me. I must have captured him completely over dinner and have only to give him some encouragement to bring him up to scratch."

Cora quickly lifted her fan in front of her lips and giggled softly. She could see why the girl might think that, but it was such a leap from dinner conversation to marriage. That was one more piece of evidence—she was sure she had Simon's secret now.

When Simon moved to rejoin her, he stopped two steps away, a glass of punch in each hand, surveying the plant at her side. "May we stand by the terrace doors?" He smiled, but the expression looked almost pleading. "A little breeze might be refreshing."

Cora gave an affirmative nod. "What a wonderful idea."

Simon passed her a glass of punch.

She stood in place for a moment, taking a slow sip of the

drink, then slowly mouthed the words. "Thank you. This is delicious."

"You're welcome," Simon replied aloud and extended his arm to her.

Gotcha!

No sooner had they finished their punch than Wetheridge appeared before Cora. "This is my set, is it not?"

"It is." She handed her glass back to Simon.

Her dance card had been nearly full all night, unlike her first foray into a Victorian ball. More than one pointed remark made it apparent that her status as an heiress had been leaked, and there were many interested in lessening her burden of all that money. *Sheesh.*

The group prepared to leave the house near midnight, early by the standards Cora had witnessed for most parties here. As their carriage made its way to the front of the line, they waited just inside the door. A devilish idea struck Cora for one last test. She hung back, so her face was well lit by the gas light in the entry. When Simon offered his arm to escort her out, she mouthed, "Olive juice."

His eyes widened, and he looked quickly around as if to see if anyone else might have heard her. During his distraction, Cora stepped out the door and walked with haste to the carriage.

Simon caught up to her in time to assist her into the coach and enter himself, abandoning Everett to assist the rest of the ladies.

"I think we need to talk," he said.

"Yes. We do but not here and not tonight. You can visit me tomorrow at Aunt Nellie's. Then I'm going home with May for a week for some events her mother has planned."

"I'm afraid a morning call wouldn't give us the privacy we might need." Simon's voice sounded tight, worried.

"I'm going to exercise early. Come at nine, and we'll have breakfast."

The rest of their party filled the cushioned seats, and the carriage jerked into movement. Although the rest of the group chattered about the dance, Simon sat very still, a grave look on his face. Cora believed that he was considering what to say to her about her little test. She leaned her head back against the squabs and closed her eyes. What had she done? She'd been so caught up in solving Simon's mystery that she'd said something she wished she hadn't. She wished she could pick up a phone and apologize.

If she had met Simon in her own time, she wouldn't have wasted a moment before getting to know him. She was visiting a fantasy world—a place where time was broken. She shouldn't even be here, but she was. And she had hurt a dear friend.

She didn't sleep much that night eager to see him the next day. She had to apologize.

The night drug on as did the morning. At nearly eleven the next morning, Cora looked out her bedroom window, her stomach twisting in nervous knots. Although Simon had agreed to come for breakfast, he hadn't. She wondered for the hundredth time how badly she'd hurt him. It was obvious to her last night that Simon was lip-reading. She also knew that the motion of the lips for "olive juice" was nearly indistinguishable from the motion the lips make to say "I love you."

She hadn't expected him to take the words so seriously, but she knew it was thoughtless. It was a common phrase between people in her century but not here. Had she ruined their ... friendship? She hoped not. A thought clicked in her mind, and she wondered if it was becoming something more than that.

CHAPTER 7

Simon Tuttle

LATE LAST NIGHT UPON ARRIVING HOME AFTER THE PAGEANT, Simon was given a message that an emergency needed his attention at the children's school under his patronage, and he had ridden all night to get there, then turned and ridden for hours again to get back.

Four hours past noon, and eight hours past the time Cora had expected him, Simon's horse, wet from exertion, stopped in front of Twickenham Manor. He had stopped by Everett's rented house in Richmond to shake the road dust from his person and saw the letter intended for Cora sitting on the mail tray. It wasn't meant to be posted, but delivered. That hadn't happened, and he could only imagine the slight she was feeling at his absence.

What would he say to explain it to her? After all, he'd given his word. He didn't have an excuse he could share, so he planned just to beg forgiveness as he approached the door.

"Miss Rey will join you momentarily." The butler pointed him to the parlor.

Simon nodded his understanding and sat on the edge of the sofa only to stand immediately. His emotions felt much too jittery to sit. He wondered if Cora would forgive his absence. He walked back and forth on the wool carpet in the small room. He would offer no excuses—simply apologize, and if that didn't work, he'd walk away with his pride. He wouldn't grovel.

He wondered what Cora had meant last night, saying she loved him. It couldn't be. But if it were, what would he do? That question had plagued him on his ride last night, and he seemed to repeat it to every tree he passed along the way. Since he hadn't kept his word to return before breakfast this morning, it was likely she didn't feel that way anymore. A man who didn't keep promises was not to be trusted with a woman's heart. He stopped suddenly and placed his hand on the top of a wingback chair. Could he have her heart? If not now, someday?

He realized that her opinion of him was as important as breathing. He wanted her love and her trust. He knew what he must do—he'd grovel.

Cora joined him a moment after his decision. "I missed you this morning."

Simon wasn't sure if he heard her right. The tone seemed kind, matching the look on her face. She continued. "Something must have come up. I'm glad you still came. We have little privacy here. Would you like to go for a walk, or shall we call for a tray?"

Simon's heart continued to race. It would be nice to continue moving for the conversation to come. "A walk, then tea."

Cora smiled. "I feel the same."

Of all the things she could say, Simon realized he could read too much into those four words. Did she feel a longing and closeness forming between the two? Did she feel the air sparking with hope?

The path in the garden was filled with tiny white seashells that crunched underfoot. Cora led him over to a bench set in a little courtyard of rosebushes. She sat, then stood and moved to the other side to be on his right.

"I wrote you a letter this morning. I hadn't decided if I would send it." She pulled a folded linen page from a pocket. "I'd like you to read it."

She placed it in his hand, and Simon read the lettering on the front. "To Cousin Simon."

His heart pinched as he stared at the word "cousin." He slid his finger behind the wafer and unfolded it, revealing a few scant lines. She sat entirely too close for his eyes to attend to the page, but he forced them to focus on the writing.

Dear—Oh, I quit. I'll never figure out how titles here work.

Dear Simon,

She had penned his name—the only one that really belonged to him. He was again filled with hope that she saw him as no one else had. He read on.

Hearing doesn't define you.

She knows. Panic flashed through his chest. To have his impairment openly revealed, after he and his family had carefully covered it for the past few years, left him vulnerable. If others came to know of his condition, would he be ostracized? And what of his sisters—would his injury ruin their chances?

Simon reread the line. *She knows but isn't repulsed by me. In fact, it sounds hopeful.* Was America truly such a different place that she would overlook what he saw as a serious limitation? He refocused on her words and finished the letter.

Sincerely,

Cora

P.S. Olive juice.

Simon read the last two words. Had he read them right? He looked again and felt his brow scrunch with confusion. Cora's hand came to rest on his arm, and he turned toward her.

She didn't meet his gaze but continued to tap the fingers of her other hand against her knee. "There's no easy way to say this. When you said that you were acting as my near relative, I guess I relaxed around you. Too much." Her eyes lifted to his. "I'm sorry I teased you last night. You've been a puzzle, a mystery, and I thought I had all the pieces, so … so I was testing you. I'm sorry. I wouldn't have risked our friendship for the world. Please say that you forgive me."

They sat silently, Cora looking eager for his reply.

"What does *this* mean?" he asked, pointing to the last line. "I know what it is, just not why it's in your letter."

"That says 'olive juice.'"

This time, Simon saw the movement of her lips, and since she sat very near him on the small bench, he heard the words. He nodded and looked away. She hadn't been offering him her heart. In fact, she firmly considered him either family or a friend—a friend who would help her find a husband. A friend she could tease without worry of being taken seriously.

A fireball of pain volleyed through his chest. She knew his secret and didn't consider him a candidate for herself. For months, since deciding to return to society, he'd worried about what would happen if someone found out. Now he knew—despair. If he was honest about it, he would admit that this was just what he expected.

Simon, realizing that his shoulders had slumped, and his head hung down, sat up on the bench. "Of course I forgive you. I never imagined that you offered me an insult."

She also hadn't offered him her heart or her future. He would re-correct his course—he would marry for convenience to gain an heir. Nothing more.

He stood and helped her from the bench. When Simon began to turn back toward the house, Cora asked, "Shall we see if the hollyhocks have bloomed before we go back?"

They walked several paces, Cora's small hand tugging gently with each step before he said, "You very cleverly failed to answer a single question I asked in my last letter to you." Simon gave her a sideways smile. "Perhaps you could bare your soul as we walk."

"I don't have any stories as good as yours. I wish I could have seen the frogs at the birthday party."

"It's not something one is likely to forget. To this day, I can't hear the word 'frog' without imagining the creatures plopping into the punch or some rather expensive cake."

"And to call yourself the ugly duke-ling ... " She laughed.

Simon enjoyed the bright smile with it and the crinkle around her eyes. Yes, if she offered friendship, he'd accept it. "No more about me. We are halfway through the garden, and I haven't learned anything new about you. Start with an easy one—your town or your home, perhaps."

"Hmm, my home. We lived in a red brick home on Quail Run Road. We lived removed from other children, and my best friends were my horses. I spent long hours playing music, too. It was a passion of my father's, and it made me feel closer to him. He was all I had. My mother died when I was young, so after that, it was just my father and me."

"I'm sorry for your loss." Simon interrupted. "Do you remember her?"

"I remember her hands, gentle and expressive, and a few other things, but as time goes on, I doubt all of them. Sometimes I find that a memory of her was just a picture I'd seen of her."

"Your father raised you?"

"Yes. We were very close. I lost him three years ago." Her eyes glanced away from him and blinked quickly.

"I'm sorry. I chose a sad topic."

She shook her head. "Not sad, just precious." She smiled, then continued. "It's funny—though I miss him every day, I think more about the good years we had together than when he died."

Simon watched as Cora paused to pull a weed that was encroaching on the pathway. As if she thought nothing of the helpful act, she continued her story. "He was a scholar. He loved to study ancient peoples. He had heavy leather-bound books about the places around the world, and while other girls were being tucked into bed with lullabies or fairy tales, he read to me about ancient Roman aqueducts or the production of silk in China thousands of years ago. I don't remember most of what we read, but I'll always remember how it felt."

Together they turned the last corner and headed out of the garden back to the house.

"He sounds like he was an interesting man. I would have liked to meet him."

"He would have liked you, too." Cora stopped then, her eyes nearly squinting with thought, perhaps debating what she was going to say next. Simon could see it in her eyes when she decided to trust him. "My father had normal hearing, but my mother was Deaf from birth. I'm CODA, Child of Deaf Adult."

Simon felt his mouth drop open. He couldn't imagine Cora's mother getting a chance to marry and have a family. And she married a scholar. That wouldn't have happened here. Is that why Cora was comfortable with him even knowing his secret?

She began walking again. "That's part of what I meant when I wrote that your hearing doesn't define you. It just doesn't. You're more than sound waves and ear drums."

"Thank you." He felt a relief to have his secret known by someone and to be accepted. He was sure that wouldn't be the reaction he always received.

Simon swallowed, dragging courage from his chest. "I only recently lost my hearing. Three years ago."

"Late deafened. That's what we call it."

Simon nodded. "I had an injury followed by a severe fever. I lived, but my hearing wasn't the same. My family sent me to Scotland. I doubt they ever expected me to return, but then I had to assume the role of duke." It felt good to tell someone, especially her.

Cora's hand covered Simon's with a gentle squeeze. They stopped, this time gazing at each other. The air seemed thick between them. Although Simon knew he couldn't, *shouldn't* kiss her, he also knew that's exactly what he intended to do. Cora's lips parted, and just the tip of her pink tongue peeked out above her teeth.

Before he lowered his head to hers, she broke the connection and took another step toward the house. "You also asked what I do with my time. Will you keep my secret if I tell you?"

"If you will keep mine." Simon cocked his head and smiled broadly through his pain. She really didn't have amorous feelings for him. However, he would gladly take what she offered.

"Deal," she said, giving him a firm handshake. They continued across the lawn. "I'm a teacher. I teach students who are differently abled than most children. Some are hard of hearing, and some mute. Some have difficulty learning or interacting with others. They are my children for as long as I'm allowed to teach them. Although I don't need to work, it gives me great joy."

Simon was stunned. She worked. He strangely found that he admired her for it. Perhaps because it was something else they had in common—wishing all children to learn and caring for those society would shun. Before he had a chance to tell her about his school, the door to the house opened, and her American friend Reese came out. He hadn't been in the company of the other Americans since Cora was spending most of her time with Lady May Cottrell.

"Are you staying for tea?" Reese asked Simon.

"I am."

"Cyrus, Jem, and Kaitlyn are here. It's almost like a little party." She walked with them into the manor house.

After the group had been served, Cora gave a dainty cough. "I seem to have a *frog* in my throat."

Simon was grateful he hadn't moved his teacup away from his lips as he struggled to swallow the tea before he laughed. Cora met his eye. She looked guilty, like she had done that on purpose.

Polite conversation continued about the fair weather they'd been having and the beauty of the home. When the conversation turned to comparing England to the United States, Cora asked, "'The Ugly Duke-ling' is quite a popular tale there. Is it common here? I mean, duckling."

Again, Simon had just lifted his cup to his mouth. Her cup was in front of her lips as well, but just to hide a smirk, which he could clearly see. Cora's eyes danced with delight above the rim at the private joke. The air nearly left his lungs—she could do that to him with only a glance. He thought of the happiness he would win if he could look across the room at her face for the rest of his life. She'd made it clear that she considered him a friend, but she hadn't explicitly ruled out being something more. He hoped the possibility might yet be there.

CHAPTER 8

Cora Rey

Cora winced as she sat heavily in the chair on the veranda at May's home. She would be spending a few days with the Cottrell family and get to see more of England.

The backs of her thighs and glutes were tight. She had put herself through an exceptionally tough workout that morning. She'd been slacking lately, and she'd only been here a couple of weeks. Missed days here and there were adding up. She'd made up for it today—a full hour of fast-paced high jumps and kicks, duck, weave, strike, lunge—she knew she'd feel it in her legs. Honestly, it was the time spent on squat jumps that turned her legs to jelly.

May, sinking slowly toward the cushioned chair, looked every bit as sore as Cora felt. She scowled all the way down. Although she hadn't the rigor in her workout that Cora had, she'd had enough. From the comfort of the seat, she said, "Thank you for enlightening me with a new way to 'take a walk.' I'm now aware of muscles I didn't think a lady even had."

"It won't feel so bad tomorrow." *Or it will feel worse.* Cora took a deep breath and blew it out. *Fine. If I just sit here, I'm fine.*

Tomorrow? May mouthed, and Cora nodded enthusiastically.

Lady Cottrell, trailed by several women, stepped onto the terrace. May and Cora grimaced and stood to greet them. Both the young women's lips pressed in a straight line to approximate a smile, but it didn't work. Cora suspected they looked pained. They were joining Lady Cottrell for a light meal with her closest friends. Just as the burn was leaving Cora's legs, Mrs. Cottrell motioned her attention to the women. "We won't stand on formality with this group of friends." She leaned toward Cora and said with a conspiratorial whisper, "You'll see why soon." The servants were dismissed, then Lady Cottrell continued.

"Cora, may I introduce you to my best friends, Cassia, Shamay, and Idelisa."

"Hello. It's a pleasure," Cora replied.

Shamay, a woman with rich brown hair and eyes, stepped toward her. "Pleased to meet you, mon petite." She kissed Cora on each cheek and stepped aside as Cassia moved forward.

The large black-haired woman had a mischievous smile and eyes that twinkled. "Salve. You are among friends," Cassia said.

Idelisa smiled. "Welcome. I'm pleased to know you." Her accent was thick and lilting with a song-like cadence.

Lady Cottrell led the women to be seated, poured out cups of tea, and then pinned Cora with a look. "Each of us traveled through the ley lines to this place. As you did." Lady Cottrell took one sip. "My name is *Bethany* Cottrell. I'd like you to call me Bethany."

Cora scanned the women's faces. Each one seemed to be gauging her response. Then she looked at May. "You knew this? About me?"

"I thought it was possible, and then I asked my mother, and she confirmed it." May answered. "You just seemed so new to all of this that it could make sense. Not only that you didn't belong in England, but you didn't belong in this *year,* either."

"I'm glad I was visiting Aunt Nellie the day you arrived. We actually have a lot in common. I'll get to that later," Lady Cottrell added. "And since you and May seemed to have become fast friends, I decided to invite you here to meet the others. We use first names when we gather though we use the names society demands outside of our private meetings."

Cora's thoughts began to unscramble. Of course she knew there had been others to make the trip as she had. Nellie had a whole room that looked like a costume rental business. She just hadn't thought about it past that. "Where are you from?"

Bethany spoke up first. "I'm from Arizona. I was twenty years old when I came to England for spring break in 2011." Cora gasped, but Bethany continued her story. "That was nearly thirty years ago. I've been back to my century four times for the birth of each of my children."

May laughed softly. "I'm officially a U.S. citizen. I fell back through time while my mother still carried me. As an infant, I came through with Mum, so I have a portrait I can pass through."

"We should be about the same age," Cora said to Lady Cottrell. "That's a little more than crazy. I'm also about the same age as your daughter."

"Yes and no," Bethany replied. "We would have been similar in age had we both stayed in the same century, but I've accumulated more years because I went back in time farther than you did."

Cora looked at the group. How often had this happened? Obviously many more times than she'd ever considered. That explained the large room of historical clothes at Twickenham Manor.

Idelisa reached across to Cora's arm. With a rich accent she said, "Since you and your friends have come, I'm not the newest anymore. I've been here a little less than a year. My old place was a land you call Ireland. I came forward in time more than two thousand years."

Cora imagined that her expression looked thunderstruck. She felt it. She imagined it had taken a whole pot of Aunt Nellie's tea to sufficiently explain Idelisa's time shift to her.

"I came forward, too, almost that much, just under two thousand years for me," Cassia said. "I'm Roman. I traveled with the army that invaded Britain. I've been here nearly twenty years."

Shamay returned her cup to the saucer. "I was born five hundred years ago in France. My father brought me to England to escape the Black Death. The ley lines took me even farther away, but I'm happy to have come forward in time. Life is so much better now." Cassia and Idelisa nodded in agreement.

"How could we all come to this time and place?" Cora asked.

All five women answered in unison, repeating Nellie's explanation. "Time is a fuzzball." The women laughed together.

They settled into lunch and conversations about the upcoming events planned at the Cottrells' home this week. After the lunch, the ladies said their goodbyes, and May and Cora followed Lady Cottrell to the morning room for visits.

Cora wondered about what Lady Cottrell had said—that she went to her own time to have her children, and then came back. That eased her mind about Aunt Nellie being able to send them all back on the next full moon. She still had half a month to enjoy this vacation.

May sat on the sofa near the windows and took up her needlework while Lady Cottrell did the same in a chair near the fireplace. Cora's fingers still hurt from the clumsy attempts she'd made at needlepoint at Nellie's house.

"Do you play?" Lady Cottrell asked.

Cora's mind blanked. How could she redirect that question without being rude or lying? She couldn't. "Sometimes."

"Would it be all right if you played a song or two? I find it so relaxing. It's been a very busy day, has it not?"

"What would you like to hear?" Cora asked, her hand resting on the corner of the piano. She was stalling, partly grateful that she hadn't had much time to think about the performance. Still her hands shook beside her, and she fisted the material of her skirt in her palms to stop it. However, she knew it would stop as she continued to play—getting started was the worst part. Her stage fright was more intense in anticipation than in the performance.

"Nothing too complicated. Just some background tune to soothe us all," Lady Cottrell answered.

Cora nodded her assent, sat, and adjusted the seat. She began Chopin's "Prelude in E-Minor." The beginning movement was tentative and clear, easing her into the music. Her fingers seemed to limber up with each note, and her back relaxed.

In moments, the notes and rhythm absorbed her, her fingers striking the keys, but her heart revisited her memories. This song had always reminded her of her family. The rhythmic notes from the left hand steady and sure like her father. Then the right hand began speaking, almost pleading, much like herself as a child, trying, learning, growing. In the last movement, the emotion took on a sad, contemplative stance. And then there was silence, and Cora felt alone in the world. She completed the prelude, then without interruption slipped into another Chopin piece and another.

When the resonance of the final key faded, Lady Cottrell whispered, "Thank you."

Cora, suddenly aware of the audience, faced the women, noticing the unshed tears in their eyes. Cora, too, had to regain her composure like coming out of a dream—the music and memories still swirled within her. This alone made it worth playing the piano and facing the fear that tried to push her away from it.

After their time in the parlor, May and Cora went for a walk in the only bright sunshine they'd had that day. An hour later, when they reentered the parlor, they were surprised to see Lady Cottrell chatting with several young men. The guests stood abruptly and greeted May and Cora.

"I just ordered a tea service. You'll join us, won't you?" Lady Cottrell asked with a smirk that said she found this sudden interest of so many eligible gentlemen very entertaining.

"Yes. Of course." May nodded to the room full of men. "We'll just freshen up and come back down." She stepped into the hall, pulling Cora by the hand. "Excuse us." They walked quietly around the corner and up the grand staircase.

At the top, Cora broke the silence. "Were you expecting them?"

May paused. "Not specifically, but I thought it a possibility because you came. There's quite an interest building among the gentry and some nobility to attend our little luncheon auction tomorrow. Of course, we sent out more invitations than we thought might be accepted, but Mother's been receiving an unusual number of acceptances the past two days." May turned into Cora's bedroom instead of her own. "From men." She pulled off her bonnet.

Each woman smoothed her hair, shook out her dress, and returned downstairs. The men jumped up again. Cora wondered if she would ever get used to that. Although an outdated and abandoned ritual of chivalry in her century, Cora found she liked it. It was nice to be acknowledged whenever she entered.

The tea and cakes had been delivered in their absence, and May's mother poured them each a cup. The men approached the young women, announcing their names and greeting them. Cora wished she had noticed who had been sitting where, so she could take a seat and not displace anyone. In the end, she and May choose a settee together. Most of the men crowded around—some in chairs, some standing.

"Miss Rey, will you be staying for the charity event?" asked the Honorable Vernon Shelby. He was wearing a red coat with yellow-and-red striped pants. Cora could see why Simon had referred to him as a fop. It wasn't just the colors. He had a matching silk hankie peeking out of the pocket on his left breast. Each button on both the coat and vest were jeweled, and he wore several rings. Finally, his necktie was trimmed with lace—lots of lace.

Cora pulled her attention back to him. "Oh, yes. I can hardly wait. Will any of you be attending as well?"

The men's answers chimed over each other's, some asking to escort Cora or May, and some suggesting other diversions.

May answered, "We won't make any promises for partners.

We'll just have to see how it falls out tomorrow. You'll have to bid for the favor of our company. It's for charity, after all."

The conversation continued on benign subjects, and Cora's attention drifted, taking in the men in attendance.

Lord Wetheridge slouched in the chair beside the fireplace, looking utterly bored. He roused himself once or twice to laugh or sigh at a comment made in the group. Cora caught him staring her way a few times though. *Why was he so antisocial?* Not that she thought that every man should pay court to them, but since he knew her, and he was here, it seemed rude to ignore the company.

On the other side of the room, the Honorable Michael Wyndham stood near the doorway. Occasionally, he looked as if he might join the conversation. But just as often, he looked through the door, perhaps planning his escape. He was very young—too young, Cora decided, for either May or herself to be interested.

Although suitors surrounded Cora, her attention was not fully given to them. She wondered why Simon hadn't come that morning—well, afternoon. She would never get used to the idea of sleeping until noon and having breakfast. And morning calls, they were in the afternoon, too.

When Cora refocused on the conversation, she realized that she and May would take a morning ride with Lord Bellion and Mr. Echols tomorrow.

Lady Cottrell spoke up. "I'm sure my son, James, will join you as well. I expect he'll arrive before supper. There's nothing like a ride in the morning air to make you appreciate a warm breakfast."

"I look forward to seeing Lord Cottrell again," Lord Bellion replied.

Cora noticed Lord Bellion's slight reaction before he smiled and responded. Was it a surprise that May's brother was expected? Or was he affronted that Lady Cottrell felt the women needed that type of protection?

The next morning, May and Cora donned riding habits and headed downstairs.

"Are you sure you won't join us?" May asked her mother as May walked with Cora to the stables.

"Not this time. Your brother will take good care of you on the ride, or perhaps Lord Bellion will misstep treating you properly, and James will shoot him." Her words came out with a little giggle. "With Bellion's reputation, I doubt it would be much of a surprise to our other guests, but it could dampen the mood at the picnic. Anyway, I have much to do to be ready for the party this afternoon."

"Thank you for loaning me a riding dress." Cora loved the navy blue wool suit fashioned with a split skirt that would allow her to ride astride.

As Cora and May approached the small paddock just outside the stables, five horses stood near the fence—three beautiful stallions and two equally beautiful mares.

"All Thoroughbreds." Cora gave a soft whistle and asked May with a bit of awe in her voice, "Which horse is yours?"

"The pretty chestnut mare on the end. Her name is Taffy."

Cora noted that the horse didn't sport a sidesaddle. "And which belongs to James?"

"Well, technically, they all do, since my brother fancies himself a horse breeder. They're part of James' breeding program. His favorite is the tall black next to Taffy." May pointed her crop toward to the far right. "He's aptly named Satan."

He and a gray appeared high-spirited, dancing in place as they approached. Two of the horses had been chosen for the ladies and one, presumably for Cora, was already prepared with a sidesaddle. "Apparently, I'm to ride the other mare."

May shook her head slightly. "You're here first. Choose the one you want."

May approached Taffy, murmuring softly and pushing her hand from the muzzle to forehead and back again.

If Cora had known there were horses like this in the stables, she would've been out for a ride every day. She planned to make good use of the habit she'd borrowed. She doubted it was quite the thing since it was a split skirt. Apparently, the women in this family didn't ride sidesaddle either.

Cora approached the dapple gray. "What's his name?" The horse, its coat like liquid silver in the sunlight, stood at least seventeen hands high.

"Cricket. He's quite the jumper."

"Great. He's mine." Cora led him to a mounting block and swung into the saddle before a groom could stop her or help her.

The groom rushed to her side. "He's a spirited horse. I have a gentler mare you could take. May I help you get off?"

"Maybe in an hour or two," she responded.

May sat atop her mare and turned her to approach Cora, calling over her shoulder to the groom, "You'll need to change out that sidesaddle before the men join us." The ladies walked their horses to the far end of the paddock when the gentleman arrived.

James called out, "May, how did you find another hoyden to befriend?" Then he said toward Mr. Echols, "Sorry, old man. There's only a sidesaddle left. You don't mind, do you?"

Lord Bellion laughed along, but Mr. Echols seemed affronted by the suggestion.

The groom, with the precision of a NASCAR pit crew, quickly exchanged the saddle, so Mr. Echols could join them.

As they rode out, James placed himself between May and the cad, Lord Bellion. Cora and Mr. Echols followed behind for several minutes. She could tell that her horse didn't like to be in the back. His ears twitched while he strained at the reins. Though she held him to the walk, he would have none of it. He danced a little to the side and snorted, tossing his head.

"Cricket doesn't really like being in the back, and it looks like your horse agrees. What do you think, Mr. Echols? Are you and Homer ready to take the lead with us?" she asked. Without waiting for an answer, Cora nudged her horse forward to trot in front of the other three.

Behind her, Mr. Echols called, "You don't know the lay of the land." However, she knew he must have followed her forward because he continued his argument quite close to her and much louder than necessary. "It seems *prudent* that we should *stay* in the *back*."

Cora wondered if he knew he was annoying as he chastised her or if he did it unconsciously. "Oh, well, it looks like it's too late for that." She patted Cricket's neck. "See how happy he is when he's the leader?"

Cora twisted to talk to the group behind her. "Shall we give them their heads, and run a bit?" She heard Mr. Echols snort beside her, but she didn't look his way. It sounded like a good idea to gallop and not be expected to converse with the man beside her.

"I won't be running today. Taffy and I never do," May said.

"We'll just enjoy the scenery and conversation, then" Cora answered but doubted it was possible.

Mr. Echols asked, "Are you enjoying your trip so far, Miss Rey?"

Cora could think of a thousand different ways to answer that question, and none of them would be truthful. Yes, she was enjoying it, but it was so much more than she had ever imagined her trip to England might be.

"From what I've seen so far, England is a beautiful country. Perhaps the best part, though, is making a dear friend."

"Of course girls need their little friends, don't they?" He chuckled.

Cora turned and looked at him, but there was merriment in his eyes, and she thought perhaps she had misunderstood him with the cultural gap.

"Why did you come to the house party, Mr. Echols?"

"Oh, to snap up one of the young girls. I have need of a wife, and I hope one attending might do."

She wasn't about to follow that line of questioning—new subject. "What are your interests?" she asked.

"Nothing a woman would be interested in, really. I'm not much of a dancer. I don't give a fig about fashions, and the latest gossip is of no interest to me." He nodded his head with a firm shake on the last phrase as if he were punctuating the end. Did he think that's what she was interested in?

A Victorian dating game was obviously harder than she'd thought it would be, but she tried again. "Now that you've said what you're *not* interested in, what is it you do?" Cora asked.

"I doubt you'd understand—financial interests, land management, seeing to the needs of the peasants."

Cora rolled her eyes. *I doubt he has peasants.*

"But I do enjoy a bit of good horseflesh. It is the right of man to subdue all those around him, and subduing a horse is possibly one of the highest achievements—next to matrimony, of course."

Cora wondered if there was any way to keep him from talking about women. "Do you keep horses, Mr. Echols?"

"One of the finest stables. Though I don't say so myself, but it has been bandied about that I keep one of the finest in all of Suffolk County. Of course I would never say that myself, but many have said so about me. Many of the finest horses in all of England can trace their roots back to sires on my property with thanks as well to my father and grandfather and his father before him."

This seemed like a safe topic—keep him talking about horses. "Which breed do you have, and how do you train them?"

"I don't. I hire men to train them." He paused, and Cora racked her brain to think of another question that he might like to answer. Before she could, Mr. Echols added, "It seems unbecoming and vulgar for a woman to show interest in horse breeding and training, but then, you are an American."

Jerk! Cora decided to enjoy the ride and ignore the man. She again twisted back toward May. "I think Cricket would like a challenge. What's beyond the curve in the trail in front of us?"

However, it was James who answered. "There is a course of sorts—gates to jump, hedges, fences, a creek, and that sort of thing."

"Is the course clearly marked?" she asked. James nodded, and Cora added, "Then let's have a contest before we head home. It will add a little excitement to the morning. It seems my horse is too spirited to settle for a sedate walk."

Mr. Echols sniffed in prelude to a comment Cora was pretty sure she didn't want to hear. "Women are delicate and fragile. To goad one into a competition is ungentlemanly. I would never disgrace myself in that way."

Called it. Cora couldn't help but wonder if he would think her roundhouse kick was delicate. "Since I am just an American, as you say, it seems that you would hardly be racing a *lady* at all."

Lord Bellion commented on his way past the pair, "Echols, do you merely sell horses, or do you ride them too?"

Cora heard the challenge in his remark.

Echols replied, "Who am I to disallow a lady to have a little pleasure?" He nodded toward Cora as he doffed his hat.

James rode up between Cora and Mr. Echols. "Let's start at that lone tree beside the road. Lord Bellion and I will go first. Then the two of you will race."

May chimed in. "I'll be the judge and await the group at that hill. I'll ride along the course, so you can see it. When I wave, the race starts."

When May settled at the end, James and Lord Bellion ran the course.

Cora watched the men swing to the right and the horses jump first a pole fence, then a pile of logs before the trail turned back on itself. The obstacles along that stretch were a hedge and a hill with a stack of logs on the downhill side. The final leg of the course required the horses to jump a fence, land in water, and then jump back out over a pole. The end of the race was marked with a narrow gate that would only allow one horse through—Satan and James were the winners.

May made eye contact with Cora as she held her horse side by side with Mr. Echols. With a wave, May signaled the start of the race.

Cricket and Homer jumped anxiously into the race, neck and neck through the fence and log jumps. As they rounded the corner,

Mr. Echols took a slight lead heading toward the hedge. He kept that lead as they ran toward the final obstacle, and by the time his horse descended toward the water, Mr. Echols was far out of position, leaning forward instead of back for his horse's landing.

Cora concentrated on her own position, leaning well back on her seat. From the corner of her eye, she saw Mr. Echols tumble over the front of his horse into the creek as her horse leaped out of the water on the other side, then went on to finish the course.

On the way back to the house, May rode beside Lord Bellion. James and Cora chatted happily. Mr. Echols was completely silent. Cora wished she'd thought of this earlier. During the ride home, she admitted that she wasn't playing the bachelorette game very well, considering she was finding reasons to disqualify each potential suitor. Again, none of them compared to Simon. He was the spoiler—the Mr. Darcy to make everyone else pale into a Mr. Collins.

When they returned, Lady Cottrell paused while walking past the stables with several gardeners following in her wake carrying baskets of vegetables. "How was your ride?" she asked.

Cora looked toward Mr. Echols, then back to Lady Cottrell and said with a wink, "Bruising."

Cora changed into a deep green dress with small colorful flowers lining the neck and hem. She also picked up the bonnet with the bright orange bow Simon had teased her about.

May likewise changed and met Cora in the hall then walked with her to the parlor. When they entered, Lady Cottrell rose. "We're all here. If you'll follow me to the dining room, we'll get started." More than a dozen young women chatted excitedly at they walked together.

Silk flowers, bright ribbons, and small crafted birds and animals littered the dining table. Spaced along the edges sat fifteen baskets. Each basket was identical.

"Today's box lunch will be an auction. The gentlemen will pay for having the favor of eating with you ladies. The meals will be the same, but you will decorate a basket," Lady Cottrell announced. "They will be presented by the servants. None of the men will know which basket belongs to which lady, but by purchasing the basket, they arrange to have lunch with you."

A few of the girls giggled with excitement. Clearly they were enjoying the mystery of this as much as they hoped the men would. More than once, Cora heard the names "Hertfordshire" or "Albans" whispered. Apparently, she wasn't the only one who wished for Simon's company that day. It was possible that another man could win her basket. She had a hard time imagining which of the gentlemen she would rather sit with for the picnic. None.

May got right to work. She walked along the table choosing anything that was pink—pink lace, pink bows, pink flowers, and even a pink ostrich feather. She gathered her arms full, taking all the pink with her, before returning to a basket at the end of the table. She methodically began choosing arrangements, holding this grouping or that grouping up for scrutiny. When she was satisfied, she tied them onto her basket.

Cora realized that May's dress was completely pink as well. She was certain the color was meant to signal Lord Saalfeld to purchase May's basket. It was a brilliant idea.

How could she signal Simon? She looked down at her dress—too many colors. That wouldn't work. Then she recalled his fascination with her little purse at Nellie's picnic. Cora left the dining hall and bounded up the staircase to her room. Searching through her trunks, she found the little yellow silk purse and hurried back downstairs.

Cora chose one flower of each color from her dress and tucked the stems inside the little purse. Its strings were wound around the top of the handle of the basket. It hung down like a dainty potted plant. She pulled the orange ribbon from her bonnet and tied it on top of the handle in a large bow with the tails hanging down to each side.

When all the baskets were completed, Cora was impressed with the talents the women displayed in the floral arrangements. The servants came in and picked up the baskets, carrying them outside, the ladies following behind. At Cora's side, May was wearing the pink ostrich feather in her hat.

The baskets were arranged on a long table, and Lord Cottrell stood before them to explain the auction. "Thank you, ladies. The baskets are lovely." He nodded with acknowledgement to the women. Toward the men seated a few feet away, he said, "The highest bidder among you will win the corresponding lady's company for lunch. When a basket is purchased, the lady belonging to that basket will stand and take the basket to the gentleman. Then they will find a blanket where they will enjoy their meal al fresco." He waved his hand toward the blankets arranged in the shadows at the edge of the woods.

Lady Cottrell added, "I'm sorry to say that there are more gentlemen than ladies this afternoon, so bid to win. Remember, this charity event will provide children with warm coats, blankets, and shoes for the coming winter. With all my heart, I say that your generosity is greatly appreciated."

Lord Cottrell placed his hand on the small of his wife's back and was rewarded with a loving smile. The warmth of their relationship was clear to Cora. She could see why Bethany chose to stay. She chose *him*, and he happened to live in the nineteenth century.

The Cottrells' butler ceremoniously held up the first basket. Cora was impressed that none of the women gave away the ownership. The bidding started at two pounds and sold for fifteen. As if that set the going price, each basket sold for between ten and twenty pounds, but the men made a sport of it, bidding such and such pounds and so many shillings.

May leaned toward Cora. "That amount of money probably doesn't mean much to you, but it's roughly the cost of the yearly salary for a maid." Cora gave her a surprised look, and May replied, "They are being extremely generous. Mother will be thrilled."

Several baskets were dispersed. Cora was glad to see that Mr. Echols and Lord Bellion won bids on lunches early.

Next, the butler held the very pink basket aloft. Lord Cottrell looked at his wife, who hid a smile behind her hand. They knew their daughter well. "Where shall we start the bidding this time?" he asked her, teasing their daughter and the audience. She whispered something in his ear, and he smiled broadly. "Excellent idea. The bidding will start at twenty pounds, which I bid myself. I think I should quite enjoy this little meal."

The crowd laughed, but May's countenance was quizzical.

"Are there any other bids?" Without waiting for a response, he said, "If not, I should like to—"

"Fifty pounds."

Cora saw May gasp. All eyes turned toward Lord Saalfeld, who had been sitting beside Everett and Simon but now was standing, boldly eyeing Lord Cottrell.

Before Lord Cottrell could give another bid, Lady Cottrell shouted, "Sold to Lord Saalfeld. The children thank you."

After a moment of stunned silence, Lord Cottrell said, "Yes, well, that's the spirit," though Cora thought his sentiment was more like *"Well, should I suspect your motives?"*

May jumped up without looking toward her parents and retrieved the basket, then the couple retired to a blanket to watch the rest of the bidding.

There were only three baskets left. The butler stepped over and raised Cora's basket as Lord Cottrell shouted, "Who'll start us off?"

"Twenty pounds." That was the first bid Wetheridge had made on any basket yet. Did he know it was hers?

"Fifty pounds." All eyes swung toward Simon at the other end of the men's group. He obviously didn't expect to be challenged on his bid and gazed expectantly toward Lord Cottrell to grant him the purchase.

"Fifty-five pounds." Wetheridge turned to face Simon.

Seemingly without thought, though Cora saw Everett tap Simon's boot with his own, Simon bid. "Sixty pounds."

Wetheridge paused. His jaw was set, and he clenched it twice before speaking again. "Sixty-five pounds."

The watching audience was completely silent. Cora sneaked a look at May. While many people's faces had the look of watching a carriage accident, May had a broad smile, and she was nearly strangling Lord Saalfeld's arm with excitement.

Simon stared straight ahead, calling out, "Seventy pounds." Cora made eye contact with him. Just one side of his lips tipped up in a smile, but she quickly glanced away not to give away her own elation.

Wetheridge had considered each time he'd countered Simon. He paused, and the whole group waited to see if he would raise the bid or wave off the auction. "Seventy-five pounds." His voice was not as strong as it had been just moments ago.

This time Simon stood, making direct eye contact with Lord Wetheridge before calling out, "One hundred pounds." He looked expectantly at the man. There was no doubt to Cora, or possibly anyone watching the scene, that Simon planned to win the lunch at any cost, and that price would be above what Wetheridge could afford. Maybe it already was.

Some anger shown in Wetheridge's eyes, or maybe it was disdain. He called out, "I concede to His Grace. May you enjoy the spoils with lovely company." To the rest of the group, he said, "It must be nice to be a duke."

Cora picked up the basket and made her way to Simon, who stood with the kind of smile she'd witnessed on Lord Cottrell when he looked at his wife. Immediately, Simon took the basket from her hands, offered his elbow to her, and escorted her to the blanket with Saalfeld and May.

As they approached, Cora could feel the stupid smile she must have on her face but couldn't remove it. May jumped up and hugged her. Saalfeld just raised a quizzical eyebrow toward Simon.

Without being asked, Simon justified the purchase by saying, "It was rumored that the plates in *this* basket were gold."

"That must be American gold." Saalfeld laughed and added, "Or perhaps it was rumored that it belonged to a certain American with golden hair."

Everett purchased Lucy's basket. Twice he bid against himself to raise the price to the delight of both Lucy and the gathered crowd. He and Lucy joined Saalfeld and Simon on their blanket.

At the end of the auction, Lady Cottrell stood before the group. "Thank you for your generous donations to the children's school. If you were not lucky enough to purchase a basket, the earl and I invite you to dine with us. If you would like to make a small donation, please speak to Lord Cottrell before you leave this evening."

After her speech, Lady Cottrell approached Wetheridge. "It's so good to see you, Charles. How is your mother?" She led him to a blanket with a large basket and several other guests. Lord Cottrell did the same with other guests.

The men seemed starved, digging into the baskets and laying out the goodies they found within. Simon peeked inside a linen napkin and showed Cora the fruit turnovers. He set each new item out within arm's reach. A miniature banquet littered the blanket—a variety of cold meats and cheeses, grapes, biscuits, and a tub of stewed berries. From the bottom of the basket, he retrieved plates and silverware, and then began serving.

Cora could feel her heart bobbing against her ribs. It didn't just feel good only because he purchased the basket for a large amount, but because it was worth it to him to sit with her for a luncheon. And she knew she was returning that regard.

For the sake of sparing them both when she left, she hoped she mistook his glance. She hoped she was reading more into it than he was feeling. But a little voice whispered behind those thoughts, saying she hoped he was falling for her the way she was falling for him. With that, she stopped herself. *I won't let it go any further—just friends.*

Cora thought she saw more than appreciation in his eyes as they sat next to each other enjoying lunch. It was heady to realize that such an amazing person wanted her company. A small bit of doubt and guilt quickly sank into her chest. Would she break his heart if she left? *When* she left? With this game of bachelorette, was she playing with Simon's feelings?

After they had eaten, they were invited to enjoy the garden or to wander the path through the forest, or the woods, as they called them. Couples joined together to take a walk around the estate. Cora accepted Simon's extended arm without even a thought until she reflected on how natural it had been to take it, one hand on his bicep and the other on his forearm. His face smiled down at her. The warmth in his eyes made her heart flip-flop. She had no words for the desire she felt. He cleared his throat and inclined his head for them to follow Saalfeld and Everett on the path at the woods' edge.

Although they began walking, Cora still felt a strong connection to Simon, hyper-aware of his nearness, trying to distract her mind from him. "I see those small flowers everywhere." She noted clumps of small bluish flowers, so much like daisies except having petals that were lacy at their blunt ends.

"Chicory. It's the official flower of my home county." Simon picked several and paused, watching her face as he tucked them into her hair.

"Thank you. I believe this is my favorite flower now." She pulled his arm closer to her as she held it.

After they had made several turns Cora noticed that May and Lord Saalfeld were no longer with the group. There was more to that relationship—she was sure of it now.

CHAPTER 9

Simon Tuttle

"Right sporting of you to allow other men to court your wife." Everett's words felt like blows, but Simon noticed his friend busily engaged in cleaning his gun for that morning's shoot.

"I don't have a wife." Simon's response sounded surly even to himself. Cora's face filled his mind's eye—waking up with her each morning, her rosy lips, her teasing smile, and her laugh being the music behind it all. *Wife.* He had to admit there was more than a little charm to thinking of her that way.

"Seems that Cora is considered a diamond with the bachelors we know." Everett's voice held a note of sarcasm in it. "Isn't it wonderful?"

Everett only seemed to be studiously cleaning and reassembling his rifle. Simon saw it for what it was—baiting him. "Wonderful," Simon agreed without a smile, returning to work on his own gun.

Everett kept his eyes trained on his work, but Simon looked at the man. "Why bring this up?" What was he playing at? Simon determined to remain indifferent to the conversation. "And why would she not? She's beautiful and intelligent. She ..." Simon held back the thought that she deserved the best life offered—love, loyalty, security. How had *this* group of men infiltrated her life? Not one of them was worthy of her. "Cora's being pursued by fools and rakes." His voice grew louder. "She won't take any of them seriously."

So much for proving his indifference.

Everett's head tipped up, and his gaze locked with Simon's before he asked, "Why do you care?"

He threw his cleaning rag to the floor and stood with his gun. "I don't." Simon stalked to the back door to join the rest of the men.

"It sounds like you do," Everett commented as they strode across the veranda.

The gentlemen gathered on the back lawn. Not long after, a dozen young women in walking dresses assembled behind them. Although Simon stood quietly with the group of men, a roaring conversation filled his head.

If I held her in special regard, I would have singled her out. I would have changed my plans for her. I would gladly accept her company at whatever personal cost. Simon thought back to the moment he'd met her behind the curtains in the music room and every moment since then. He sighed. *Everett is right—I've done all of that.*

Cora was just outside his view, but he knew her exact location within the women. He couldn't hear her words, but recognized the tone that was uniquely her, and now and again her laughter. If he were to look, he'd see her confidence in the way she stood. He would recognize her quick humor by the twinkle in her eye. From a glance as the women walked up behind him minutes ago, he knew she was wearing the palest green and carried a parasol as did two other women though he couldn't say exactly who.

Something about Cora stayed with him long after she was no

longer in his sight or location, like looking at the flame of a candle, then closing his eyes.

The image of Cora's face disappeared when Everett jabbed his elbow into Simon's ribs. He noticed the group beginning to move toward a thin tree line that separated the back lawns and gardens from a field beyond. They weren't going far from the house, but the group seemed to be walking inordinately slowly. Many of the men looked behind them toward the women.

"What's the quarry today? It's a competition, right?" asked a woman directly behind his right shoulder.

Cora replied loudly enough for Simon and probably all of the women to hear. "Yes, it is. For us, like every day, the quarry today is men." Giggles broke out among the women, completely capturing the attention of many men.

Simon noticed Wetheridge step off to the side and stop as if to wait for the ladies. Simon guessed he was waiting for Cora, and quickly did the same. The entire men's group came to a halt.

"May I escort you to the field, ladies?" Simon asked Cora and the woman next to her. From the corner of his eye, he saw Wetheridge scowl in his direction. Simon wondered if it was bad timing to anger a man right before handing him a loaded gun.

"Of coursc," Cora answered, resting her hand on his extended arm.

For the last few yards, the gentlemen escorted the women.

When they arrived in the field, Lord Cottrell stood in front of the group. "Three teams have volunteered for this competition. You may use your own guns or one of those provided on the tables. Members of the team will take turns at the shots in a set rotation. A kill point will be awarded for any broken glass bulb. We've made an innovation this year to our contest. Instead of throwing the glass balls into the air, they will be launched via slingshots to throw them at an angle better simulating the flight of a bird. Our gamekeeper and his assistants will toss the globes for us."

Wyndham and Wetheridge joined with May's brother, James, as the first team. Simon, Lord Saalfeld, and Everett stepped up as the third team. The table for the second team was yet unattended.

Lord Cottrell called the group's attention. "On the women's team this year will be my wife, Lady Cottrell, my daughter, Lady May Cottrell, and Miss Cora Rey."

James groaned, then said to his team, "My mother and sister shoot very well, but perhaps Miss Rey can't shoot. Then the other teams may have a chance." His voice lifted at the end as if he were asking Cora a question.

Her eyes brightened, but she offered no clarification. The flat smile across her lips told Simon she was holding back a laugh. He knew—she could shoot, expertly.

Wetheridge asked across the table that separated him from the women's team, "Are you a crack shot, Miss Rey?"

"I shoot, and today, we'll find out how well." Though her voice was teasing, Simon heard confidence.

Lord Cottrell listed the rules. "The first team may take a shot at the globe during the ascent of the target tossed for them. If they miss, the next team ..." He smiled warmly at the women. "... may take a shot at the ball on its downward arc to steal the point. If both teams miss, the third team may take a shot after the second. If the second team fails to make an attempt before it falls to the ground, the last team is awarded a point by default. We'll declare a winner after three sets of three rounds each."

Lord Cottrell lifted one finger and announced, "If anyone cares to make a wager, I'll act as the bank and hold the vowels for it. Again, any proceeds earned by the bank will be donated to the children's home."

Simon noticed that although he tried to sound nonchalant, Lord Cottrell, too, was confident. James boasted among the men that one weak member of a team was all the women needed for a loss, raising bets for the men's teams to win.

Simon called out, "I'll double the bank's position. If your team should win the bet, the award will be paid twice." That encouraged the stakes to rise.

When the teams and spectators returned to their positions, May waved daintily at her father. "Would you permit Cora to take a practice shot before we begin the competition? She's never shot this type of gun before."

He gestured to the men's teams, and they agreed. May carried a glass goblet out into the field at an even distance to where the gamekeeper would be throwing the orbs, set it on the ground, and walked back to her team.

Cora sighted down the barrel to where the wine glass glinted in the sun. Simon considered how that angle would affect the trajectory if the sights were inaccurate. Apparently, she did too. The better position for the practice would have been prone on the ground except that her arms wouldn't have been free to move. Besides, she could hardly do that in the contest. Instead she knelt and sat on her right foot while holding her body at a forty-five-degree angle to the goblet as she leveled the gun.

Simon wished he could have the stability Cora demonstrated in that position. She would make an army marksman proud. The children's home was going to add another sizable gift to its coffers today.

"I wish to change my bet," called one of the gentlemen.

With the butt of the gun against her right shoulder, Cora pulled the trigger very slowly. Neither the explosion nor the recoil seemed to bother her, and she watched steadily to see where her bullet hit in the ground—about a foot short.

"On second thought, I'll double it," the same man called out.

"I'll take that bet," Simon called back, and then he smiled at Cora and nodded to Lord Cottrell. *She now knows by how much she needs to adjust her shot. She's brilliant.*

Everett nudged him. "You're betting against us."

"Quite."

Lord Cottrell called for the teams to take their positions. Lady Cottrell stood in front of May, who stood in front of Cora. On team number one, Wetheridge lined up even with Cora as the third shooter for his team. Simon stood in the front of the line for his team.

Lord Cottrell called out, "Shooters, to your mark."

Simon, Bethany, and James stepped forward and raised their guns. A glass globe filled with feathers was launched into the air, and James took the first shot. The glass burst, sending shards glinting in the morning light and feathers floating on the wind.

"Point," called Lord Cottrell. The spectators clapped. The next two tosses ended with the same result. Following Lady Cottrell's kill shot, the women in attendance cheered. During the second round, Wyndham missed his shot, and May was able to score that one and her own as a kill for the women's team, making them the leaders.

Cora stepped into position for the third round. Simon watched her steady hands and the concentration on her face as she followed the orb tossed for Wetheridge until his shot broke it. Cora scored a point as well on her turn. Lord Saalfeld missed his shot, and Wetheridge waited until the ball nearly grounded to take a shot. He missed it, but Cora didn't have a chance to fire before it shattered.

"So, that's how it's going to be?" she asked Wetheridge.

"Strategy is part of battle," he replied to the amusement of several men.

Simon saw her smile and nod but knew it was not an agreement, just acknowledgment that she could play that game.

In the next set, James, Lady Cottrell, and Simon all made their shots. Wetheridge was up for the first shot of the second round. The gamekeeper slung the glass orb into the air as May stepped behind Cora and tickled her, causing Cora to giggle and draw the attention of every man, including Wetheridge, whose shot went wide. Cora quickly sited her gun and squeezed the trigger. The ball blew apart.

"Your behavior borders on being dishonorable," Wetheridge barked out toward the women.

Immediately, Cora replied, "Strategy is part of battle."

Simon considered how lovely that sounded coming from her lips. He loved her wit.

In the third and final set, the women's team was ahead of James' team by two points and even with Simon's team. The last competitor, Everett, missed his shot. Wetheridge waited as the ball descended. Waited. Waited. Everyone knew that if he missed, it would be inches above the ground. Again Cora knelt and pulled the trigger as soon as Wetheridge's gun discharged, her shot blasting the ball apart just before it disappeared into the grass.

Simon cheered. Lady Cottrell and May hugged her. Simon wished he were able to put his arms around Cora in celebration. That he was able to pick her up, twirl her ... kiss her.

Everett was right. He'd chosen his wife—she didn't know it yet, but now he did.

He'd not shown interest in any other lady, and he knew he wouldn't. She completely anchored his heart and soul. There was certainly no commitment or understanding between them. There had been no talk of courting, even. As far as the rest of the world knew, he wasn't partial, but Simon knew he couldn't fool Everett, who might know Simon's mind better than he knew his own.

The women came from the sidelines and hugged their team, cheering and shouting. When the celebration calmed, Lady Cottrell shouted, "The children's home thanks you for your generous donations, gentlemen."

CHAPTER 10

Cora Rey

The next day was completely unplanned for much of the time. This gave the newly forming couples an opportunity to take a walk, go shopping, or be otherwise engaged in courting. May and Cora opted for sewing and reading in the morning room with Bethany until their—*dates?*—arrived.

At precisely one o'clock, the door to the morning room swung open, and the Cottrell's butler announced, "Lord Saalfeld and Mr. McElroy to visit, my lady."

Cora noticed May quickly dabbed her eyes and then stood.

"Might we collect the young ladies?" Mr. McElroy asked, bowing over Lady Cottrell's hand.

"Of course. We've been expecting you." Mrs. Cottrell looked toward May and Cora. "Have a lovely drive, girls."

After the ladies tied on their bonnets, both couples descended the front steps toward a lovely black phaeton just outside. Cora couldn't help but think that it looked a lot like a pram.

Lord Saalfeld sat beside May in the forward-facing seat while Mr. McElroy sat next to Cora on the aft-facing cushions. The open carriage allowed the sun to warm her arms. Cora considered that the weather in England was quite unlike the blue skies she grew up with in Texas. Days like today with clear and sunny skies were to be treasured here.

"You've certainly arranged a perfect day for a ride," Cora said.

Mr. McElroy swallowed deeply, his Adam's apple bobbing nervously up and down against the top of his necktie. "Well, we did our best. Aye, Saalfeld?"

Lord Saalfeld, however, wasn't listening—his attention wholly on May. Cora watched with some surprise to see him extend himself at all. The bored lord persona was gone, and he looked—besotted. He turned toward May and spoke so low that Cora couldn't hear the words. But by the smile May was failing to suppress, the pink glow to her cheeks, and the flirty glances she gave him, it appeared that May was enjoying the attention.

Cora turned to Mr. McElroy. "I guess we're on our own."

His face visibly paled. "The ... um ... property on our left belongs to my great-uncle. Um ... when he ... I mean, should he die ... I stand to inherit. There are no other heirs."

"That's wonderful. What will you do with the property?" Cora asked, wanting to keep the conversation going to allow May a small amount of privacy.

"My uncle has begun my training. I suppose I will continue to do what he has done."

"Oh, and what is that?"

"His investments are in the manufacturing of cotton fabrics." Mr. McElroy glanced at Cora. She thought she saw fear in his eyes. "Our money is based in trade." His voice sounded a little shaky when he added, "I hope that doesn't offend you."

Oh, goodness. It's like he's at a job interview. I don't need to hear his resume like it's an application for a marriage contract. Cora answered,

"No, it doesn't. I'm American—capitalism might be our national religion. I'd like to hear more about textiles."

For the next thirty minutes, Mr. McElroy talked nonstop with growing confidence.

Cora listened to the beginning of each of his orations, but tuned out much of the rest as her mind considered the outcomes of each.

"The growth of the textile industry, particularly cotton production in the southern states of the colonies, has changed the potential of the industry ... Or their factories in the north of England show particularly promise for long growth rewards ... The power looms have greatly increased profits for ... The economical cost of importing cotton from America is dependent on low labor costs, thus making it feasible to make the cloth we ship abroad ... Not really the sort of thing I'd expect you to worry your pretty head about."

Cora strained to remain polite and silent. Did he not stop to think that his industry had long supported and exploited slave labor? She bit her tongue and reminded herself that this was a different time. And they were already on their way back to May's house. It wouldn't be long now.

As they neared the home, she said, "It sounds like a complex business interest for sure. England must have figured out a way to minimize the dangerous working conditions, child labor abuses, and even the appalling poverty of the workers receiving low wages for the long hours they work. Maybe next time, you can tell me about your solutions. America hasn't figured that out yet. By the way, you are financially incentivizing slavery."

Mr. McElroy's mouth dropped open and shut several times. Perhaps he hadn't knowledge of that, or it could be he saw nothing wrong with it. Maybe he believed a woman should not know about or speak of it. Whichever, he was out of the running for this bachelorette.

From the corner of her eye, Cora noticed that the whispered conversation just across from her had gone silent but not because they were paying attention to her. The couple's heads leaned slightly toward each other until the phaeton rumbled to a stop. When they said their goodbyes, Lord Saalfeld bowed deeply, and May's curtsy matched it. Cora wondered at the full story they were hiding that made something as mundane as a bow sizzle between them.

The ladies entered May's house, and the gentlemen left. Cora wondered if it would be an intrusion to ask May about the tears she'd been blotting that morning. On one hand, May hadn't offered to confide in her. On the other hand, Cora considered her a dear friend.

"I noticed you were sad before we left this morning. Is there anything I can do?" Cora asked as the women ascended the stairs.

May shook her head but said, "Just before you arrived at Aunt Nellie's, I'd taken a 'vacation.' That's what I tell Saalfeld whenever I go to my other century. I miss him. He misses me. I can't give an explanation of what I'm doing, but he wants one. It's the same every time." May sighed. "I don't always come back out in society the exact night I return because there's a change in me for the time I've spent away, so I skip a month. He would notice if I were suddenly tanned or my hair were sun-bleached." May stopped in the hallway outside Cora's door. "I was thinking about it and about him. I was pretty emotional right then. I'm okay now. It was a very good day."

Cora hugged her friend before she went into her room to change. She knew there was a lot more to that story, but she hoped May sensed her support and concern for her.

The following morning after a cup of bitter chocolate—the taste was growing on her—and dry toast, she dressed for the day and made her way to the music room to practice. The dozen or so ladies still staying at the Cottrell's had been bundled off to do some shopping, but Cora had awoken with a headache and begged off the trip. Of course her decision to play the piano for Simon had caused the headache in the first place. She kept telling herself,

"Just Simon, not an audience," but butterflies continued rioting in her stomach.

She spent an hour playing songs from heart before she committed to choosing one that was perfect for her private concert.

Cora noticed him straining to hear the instruments at balls. He often turned his right ear toward sounds but still had a look of irritation on his face. To anyone else, he might have just looked nervous, displeased, bored, or as if he were fidgeting. But she knew it must be frustrating for him to only hear some of the notes. He strategically positioned himself near the musicians to be able to dance. He even admitted to her that he used to enjoy music, meaning he no longer did—but maybe he could again.

She had experienced it in a college class. The students inserted noise-cancelling plugs in their ears, then used conduction through their jawbones to hear. In the experiment, she held a stick between her teeth and then pressed the other end of the rod to the soundboard of a piano, much like Beethoven did. The music was softer but surprisingly sweet as it vibrated through her jawbone and into her ear.

This could work. She didn't want to subject Simon to another musical failure, but what if it was possible?

Cora paced in the music room on shaky legs, back and forth across the red carpet—her performance anxiety in full swing. She found she couldn't ignore the irrational thoughts plaguing her. What if she missed the notes? What if he hated it? What if he couldn't hear it, and she failed him? Her mouth felt dry even as her body felt sweaty. She had to get a grip to make it through this.

She closed her eyes and chanted internally, "He's not coming here to judge me. It isn't helpful for me to judge myself a failure before I even start." She took a cleansing breath between each repetition of the phrases. The squirmy feeling in her stomach was easing. It was going to be all right. Or not.

Maybe if she worried about something else, it would help. Was this the right thing to do? In her own century, there would've been no decision to make. She would have simply invited Simon to come sit beside her at the piano. But in this century, what she was proposing would be a clandestine meeting. Under the best of circumstances, if they were caught, she would be asked to leave the house and no longer be a guest. Under the worst circumstances, she would be expected to marry Simon quickly.

She had decided it was worth the risk. If he could have music back in his life, she would do it.

An hour later, at her request, Everett and Simon entered the music room.

"I have a special request of each of you. Simon, I've prepared a private concert for you. And Everett, I wondered if you would guard the door. Although everyone seems to have gone shopping, I'd feel better knowing that no one will disrupt us."

Cora would have laughed out loud at their expressions—Simon's full of curiosity and a bit of fear, and Everett's of surprise quickly turning to mischief—had she not been so nervous that her stomach was tying itself in knots.

Everett was the first to recover from the odd request and saluted Cora then left, shutting the door behind him. Simon stood, rooted to his spot. It wasn't often that Everett left Simon to make his own way, and Simon looked a little unsure about what to do.

"Will you join me?" Cora asked, then turned back toward the piano, staring at the landscape of white and black keys that seemed to sway. She wouldn't let this stop her. She looked straight into Simon's eyes and motioned for him to sit beside her. With a huge grin, he sat to her left as if he would be turning pages. That was exactly what she needed. His expression hinted that he accepted her and trusted her. She could do this.

"I chose this piece because it uses so much of the keyboard. I thought you could tell me which parts you most enjoy and which parts are hard to hear."

Simon nodded curtly, obviously still uncomfortable with someone knowing his secret. Cora had hoped that he was confident enough in her to know she had considered this before extending the invitation. He was still sitting on the bench, so that was something.

Cora's left hand hovered above the ivories with her right above the ebonies. There was no easing into this piece—she would strike the keys quickly again and again with triplets on her right and a staccato beat with her left. She'd been this nervous to perform a piece of music before—many times before—and pushed the feeling down. The opening notes rang through the room, and she saw Simon's head gradually lean forward. He also turned his head slightly away from her, his right ear toward the keyboard.

The notes at the beginning played along the higher register. The rhythmic, almost prancing cadence of the left hand was much lower, especially toward the end of the short piece.

She noticed Simon lean forward more as the song continued until his forehead was nearly to the backboard, his eyes closed in concentration. When she finished the piece, she turned to him. Leaning close, she asked, "What could you hear?"

Simon motioned to the notes left of middle C. "These I hear clearly." He motioned to the middle of the keyboard. "These are muted." And when he pointed to the farthest right, the highest notes, he said, "I don't believe ... I can't ... I ... barely hear those ... at all." His eyes closed again, this time in resignation.

Cora recognized the longing in his voice, the desire to hear what once was his and was now denied him. She reached up to touch his cheek. His eyes snapped open, and his hand covered hers.

"Simon, I have a challenge for you." She stood from the bench, her hand slipping from his, and walked to a simple oak chair near the window and lifted it. Immediately, Simon was next to her, taking the chair into his hands. "Please set the chair next to the piano." She walked back and pointed to the floor. She hoped she didn't sound as wooden as she felt. Combining her fear to perform with playing for someone she cared for deeply made her stiff. "Here. This chair is for you." After Simon sat, Cora asked, "May I position your head?"

He nodded, and Cora, placing one hand on each side of his face, guided it to lean against the piano case. His eyes widened, but he allowed her to move him to the location she'd determined.

She liked the feel of his skin under hers. "Please rest your jaw here." She tapped one finger against the piano case. "The soundboard connects here and amplifies the vibration." She had one hand still on his face, reluctant to move it. This alone calmed her.

When she stepped back toward the bench, Simon raised his head. Cora commented, "I'd like to play the song again, but you have to promise that your jaw will not leave the casing until I'm finished."

"I agree," he answered, but there was questioning in his eyes. And his jaw had already left the wood.

"Please ... " Cora's finger motioned him to place his jaw back against the case. "I hope you'll be able to hear the higher notes better."

The moment she began the fluttering melody of Chopin's "Black Key Etude," Simon's eyes widened with a bit of a startle, but she kept playing, and he stayed rigidly in position with an ever-widening smile on his face.

Deep emotions of excitement and gratitude swelled in her chest—it was working. When his eyes closed, she knew this was a profound experience for him. Near the end, one tear escaped his eye and rolled past his cheek before he swiped it away.

Cora's hands rested on the keys as the final notes faded. Her consciousness slowly expanded beyond the meter and notes, beyond the vibration that had engulfed her. The world that had faded behind the melody and beyond where she sat with Simon became sharper and real again. *Had he felt it? How music lifts you to another place?*

A complete minute of silence passed between them. Cora could see Simon taking a deep breath and wondered if he needed a moment to collect his emotions. His voice was soft and somewhat broken when he asked, "Would you play it again—once more?"

Cora welcomed the chance to weave a cocoon around them.

She leaned across the corner of the keyboard and laid her hand on top of Simon's. "I will play it for you as many times as you wish." She could barely whisper as her voice cracked on the simple words too.

Simon resettled against the piano as the opening notes rang out. After it was completed, Cora played another piece she knew by heart and watched the joy apparent on Simon's face, the unshed tears in his eyes. She would not have been able to see the music sheets since her own eyes were also filling with tears. She didn't want to stop, so she pulled music in front of her, wiped the tears away, and played three more songs.

When the last vibration ended, Simon's gaze moved to hers. He stood from his chair, and Cora stood from the bench. A smile creased Simon's face. "I have never had such a gift. Thank you, Cora."

It seemed the right thing to do—Cora's arms ached to hold him and share the happiness they both felt. She stepped to him and wrapped her arms around him. His arms likewise circled her. Her cheek pressed to his chest, and she felt his arms tighten.

Her hands were beneath his coat and pressing against his back. His pulse raced under her cheek. One of his arms held her closely while his other hand lightly caressed the side of her face, her ear, her neck.

"Cora," he whispered.

Her body reacted to the one word with a blast of tingles. She found it difficult to breathe, not because of his hold but because of his touch. She had only imagined how it would feel, and now, the reality of it was like a dream.

When she looked at him, he placed one finger beneath her chin, lifting it slowly. His lips touched hers, not yet a kiss, just a touch, but she wanted more. She sighed. Her hands slipped around his neck, and he lifted her closer as she rose to her tiptoes to press her mouth firmly against his and threw herself into kissing him. His obvious passion matched her own. They kissed until they were both breathing heavily and looking flushed.

Simon leaned away and looked into Cora's face. A smile grew. He pulled her in for a hug, giving her comfort and acceptance.

Cora relaxed in his arms and realized that the phobia of playing for someone was completely absent after the beginning moments of this recital. Choosing to give music to another person must counteract the phobia—that or the recent lip therapy completely erased any memory of it.

The door to the music room flew open. "Who was playing—ack! Your Grace?" Lady Radnor's smile soured as she stood in the doorway, gaping at Simon and Cora, who both jumped back immediately. "Misalliance, that's what this is. Oh, the shame. You were—"

Cora cut her off before she could finish. "You must be mistaken. I was simply leaving." She nodded to Simon and brushed past Lady Radnor as she left.

Everett was jogging toward her with a scone in his hand before she reached the staircase. "I only left the door for a minute."

All she said in passing was, "Nothing happened." She continued up the stairs to her room and closed the door behind her, then sat heavily on the side of the bed. Had she changed his life? Damaged his reputation?

Cora debated missing afternoon tea but knew her absence would be akin to an admission of guilt or a license to gossip. At the appointed hour, she put on a smile and walked into the parlor. May greeted her at the door and led her to a seat to the right of her mother.

"How was your day, Cora?" Lady Cottrell asked, handing her a teacup.

"I practiced piano for most of the time, so it was wonderful." Cora noticed Bethany's eyes sparkle with curiosity at the reply. Instead of questioning her, Lady Cottrell nodded and nibbled on the cookie in her hand.

Cora heard Lady Radnor harrumph. Maybe she was hoping for public humiliation or at least an interrogation. Cora continued the dull conversation she had witnessed so often at these teas.

When everyone left to prepare for the evening, Cora hung back and approached Bethany and May. "I need to let you know what happened this afternoon."

"I heard a bit from my lady's maid, but I'd love to hear the whole story," Bethany said as she closed the door.

The women sat together on the large davenport by the windows, and Cora told them about the private concert and the moment Lady Radnor entered. "I'm sorry if this causes problems. Will this reflect poorly on Simon or either of you?"

"No. Our status is above such a thing causing any social bruise. It might for you if you cared about society's censure," Bethany assured her.

A knock on the door ended the conversation. "Mr. Everett Hawley, my lady," the butler announced.

Everett entered and greeted the women. "I know I'm interrupting, but I have a question for Cora."

Lady Cottrell began walking toward the door. "I've promised to find Lord Cottrell."

"Would you care to take a walk?" he asked Cora and May.

Both women rose and followed him.

Everett, Cora, and May walked down the stairs to the gravel drive surrounding the park in front of the house. Along the tree line was a bench where the three sat.

Everett lowered his voice. "I was hoping to talk with you about what happened earlier—with Simon."

Cora nodded slowly. This was an odd request, and she didn't understand why Everett would make it. Perhaps it wasn't, though. Everett was Simon's wingman. He'd made a commitment to protect his friend, and he was continuing that duty. "And?" she asked.

He looked down at his hands and folded them in front of him. "And I need to be assured that your waltz before the midnight supper wouldn't be available for Simon." He looked her in the eye. "May I request the supper dance?"

He was an amazing friend. It was true that Cora had no use for the rules of this time period. In her mind, it was impossible for her to be ruined. A soft understanding glanced through her thoughts. Everett was acting to preserve Simon's reputation—not to be labeled as someone who would ruin a woman or use her badly.

She yearned to spare Simon any humiliation from society as well. She nodded in acceptance. "What do you suggest I do?"

Everett squared his shoulders. "If you would accept only one dance from Simon, and preferably a country dance, it would go a long way to silencing the rumors Lady Radnor is whispering about."

"Of course." Cora stood and was followed by May and Everett. "Thank you. I'm looking forward to this evening."

May linked her arm with Cora's. "We should start getting ready." They walked back to the house and into their rooms.

After a two-hour ordeal, having been bathed, dressed, coiffed, and dressed some more, Cora was pronounced acceptable to be seen by genteel company.

The ball was the final day of Lord and Lady Cottrell's house party, and the guests would go their separate ways tomorrow. Cora and May had accepted the invitation to travel to Everett's home for a week before returning to Aunt Nellie's. A little bundle of sadness settled into Cora's chest. She knew it wasn't waiting to go back to her own time that caused the sorrow but because she would be leaving—Simon specifically. She wanted to make the most of the time she had left. She would only give him one dance as she'd promised Everett, but she could spend time with him without dancing.

The ball began shortly after a dinner with the houseguests. That had been two hours ago, and Cora had yet to see Simon. More people arrived every minute, none of them Simon. Wetheridge had already claimed one dance from May and Cora, but continued to hover around them. Most of the other men Cora had met during her stay had already danced with her as well. May continued to introduce Cora to new gentlemen as they arrived. They filled her dance card, leaving her with no time to stand along the wall. She had little time to miss Simon, but she did.

A waltz began playing signaling the midnight supper was next. Wetheridge appeared in front of Cora, and extended his hand confidently, "May I have this dance?"

"No ... " was all she was able to say before Everett appeared with his arm extended. "I believe this is my dance, Miss Rey," he said, and then turned toward Wetheridge. "Sorry, cousin."

Cora accepted Everett's arm, leaving Wetheridge red-faced. She saw Simon out of the corner of her vision escorting Lucy to the dance floor. A quick thrill shot through her. Evening clothes accentuated every feature of the man, heightening her appreciation. He didn't dress in extreme fashions or colors, but his traditional masculinity radiated from him like a pheromone.

"From the look on your face, I suppose you've noticed Simon's arrival." Everett turned her into dance position as the music started. As he leaned into the first step he said, "His mother and sisters stopped by on their way back from Bath to London and decided at the last minute to attend this ball."

"His family is here?" Cora's head swung to look around the room, but she realized she wouldn't recognize them anyway. "Who are they?"

Everett turned her and replied. "Over my left shoulder. The older woman in green is the dowager duchess of Hertfordshire. Simon's sisters are on either side of her.

"I had no idea they were coming. Simon didn't say a thing."

"He had no idea, either, until he received a note from his mother accusing him of accosting an American and shaming his family." Everett looked in Cora's eyes. "He asked me to tell you that he will only offer you one dance this evening. Simon is in a tough spot and doesn't want you to be as well."

"I'm so sorry." Then Cora quickly added, "Not for the private recital but for not realizing the full impact the situation would have on him."

"I know Simon doesn't regret the concert or your company."

Everett had taken a breath as if he had more to say, but instead, his mouth snapped shut and his eyes swept away from her.

"What are you not telling me?"

Everett seemed to debate momentarily and then spoke carefully. "Simon had a childhood that left him vulnerable. He was treated with indifference, if he was noticed at all. Most times when we took a break from school, he would come to my home instead of his own, and his parents preferred that."

Cora remembered the lonely tone on occasions when Simon wrote or spoke about his family.

"He has a tender heart, though. They couldn't take that from him. For all he's been through, he guards it and rarely reveals it." Everett deftly sidestepped another couple on the floor. "You, however, have pierced his armor. It's as if he can't hide himself from you."

Cora vacillated between hope and despair at what she was hearing. She had only hoped that if she were ever to marry, it would be to someone who loved her as wholly as her parents had loved each other. That same hope was tarnished with a thick edge of gloom. Simon lived in a different century, literally dying before she was born. Her heart twisted, and she had to blink back tears that crested around her lids.

The song was nearly over. As the closing notes rang out, Everett gave a small bow and motioned them to move toward the supper prepared in the grand salon next door. He cleared his throat from strong emotion.

Cora was so glad Simon had such a friend.

He continued his tale. "Simon has never let himself dream that he could be loved for himself or have an affectionate wife and family of his own. He doesn't think himself worthy. He hoped that his wealth or title would attract a woman who would help him fulfill his duty and not cuckold him before giving him an heir. You said that you came here to find a husband. If love is your aim for a marriage partner, I'll give my blessing to your union with Simon should it come to that. If a love match isn't something you can give him, please don't include him in your hunt."

His blunt words seemed to bounce around in Cora's chest and soured her stomach. She would be gone in a couple of weeks. The closer she became to Simon, the more the separation would hurt them both. "Thank you, Everett." Cora could barely push the words past the lump in her throat. "I understand."

After seating Cora, Everett left to retrieve plates for them. She sat, head bent in contemplation. Did she see love in Simon? She had to admit that there were tailings of love sprinkled all through their interactions. Cora admired his determination to move forward in his life though she thought it might take incredible force and courage. She appreciated his intelligence and his loyalty. If it wasn't love yet, it could easily become so.

Simon seated Lucy in the chair next to where Everett would be, making Simon three seats to the right of Cora. May took a seat near Cora before Lord Saalfeld left with Simon.

"Are you all right?" May leaned across the chair between them and pressed her hand to Cora's shoulder. "Sorry, but you look terrible."

"It's nothing a little rest won't cure." Cora forced a weak smile. She noticed May looking at her, then at Simon and back again. "We'll talk later," Cora added.

The other gentlemen arrived with dinner plates, allowing Cora to turn her attention elsewhere. She wasn't hungry. She pushed the food around her plate to approximate eating and was happy that she wasn't required to hold a conversation. Everett had turned to Lucy, and May conversed with Lord Saalfeld. She didn't see any movement from where Simon sat, but she didn't really look that way, either.

At the end of the meal, Cora looked at May, who mouthed the word "Surprise," as Lord Saalfeld lifted his glass toward Cora and spoke to those seated at the table. "Miss Cottrell tells me it is Miss Rey's birthday." The other guests raised their glasses as well. "To your health," he said, tipping his glass toward her, followed by the same wish from the others around the table.

Except from Simon. Cora's ears were attuned to his voice, a clear timbre through the muffled words around her. "To your happiness."

"Thank you for the wishes." Simon's toast wasn't so easy to dismiss. It made her wonder what would cause her happiness. She believed happiness was a choice. She'd had some big disappointments and sorrows in her life, and she chose to look for the good that came from them. Although her parents were taken from her too early, her mother *much* too early, she had memories and gifts from each of them that gave her joy.

Her mother had given Cora her face. Each day when she looked in the mirror, she could remember what her mother looked like. She had also given her the gift of books and the love of reading. Her father had given her music and an appreciation for learning and teaching. Much of the pleasure in her life came directly from them.

What of Simon? Just being around him or planning something special to do for him filled her with exhilaration that she'd never before experienced and that she felt she could never get enough of —it whispered of happily ever after.

When the dinner was finished, the guests began moving back to the ballroom.

Cora stepped up beside May and hugged her friend. "Thank you for wanting to lift my spirits, but it isn't my birthday for several months."

May replied, "That's what made it a surprise. I thought you could use a little lift tonight."

The two women walked arm in arm to the open doors near the terrace. "You don't need to stay with me. Go enjoy your party." Then with a wink, she added, "and Lord Saalfeld."

"He'll be playing cards for a while. It gives me a chance to 'hang with you' as my mother would say." A cool breeze floated through the doors. Before May could say another word, a gentleman bowed toward her.

"Might I have this dance?"

Though her answer was slow, May accepted and was led into the dancing crowd.

Cora turned to look outside but heard, "Miss Rey, would you care to dance?" Wetheridge again stood before Cora.

It was just another piece of evidence that she would never make it as the star of a bachelorette series. She wasn't interested in leading men on when she had no interest in their attention. Before answering, she looked around to make sure there was no one who would overhear. "No. It would be untruthful to show you any partiality. I wouldn't want to give you or the guests here the wrong impression that I favor a suit from you. I don't. Please don't ask again."

Wetheridge's jaw clenched, and fire seemed to light his eyes. Without a word, he spun on his heel and exited through the open doors onto the veranda.

Cora fixed her gaze on the dancers before her, but directly across the room was Simon, his gaze on her. He stood next to his mother and one sister. He whispered something to his mom and stepped to leave them, his eyes never wavering from her own.

Her reasoning warred with her emotions. She wanted desperately to dance with him. She craved the riot of pleasure just to be held in his arms, to earn a word or a smile. Equally as much, though, she didn't know what she really wanted. *One dance wouldn't hurt. No, in fact, it would be just the opposite—enough pleasure to muddle my judgment.* She turned away from his gaze. *Nothing should be determined at two in the morning anyway. I don't even know what I need to consider.* Until she did, she'd be more cautious.

Simon continued to move around the crowded edges, greeting a few people in passing.

Cora decided not to decide but instead determined the evening was at an end—for her. She walked as quickly as she could to the staircase and ascended. From the top, she glanced back and saw Simon standing several feet away from the bottom stair.

After Cora retreated to her room and changed into a nightrail, the window seat called to her more strongly than the quilt-topped bed. There was too much to think about to sleep. Crossing the room, she saw a letter sitting on the little desk by the door. She knew it must be from Simon. Could she face it now? She'd practically run from him moments ago. It must have been written and delivered for her to find upon returning from the ball. She picked it up and held it in front of her, deciding not to open it yet. She slid onto the bench under the window and gazed out.

Though there were thousands more visible stars in the sky, she marveled that the same constellations moved across this century in the same nightly dance. The waxing moon burned a bright hole through the black satin of the western sky. Her window faced the rear of the house, overlooking the rose garden. *It's the same and yet very different here.*

Her mind knew what she should do, but her heart was confused. It was practical to return to her time and her work. Her chest squeezed painfully at leaving Simon behind. She'd never been so romantic as to believe that there was a one-and-only person to fall in love with. This situation was evidence to prove that. If she'd never transported back in time, she would have never met Simon, and her one chance at love would have been sequestered behind the folds of centuries past.

The letter in her hand now was part of the injustice. Cora fanned it back and forth. Nothing it held could be important to her. She pressed it to her lap and smoothed her hands over the top. She wouldn't be here much longer. The thought made her eyes misty.

How could the universe play a trick like that on either of them? Cora shook her head. She couldn't blame her meandering thoughts on logic. Still, her heart beat out an argument to it. What if there *were* a one and only, and this was how they were to meet?

She wondered if she would even fit into Simon's world. Her

logic jumped on that topic and rattled off unique experiences that seemed to fit. She grew up in a rural area with only her father for company most days, and her interests were vastly different than other girls she went to school with—played several instruments, rode horses competitively, hunted with her dad. Okay. There were a few things that definitely fit in this century.

The letter, weighing nearly nothing, rested heavily on her knee. She reached for it, knowing it was too late to believe that Simon was just a friend or a vacation fling. His words, his thoughts were important to her because *he* was. It was too late for her not to get her heart broken when she left but maybe not too late for him.

Cora slid her finger beneath the wafer of wax and broke the seal.

Dear Cora,

Everett, at my request, has conveyed to you about the untimely arrival and lingering of my family as a result of a few scandalous rumors, which I promise will not touch you.

With deep regard,

Simon

P.S. You must know I wouldn't risk your reputation even for my own selfish desire to be with you this evening. I will only offer you one dance. Of course, when you read this, the evening will be at an end, but I want you to know the treasure your company is to me—the relief you offer me of being myself, to put away pretense. I dare to hope that I offer you some degree of pleasure in return. Please do not consider my inattention a lack of favor, for it is the contrary that drove my motivation tonight.

Cora blinked back tears before they could fall and leaned her head against the wall. She'd muddled this up well and good.

CHAPTER 11

Simon Tuttle

It was an hour past noon when the short caravan of carriages and wagons traveling from the Cottrells' party reached the lane that would eventually lead to Everett's house. Simon signaled Everett to pull back. This smaller portion of the party was moving on to Everett's house for a few days.

Simon turned his horse off the lane and back toward the way they'd come to allow the baggage wagons to continue, and Everett did the same, only stepping back onto the road after the last of them had passed. From this distance, Everett would be able to talk loudly enough for Simon to hear without broadcasting the conversation to swell the current stream of gossip.

"You said you didn't want to talk about the incident," Everett reminded Simon.

"Well, now I do." But he didn't. He didn't know where to start. Questions swirled through his head faster than he could snatch one to consider. Instead, he blurted out, "Cora could have acknowledged what Lady Radnor saw. We were alone, embracing. It was exactly what she thought she saw." Simon glanced at Everett to gauge his response, but Everett just nodded and looked back toward the road. "Cora could have forced a marriage, and I wouldn't have fought it."

This time, Everett's gaze didn't leave Simon though he held off giving an opinion. Simon continued, "I would have considered myself lucky. We would marry, and I would have proudly announced it to anyone who would have listened. The whole country would have seen my joy. There would have been no scandal because I wouldn't have been trapped but rescued." Simon's voice softened as the last sentence trailed to an end. More to himself than to Everett, he added, "But she didn't."

Their horses clomped on the road, and the baggage wagons rattled ahead of them. What had he missed? He saw her longing. He felt her passion. He thought it was love. Had he been a fool over it all? They rode in silence until Simon asked, "Why didn't she, Everett?" He wasn't sure he wanted an answer.

He didn't want to consider what it might be though he'd lain awake the nights since trying to answer it to himself. Maybe she wasn't sure she wanted to live in England. Maybe she wanted to choose from many advantageous offers and not get tied to anyone yet. Maybe ... she wanted her husband whole. There was a prick at his mind, but it dulled quickly. He'd never seen pity on her face when she looked at him. He had to believe better of her.

What would she have to give up to marry him? On the surface, she seemed ready to give up much—her home, her friends, her country. What more would it cost her to choose him? Did she consider that price too high? Simon admitted to himself that he knew little of Cora's requirements for a husband. He knew there was friendship. He knew there was attraction. He decided that his next step would be to show her what it would be like to love him—what their life together might be like.

"That's the ticket. Thank you, Everett."

Everett smirked and shook his head, a quizzical arch to his brow. "Glad to have helped," he answered.

Simon heard the unspoken question in his reply but didn't elaborate. With new confidence and a direction, he sat taller in the saddle. Cora might have come to England with an idea of marriage, but he had a plan of his own. "Race you to the front!" Simon called to Everett and kicked his horse to a canter.

At the end of the drive was Everett's home. It seemed to lounge against a thick edge of ancient woods, dignified, old, and welcoming. The gray stone reached three stories high in the main building, but a wing only two stories high extended to the south, and beyond that, one story looked squat at the end. It was never intended to be a grand house. The oldest part began as a modest stone home, but as the years passed, and families built on, a manor house emerged. The property was never entailed, and his father had passed it to Everett along with the accompanying income and responsibilities.

Simon had met Everett at school—two thirteen-year-old boys shuffled off before their time. Simon thought fondly of the days he'd spent in the oldest part of the home. The children's wing was as far away from guests as possible. It was one thing for the home to *look* dignified and something completely different for the children to act so.

The carriages stopped on the drive along the front of the house, and the wagons of luggage trundled past to the rear entrance. A line of footmen stood at the ready to assist the visitors to alight. Simon took his time dismounting his horse and giving the groom directions for its care, all the while watching in his side vision, gauging when to approach, so he could lead Cora out. The moment he saw her, he stepped in front of the ready footman and extended his hand.

Cora's expression brightened, and a giggle revealed her surprise. Her hand in his felt as right as she had felt in his arms. His fingers tightened momentarily. She could imagine that he did so to secure her step down, but it was an instinctive response of his own.

It seemed now that he'd decided to woo her, his heart would take advantage of any touch.

With her feet on solid ground, Simon transferred her hand to his other, which safely tucked it in his elbow. And he could have—maybe even *should* have—extended his arm away from his body, but he didn't, preferring her hand to brush against his coat as they walked.

Simon leaned closer and said, "Welcome to Elder Weald, Everett's home."

Cora's gaze scanned the property as they walked toward the house, her steps slowing the closer they drew. Before mounting the stairs, she smiled up at Simon. He could have sworn his heart flipped over. When he realized she'd caught him staring at her for moments too long, he cleared his throat and asked, "Would you like some time to rest after the journey here?"

She stopped just inside the entry hall, her eyes following the staircases that arose on either side connecting to the mezzanine level and more stairs rising to the third floor. "It's been barely over an hour's time. No, I don't want to rest. Let's explore." She released his arm as they entered through the massive wooden door, and he immediately missed the connection.

"Let's," he replied and retrieved her hand, tucking it again in his elbow. He considered what might interest Cora most and began leading her across the home to the back lawns. Once outside, he added, "The stables, first?" Her eyes twinkled as she gave a quick nod, so he turned them away from the kitchen gardens and toward the large stables behind the children's wing.

"I like it here."

Simon looked toward her. "Is it much like your home?"

"Yes, but nothing like it, too. This home is much larger than mine, but I'd say the quarters for our horses could have rivaled these." She pointed toward the stables. "The paddock and barn were just behind my bedroom. I used to sneak out to pet the horses when I was younger and to ride them when I was older."

Simon noticed a wistful sound to her voice and a gleam in her eye that looked like unshed tears. He realized because both her mother and father had passed on, Cora probably came to England because she didn't have that home to live in anymore—such was the way with inheritance. A strong urge to protect her, to care for her, to make a home with her overwhelmed him.

She was in the situation that his sisters could find themselves in should he die before securing their futures. Perhaps Cora had the advantage there, being an heiress. She could still afford to make some choices for herself.

"Should you come up missing in the middle of the night, I'll look for you here first."

A tenuous smile tipped her lips upward. "It seems a little harder to sneak around these stables with so many hands employed in the care of the horses and carriages. I'll first have to make friends with them."

"You rode your horses at night?"

Cora opened her mouth, then snapped it shut.

He waited for a moment.

Then she said, "We had an arena. There was no danger to either of us on a bright night."

They wandered the stables, commenting on the horses they passed in the stalls. "This beautiful horse is mine." The horse poked his nose above the gate and nudged Simon's shoulder. "This is Hrimfaxi."

Cora nodded and said, "Frost Mane." Simon looked at Cora with surprise, but she continued, "He pulled the night across the sky. My father had an interest in that kind of thing."

When they reached the other end, they exited toward the carriage house. "May I take you for a ride tomorrow morning if I can secure a vehicle from Everett?"

"I'd like that, but even more, I'd love you to teach me to drive."

"My pleasure." He stopped walking, and Cora turned toward

him. "In the morning?" he questioned, remembering that she said she took exercise early each day. He was still selfish enough to hope for as much time as possible with her.

Mischief twinkled in her eyes. "Yes," Cora answered. "I'm sure whatever dangers lurk in these woods will not need my attention tomorrow."

Simon was pleased that he ranked above her exercise now.

Very early the next morning, a small gig waited in the drive with a groom standing ahead of the single horse harnessed to the buggy. Along with Everett, Simon had inspected the conveyances carefully the night before, choosing the right vehicle.

This one was light enough to be pulled by one horse, and with only two wheels it was easy to maneuver, making it easier to learn to drive. It was in excellent condition, and perhaps the most important factor was the diminutive seat. The two of them would barely fit if they sat very, very closely. It was perfect.

The sun had risen within the last hour, and fog sat heavily along the river that snaked through the meadow in front of the house. Simon extended his arm and escorted Cora down the steps at the front walkway.

"Well, there's hardly room for my dress let alone the two of us," Cora quipped.

Simon worried he had assumed too much and feared he had offended her.

"I guess you'll have to squeeze in closely," she said and winked at him.

With relief, he helped her into the gig, pushed her dress in, and then hopped up beside her. As predicted, their legs ran alongside each other's when they were seated. Although Cora adjusted the cape she wore, she didn't pull away from Simon's touch.

"I'm so excited to learn this. I woke up several times last night thinking about it." Cora pushed as much of her dress as she could behind her feet and under the seat, drew the riding apron into place, and sat with the same posture she had when she rode a horse.

"The first thing is to put your right foot on the footrest at the bottom of the dash instead of flat on the floorboard."

"To keep from being pitched forward, right?" Cora made the adjustment, and then looked toward Simon for the next instruction. Her full gaze smiled up at him, taking his breath away.

He dropped his eyes to see her boot peeking out from beneath her skirts. "Exactly." Again he wished he had already earned her love, and they were going out for a romantic drive—a very short drive and a stop in the woods near the ruins for a private moment.

Simon held the leather ribbons in one hand and cupped his left hand around the backside of hers, forming them into the shape needed to hold the reins, threading the leather ribbons through her fingers, securing them in her palm. Of course, he could have demonstrated the hold with the end of the reins in his own hand while she followed his example farther up, but where was the pleasure in that? He was definitely enjoying the contact even though both of them wore gloves.

Reluctant to release her hand, he began a bit of instruction. "Fingers aren't strong enough to hold back a horse if there are problems, so hold the ribbons tightly against your palm." He gave her hand a gentle squeeze.

Cora leaned toward him, the bill of her bonnet grazing the top of his head and speaking low enough but close to his right ear so the groom could not overhear her. "I think I'm going to enjoy this lesson. You have my complete attention, sir."

Was she flirting with him? He thought she might be. Her blue eyes were bright with delight. She knew she had captured his attention, too. When Simon took a breath, hoping to clear his mind, he noticed the slightest pleasant smell—sweet, like cake. He wanted to lean closer to Cora to make sure, but realized his face wore a daffy smile and cleared his throat, leaning away instead.

"This hand will hold the whip, like so." He placed the handle across her right hand. "Then these fingers are available to hold the tail of the reins beneath your left hand. With a turn of your hand, one side or the other will tighten, signaling the horse to turn." He pushed her hand toward the horse to loosen the reins, then demonstrated how to turn her hand. "The trick is to ask with your hand and command with your voice."

"Shall we go?" she asked.

"When you're ready," he replied. She nodded, and the groom at the horse's head stepped away. "Just say, 'Walk on.'"

Cora repeated the command, and the horse began to pull.

The lane to Everett's house was long and straight once they rode past where it wound around the gardens. There were no canals on either side, so if the horse left the trail momentarily, it might get bumpy but not dangerous. Simon noted how relaxed and comfortable Cora seemed as the driver. She sat straight and left some ease in the reins. Her hand gently, discreetly tipped the reins to confirm the horse's desire to walk down the road. She was gentle with a horse's mouth.

Nearing the end of the lane, Cora asked, "Right or left?"

He pointed to his left. "This way, between two grassy hills, is a rather lovely pond with a bridge going right through the middle, and that way," he said, pointing across Cora, "are some mysterious, and some say magical, ruins."

"The pond today, but I'll hold you to exploring the ruins another time."

Simon entertained the daydream he'd had earlier of holding her behind the ruins' crumbling rock—of her cheek pressed to his chest, her arms around his neck, and stolen kisses.

As they reached the crossroads, Cora looked up and down the road before she turned her shoulders and rolled her hand slightly, sending the horse to the left.

Soon after they topped the hill, Simon saw a farm wagon barreling down the other side of the road toward them. The horse appeared to be out of control by the look of the man desperately pulling at the reins. The wagon pitched from side to side as the horse ran, dust flying up when the wheels veered into the less-packed dirt along the roadside. Simon could see the bed of the wagon tip while the driver, his feet high and spread wide on the dashboard, fought to stay aboard. The horse listed to the side at an unusual angle. Part of the harness must have broken.

The man failed to stop the horse before it could enter the bridge straddling the lake, and in the next wild lurch, the front wheel left the bridge, pulling the wagon and horse after it into the water.

Simon reached to take the reins but he heard Cora yell, "Heya!" and saw her flick the ribbons against the horse's hindquarters. The animal bolted from a trot to a canter, covering the distance to the accident in seconds. When she reined him back at the lake's edge, Simon jumped to the ground before their carriage was fully stopped, kicked off his boots, and waded into the water, stripping his coat and vest as he went.

Where was the driver? Simon couldn't see the man. The horse thrashed, desperately intent on swimming though it was tethered still to the wagon, churning the water into frothy waves and obscuring Simon's search. He swam around the panicked beast and dove under the water, staying clear of the flailing hooves. Nothing. Again and again. Nothing.

Moments passed. He couldn't tell how long it had been, but he knew time was running out. If the man hadn't died in the accident, he would drown. Simon gasped a huge breath and dove. If he couldn't save the man, he would stay until he pulled him from the depths and returned him to his family. His muscles burned as he continued his hunt, weighted down by his soaked clothes.

Suddenly, the water calmed as the horse swam toward the shore. This time when Simon dove, he saw the driver and reached for him, but couldn't pull him away from the wreck. Simon surfaced, gulping air and quickly kicking under the water again. He positioned himself at the man's back, wrapping his arms around the man's chest, and braced his feet on the side of the wagon. Finally thrusting his legs out, he wrenched the driver away.

When he reached the surface, Simon towed him toward the shore. There was no movement in his arm as Simon swam. It had taken too long. The man was dead. He wondered how he would shelter Cora from the situation, but as he began pulling the body along the muddy bottom, he saw Cora, her hair wet and the skirt torn from her dress and tossed aside. She stood next to the wagon's horse, their own gig's reins wrapped around its neck, fooling it into thinking it was haltered.

Simon stood and wrapped his arms under the shoulders of the driver and pulled him closer to their own carriage before laying him on the ground. As he wrestled with what to say to Cora, she ran to the man and stripped away his shirt. She placed her cheek at his mouth and then on his now-bare chest.

"Help me," she demanded.

Simon didn't know what help they could now offer the man. His chest didn't rise with breathing, and the pallor of his lips and skin spoke of death. Simon realized he was a young man from the thin, fuzzy whiskers on his cheeks, dead long before his time. It would be a blow to his family. How could he shelter Cora from realizing the man was dead? He didn't think she was the fainting type, but what about hysterics? Was she the type to wail?

Before he knelt beside her, Cora had bent to the man's face, pinched his nose, and kissed his lips several times. It worried him that it was the hysterics.

"Take over when I tell you." She pointed at the man's head. The command in her voice was apparent, but he didn't know what to do. Maybe the stress had been too much for her, causing an irrational state.

A light rain began to fall, but Cora didn't seem to notice. "Breathe for him." Her voice was strong. She had moved to the man's chest and leaned—no, pressed—against it repeatedly. "Do it now. Share your air with him."

Simon leaned over the man as he had seen her do and exhaled into the dead man. The man's chest rose with the breaths as Cora leaned back on her heels and watched.

"Stop for a moment." She began vigorously pushing the man's chest again. Wisps of her hair had long ago escaped their bun as she worked. "Your turn. Breathe."

They continued back and forth, stopping occasionally for Cora to check for breath. Then they started again. Simon wondered when she would accept the man's death and cease the ritual. Could she? Was there truly something imbalanced with her in this situation?

She leaned back after another set of compressions and motioned for Simon to take his turn. Before Simon could comply, the dead man spewed vomit, and Cora rolled him to his side.

"Yes! He might make it." Cora pressed a wad of her underskirt into his mouth and ran it across his tongue, then rolled him again to his back and listened at the man's mouth. "He's breathing. Let's get him to a doctor."

Simon realized the young man must be alive. His chest moved on its own, but Simon knelt rooted to the spot, awestruck by the possibility.

"What happened?" Simon gazed at Cora. "What did you do?"

Cora didn't answer but strode to the wagon and threaded one of the reins of their horse through what was left of the other horse's bridle She called over her shoulder to Simon. "Pick him up." She was quickly at his side. "Where's a doctor?" Cora grabbed one arm as Simon took the other, the man upright between them.

"I don't know, but Everett's staff will begin nursing care until we find one." They struggled to pull the man up into Simon's lap before Cora took the reins and turned back the way they came. "Cora, how did . . . I don't even know what that was."

Cora's eyes were fixed straight ahead, but Simon recognized that she was thinking. Finally, she answered. "It's rescue breathing. Sometimes it can save someone's life." And as if considering whether or not to say more, she paused, and then added, "I teach children whose health is very fragile, so one of the requirements is that I learn to do breathing for them if there is ever an emergency. I've never had to do that until today."

"I've never even heard of that."

Emotions swelled in Simon's chest for this woman who would think more of a horse's safety than she did her own. One who cared for the dying without fear, fainting, or the hint of a swoon. And one who showed great intelligence, strength, and calm in a crisis. Cora Rey was a remarkable woman.

"It seems nothing short of a miracle," he said.

He saw her bite the corner of her bottom lip. "I'd rather not make a big deal out of it." Though not a question, it sounded like one, the way she said it. "I feel comfortable saying that he went into the lake, and we pulled him out." He thought he saw fear in her eyes, pleading with him. "We can talk about what happened later. Please don't tell anyone."

Simon nodded but internally questioned the request. They rode in silence to Everett's home.

A whirl of activity ensued when they reached the estate, and a groom was sent to fetch the doctor. While the servants were busy with the young man, Simon assisted Cora from the gig. She had adjusted the ripped skirt of her dress to be held up by the riding apron and concealed that beneath her cloak. Her arms crisscrossed her stomach, and one could easily think she was having an attack of nerves instead of holding her clothing together.

As they entered the house, May approached with a worried look for Cora, no doubt because of her disheveled appearance and being soaking wet, and a scowl to reprimand Simon for mistreating Cora so.

"Will you help Cora to her room?" Simon said before May asked a question.

Cora added, "Yes, please." Then she whispered something to her friend.

May placed her arm around Cora's waist, and the women began to climb together.

How would Cora explain the ruined dress? She probably wouldn't have to. May was the kind of friend who would help her dispose of the evidence with no one the wiser. The women made slow, measured steps. Only at the top of the stairs did Cora turn around. Simon saw some sadness to the look in her eyes.

His every nerve and muscle surged with energy. He wanted to

charge up the stairs and take her in his arms. He could hold her until the hurt went away. He knew Cora had done the right thing, a heroic thing, yet she seemed pensive. Surely she didn't regret saving that young man's life. Maybe she felt the weight of the man's survival. For a long moment, they gazed at each other. His heart pressed for him to love her, to claim her, to protect her. She smiled at him without the usual sparkle of her real smile, then disappeared down the hall to her room.

CHAPTER 12

Cora Rey

When Cora turned back at the top of the stairs, Simon was still watching her from below with a worried look. It didn't surprise her as much as it confirmed to her that he was invested in their relationship as much as she was. Today once again proved to her that she was out of time and place. She had a difficult decision to make, and she questioned whether making that one decision would cause the dam to break that held others away. What was she going to do about Simon?

Inside her room, and as soon as the door shut, Cora threw off her cape and tossed it toward the bed. Before she could remove the driving apron, the entire skirt of her dress fell to the floor.

Behind her she heard May gasp, then chuckle. "Well, there's got to be a good story to go with whatever made *that* happen."

Cora turned her back toward May but didn't yet answer her unasked question. What could she say? "I can't get this knot." The sparkle in May's eyes told Cora she was busy making up a tale of her own to go with it. May wasn't typical of the Victorian period, having lived part of her life out of it. Her mother's twentieth-century background brought a progressive element to May's upbringing.

As the strings of the apron left Cora's hips, she turned toward May. "I had to rip it off to swim into the lake and retrieve the horse while Simon rescued the driver of the wagon."

"Wait. Rescue? What wagon? Start at the beginning."

Cora recounted the driving lesson, the accident, the rescue, and CPR. "I didn't think what might happen if I used it, but, well, it's a hundred years early." Cora sat heavily on the side of the bed and dropped her face to her hands. "Have I messed up the future, changed something enough to alter what should be?" Cora paused and exhaled loudly. "I don't belong here."

She felt the weight of the mattress shift as May's arm curved around her shoulders. "No." Cora looked up to see May shaking her head as she continued. "Aunt Nellie says 'time is a fuzzball.' My mother thought time was a line that ordered the world and constrained everyone and everything to a specific point." May pulled Cora up.

"Let's get you out of these clothes and into something dry." May turned Cora's back to her and began unlacing the bodice. "Time isn't what you think it is. There isn't *one* time—there are billions. We each have our own thread of time. Our threads start and stop, but they are all mixed up in the fuzzball, too. Your thread has touched this time, so you're here. Everything that you do is part of your thread. That wagon driver has his own thread. Even though your threads touched, you didn't change his thread. You can't. It's his."

Cora hoped that was true. It was hard to imagine what May described, but May was living it, and so was Cora. And she had never felt more alive than she did here.

"Get behind the partition and step out of the rest of those sodden clothes."

Cora pulled the wet fabric from her body and legs and threw them over the top. A rap on the bedroom door stopped their conversation. May opened it, and the thin voice of a maid said, "His Grace asked that we deliver these. Can I help the miss?"

May replied, "No, thank you. We're doing fine, but put the buckets on the floor by the dressing screen." Cora heard several sets of footfalls. Then the door closed again, and May approached the screen. "Are you done?"

"Yes." Cora peeked around the partition to see what had been delivered.

"Simon sent up some warm water and towels." Cora noticed a suggestive quality about the smile May wore. "That's very thoughtful, isn't it?" May handed Cora a towel, which she wrapped around herself. "Let's clean your hair first."

Cora sat on a chair and leaned forward over an empty bucket while May poured some water over her head, then washed Cora's hair. When she finished, May wrapped another towel around Cora's head and pointed her back to the screen.

"You wash now, and I'll ... get rid of your clothes."

Later, another rap on the door sounded, and Cora heard May say, "Thank you."

"What is it?" Cora asked, still giving herself a sponge bath.

"His Grace asked that a letter be delivered."

Cora looked around the screen.

"I'll just set this right here for you to read later." She placed the note on the table. "Seems important, doesn't it?"

Cora nodded but couldn't answer. Her heart and mind were overflowing with thoughts of how she felt about Simon. That was part of the problem. Not part—it was the whole thing. She dropped the towel from around her and stood on it as she sponged off her feet.

She knew she was way beyond curious about Simon. Her interest had started with that, but it had moved on to admiring his determination. Lately, she had added the qualities of loyalty, graciousness, and honesty to her growing list of all-the-things-I-like-about-him. And today she had added trusting. He had followed her lead and performed rescue breathing without questioning her. Warmth and caring sparkled in her stomach.

She didn't think she'd fallen in love—yet. Nor had he, but left unchecked, these feelings would get there fast. Since she would be going back to her century on the next full moon when the mural was completed, Cora wouldn't play with Simon's feelings. She liked him too much.

When she was with him, he eclipsed everyone and everything else that was happening. When he wasn't around, her thoughts strayed to him with great frequency. What could she do? She had to go back, but how could she leave him? Would he consider going with her? Would that be possible? Aunt Nellie was trying to figure that out. It seemed insane. For sure, he would think *she* was if she were to ask. In her time, he might be able to choose if he wanted to be able to hear. If this wasn't some cruel trick of the universe, maybe it was an opportunity for Simon to change his life.

Although to the rest of society, he didn't seem to be looking for a wife, even dodging several women's embarrassing attempts, she was certain that his feelings for her had grown beyond friendship as well. Spending their lives together was beginning to make sense to her.

No. She would stop this. She gave a determined nod to herself. A little hurt now would save heartbreak later. But deep down, she knew it wouldn't be a little hurt now to leave him.

A new chemise and drawers flicked over the dressing screen. Cora dried off and tugged them on, then she stepped out from behind the screen to a chair where she could pull the stockings over her feet, tying them above her knees. Next, she pulled the corset down, but knew she'd need May's help for this part. May crossed the room. Tossing a new dress across a chair, she stepped behind Cora to begin pulling the ties. With the corset in place, May gathered the dress on her arms and pulled it over Cora's head.

"Now, back to our discussion," she said as she began fastening the buttons. "You said you think you don't belong here. Well, I don't belong to this time, either. I was born in yours. I have a birth certificate and a driver's license to prove it. That should rip a hole in the space-time continuum, don't you think? How about this? I've ridden in a taxi, shopped at a mall, had baby shots, and drunk Coca-Cola. I've spent enough time there to earn a college degree." May waved away Cora's startled look. "All of that together must be enough to shatter the universe." She paused. "Or perhaps just theories about the universe."

May finished the buttons and brought the ties behind Cora's back to make a bow. "Both centuries are part of my own thread. They are part of my mother's and all of my siblings', too." She stood in front of Cora. "That other theory requires you to believe that time is one dimensional. Yet here you stand—so it's not."

May turned Cora to look in the mirror. "You're dressed. I'll send a maid to do your hair." May's gaze was intense toward Cora through the reflection in the glass, a rare look for her, crowding out her natural mirth, when she asked, "Do you belong here? I can't answer that question. Only you can make the choice."

May walked to the door but turned around just before she left. "How do you know where you belong until you've been there?" She stepped out, and the door shut.

Cora quickly opened the letter to read before the maid arrived.

My Dearest Cora,

I am in awe of your compassion and knowledge. Thank you for driving out with me today.

With sincere appreciation,

Simon

P.S. There are times, many times, when I feel that I'm not prepared to lead the estate. Father would take my older brothers out on estate business while I was left behind. I thought it was because I wasn't old enough, that someday I would be, but my twelfth year came and went, and I wasn't taken from the schoolroom to meet the tenants or visit the shearing sheds in the north. I was sent to school. The years passed, and I was passed over. I suppose I've continued to think of myself as unworthy and unable.

But you give me hope. Neither of us was prepared to save a man's life today. If I just follow your example and live as true as I can, without retreating from difficulty, all will be well.

Cora folded the letter and tucked it into a drawer. It touched her heart to think that Simon believed that she made him a better person. She felt like she was better with him as well. Yes, this separation would hurt them both.

***

The next day, as the ladies were in the morning room, and the men had gone out riding, a carriage arrived, delivering four women. Cora recognized Simon's mother and two sisters but not the fourth woman who traveled with them. Remembering Simon's comment about "accosting an American," Cora wanted to leave the room before the women entered but realized she'd have to scurry through the hallway and past the door where they'd enter to do so. *I don't scurry.* Instead, she watched through the window as the processional approached the house.

"That's His Grace's family, right?" Cora asked Lucy Radnor, who shared the couch with her.

"Yes, they're breaking their journey here and will continue to London in a couple of days." Lucy clasped her hands in front of her. Cora wondered if something about their arrival made her nervous. "The dowager duchess is a school friend of Mrs. Hawley's."

"Who is that with them?" Cora had to admit, the woman looked like a goddess, tall and slender with more cleavage on display than she usually saw in the daytime here. Black, glossy curls and braids surrounded a classical face with full lips and large eyes. She had the kind of poise that was typical of televised Hollywood events.

"Her two daughters. The elder is Miss Tuttle, Georgia, and the younger is Miss Virginia Tuttle. The woman wearing green is Lady Atkins. Her name is Emaline. She's the same age as Simon and Everett." Lucy looked squarely into Cora's eyes. "Everett believes she is highly infatuated with Simon's title, and has the support of his sisters to become his duchess."

Cora studied Lady Atkins. Yes, she was what Cora expected a woman with a high social ranking to look like.

May approached her friends. "What is *she* doing here?" she hissed.

"Simon's family is stopping over. Since Emaline *is* their cousin, I suppose she came along." Hearing Cora's light gasp, Lucy added, "Their grandmothers were sisters—Emaline is their distant cousin."

"Not distant enough at this moment," May said, then leaned closer and dropped her voice. "That viper was engaged to Simon's oldest brother when he died. Before the end of the following season, she married an ancient earl with a bad cough who died within weeks, leaving her with a lovely title, property of her own, and a generous settlement."

"So, now she wants an upgrade," Cora said to herself, but must have spoken aloud as May snorted, and Lucy looked at her with wonder. "She wants to raise her status in society."

Lucy nodded. "Exactly."

The butler escorted the arriving party to the morning room, and a series of curtsies began. Cora watched with fascination as lower-ranking women bobbed to those of higher rank. When the series was completed, their eyes turned to Cora, and May made the introduction.

Cora tipped her head to the side. "My pleasure to meet you." She saw Simon's sisters' eyes narrow and his mother's chin lift as she gave a sniff before averting her gaze.

"Hardly an appropriate greeting for a duchess," Lady Atkins mumbled.

May's mouth opened, but before she could speak, Cora spoke directly to Lady Atkins with a smile on her lips, and she hoped a lighthearted voice. "I'm American. We bow to no one." Then she held eye contact with Simon's mother and added, "But it is an immense pleasure just the same."

Immediately, Mrs. Hawley stepped forward and gestured to the hallway. "You've had quite a journey. I'm so happy you're here. Let's get you settled."

The group turned toward the door, but Lady Atkins twisted back and stared at Cora. Her eyes traveled down her dress, and she made no pretense that she was judging her harshly as she lifted her hand as if to cover a laugh.

Cora had had enough and flicked her fingers, saying, "Shoo. Shoo now." Then she turned her back on the woman.

May burst out laughing while Lucy appeared shocked.

Cora commented, "Well, not a very promising start. I'd guess Lady Atkins and I won't be friends. Well, really all of them."

"Oh, you never know." May shrugged her left shoulder. "Maybe they'll admire your backbone, and it will work out fine."

Cora tried to decide if May was sincere. Lucy spoke up. "Not likely that, is it?"

"Definitely not." May threw her arms around the women's shoulders and walked them back to the sofa. "There is some history you'll need to know, Cora." The women leaned together. "It's not a coincidence they have arrived, and this won't be the last we see of them. All three ladies have a scheme. Lady Atkins has her sights set on Simon, and I expect her to follow him from event to event, using her connections with his family to get close to him."

Cora pondered that. In her current state, she didn't know if that was a good thing or a bad when both options were painful.

"Miss Virginia Tuttle has made no secret of wanting to marry Wetheridge," May said.

"She can have him," Cora offered.

Lucy twisted her hands in her lap, and Cora saw the same tension she had seen in her moments before. "And Lady Georgia Tuttle would marry Everett, should he offer. I think both their mothers might want that since they're close friends."

"Don't worry, Lucy. You are firmly settled in Everett's heart," Cora said.

"I wish that was true, but I doubt—often." She shook her head slightly as she continued, her voice a whisper. "He may love to spend time with me. He may even love to kiss me." May laid her hand on top of Lucy's and gave a little squeeze. "But he has made no offer. And another season has ended ... " Her voice trailed to nothing.

The three women sat together in silence. Cora wondered if she was at liberty to tell what she knew of Everett's service to Simon as well as his plea that he desired to make Lucy his own.

No. It wasn't her story to tell. The most she could do was have a frank conversation with Everett—and maybe Simon. Which she would tonight or at breakfast in the morning. Cora was often the only female who ate breakfast when the men did. She didn't like to see Lucy feel like she was being dangled along.

May stood from the couch. "Let's get our hats and go for a walk before they return. With any luck, we won't have to see them until dinner."

Cora saw the letter on her bed as she entered her room. It simply said, "Garden maze tonight." She felt a touch of disappointment as the letter had none of their usual banter. No joke. No long P.S. with personal revelations. No signature or even a wax seal. She chided herself for being spoiled by his previous letters. He probably penned it in a hurry before he left to go riding that morning.

She tucked it into the bottom of her trunk, donned a hat, and hurried down the stairs to join Lucy and May. When was she supposed to meet him? Surely he'd give her some sign.

Cora, May, and Lucy extended their walk and returned to the Hawley estate in time to begin dressing for dinner. She didn't see Simon or any of the men for that matter. When she came down for dinner, Simon was in the salon talking with his mother, sisters, and Lady Atkins, who was worse than a cat, rubbing herself against him accidentally on purpose whenever she laughed or turned to look somewhere.

She joined May and waited, glancing at Simon all too often.

When they were invited into the dining room, Lady Atkins

began reaching for Simon's arm, but he quickly extended it toward his mother.

She tried to push it away. "We needn't be so rigid in the orders of precedence. You're a young man and needn't waste social opportunities on me. You may escort Emaline and become reacquainted."

"You are charitable to consider my feelings, but it is not a waste for a mother to take her son's arm. I rarely have the honor. I'd be pleased to escort you in." Simon gave his mother a bow and placed her hand in the crook of his arm, then led her out the door. The rest of the guests paired off and followed behind.

The seating could not have been more to Cora's liking. Well maybe, but she was satisfied. Simon sat at one end of the table to Mrs. Hawley's right while Lady Atkins sat on Mr. Hawley's left at the other end. Cora sat beside Everett with May directly across from her and Simon in plain view. The only unfortunate placement was that Lucy was seated far from any of them across from Lady Atkins.

Cora spent much of the meal trying to decide why it mattered to her if Lady Atkins married Simon. She told herself that she didn't want to see anyone used for their social position, but that seemed to be acceptable and even encouraged in this time. She also believed Simon deserved much more though she didn't know Lady Atkins at all to be able to make that judgment.

Annoyance at herself built as she failed to clear her thoughts, contradicting herself as they bounced around.

Anyway, that was Simon's call, not hers. Did she really think that when she left, she would have so altered his life that he wouldn't find someone to share it with? No. He would find happiness. She had to believe that. Then why did the motivation for marriage matter? Her soul felt deflated, and her heart was limp. At least she wouldn't have to be here to see it.

She sat in her chair, her back straight but her head bent as she stared without seeing her dessert, her spoon poised just off the table, the apricot ice molded into a rose melting out of shape. Cora was completely torn. If she met him in the maze, would she just be adding greater heartbreak when she left? If she didn't meet him, she wouldn't know what message he had for her. She wouldn't be able to look into his face shadowed in the moonlight. She wouldn't sleep at all tonight with wondering.

She realized her bone-deep sorrow and the little antagonism she felt toward Miss Atkins were because . . . She admitted she might love Simon . . . and she was leaving him.

Thankfully the women stood to leave the dining room. Much more of that apricot ice, and tears might have begun falling.

When the men entered the salon, Simon was last through the door. He immediately walked to Everett, turning them both so their conversation was private. Simon whispered something to Everett, then his gaze met Cora's. Everett nodded once, and Simon left the room. After excusing himself to his mother, Everett followed. Cora, standing near the doorway, watched as both men disappeared down the hall.

Cora wondered if he was going to the maze now. Given her realization in the dining room, was it wise to follow him tonight? After just a few minutes, when Simon didn't return, she decided to risk more entanglements in her heart for another moment with him before she left England. Perhaps love was worth it even for a few days. She slipped around the edges of the room and out the door.

CHAPTER 13

Simon Tuttle

Everett met Simon at the door to his study. "Why would Wetheridge stroll out to the garden at this time of night?" Everett asked as he twisted the key in the lock and stood aside for Simon to enter.

Simon thought Everett looked as suspicious as Simon felt.

"You don't think ...?" He didn't continue with what he thought but shook his head and gave Simon a hopeless look.

"I have no idea, but I will find out." Simon walked across the dark wood floor, his boot heels clicking with the determination in his step. "If he thinks to have an assignation with my sister, I'll beat him bloody."

Simon sneaked out the exterior door of the office, following Wetheridge but keeping to the shadows where he wouldn't be seen. He'd run the garden maze so many times in his youth that he could do it blindfolded. Neither the hidden exits nor the false turns would give him any trouble. Of course, Wetheridge could probably do the same. As Everett's cousin, he'd likely had years of practice in this maze too.

As he slid around the corner, he saw Wetheridge pause for a moment near the formal entrance. His face turned back toward the house even as silver light broke through the back door, and a woman stepped out.

Simon hissed in his breath and held it. Suddenly he wished the tryst *was* with his sister. Instead, he recognized Cora's gold dress. Throughout dinner she'd caught his attention as he admired that color against her skin and how it brightened her hair. He exhaled slowly, his gut tightening when his own eyes verified her familiar appearance—her curly tresses lifted off her neck and the alluring spiral lovelock she'd left dangling over one shoulder. Hoping he was mistaken, he felt crushed when he confirmed even by the way she moved, stepping surely though looking over her shoulder once and striding away from the party and toward the maze—toward Wetheridge.

He didn't know what compelled him to enter the maze through a hidden passage, or perhaps he clung to one hope that he was mistaken. Or perhaps he would verify it with his own eyes before he gave her up. He also questioned if he was seeking to release the pain he felt at seeing her race to meet Wetheridge. Like pressing on a scab, he had to know.

Simon shook himself and straightened his shoulders. Cora, in many ways, was inexperienced with London society and the rules it imposed. He told himself that it was for her protection that he would remain near. He would step into the maze himself rather than let her be compromised—even though she seemed accepting of the plan.

He made his way slowly through the deep shadows of the trees bordering the lawn. He forced his feet to move quietly, slowly, though his mind was racing. Had she a special interest in the man? Surely not. But she made a straight line toward the hedge. Had they rendezvoused before? He doubted it. He would have noticed

Cora missing from a dinner or any other event as her presence was a constant pull to his mind, and his eyes searched for her before he knew he wanted to see her again. It must be a coincidence. Must be.

Wetheridge was nowhere to be seen now as he'd entered straightway. Cora didn't even pause but almost charged into the entrance. He brushed off the possibility that she was excited for the meeting, thinking that perhaps she was angry. That would explain the determination and fast pace. Simon decided to go through a back entrance into the hedge where he could see what was happening. He had to move quickly but quietly to reach the fountain while she followed the twisting passageways. *If* she planned to go to the fountain.

Pausing at the last corner, Simon glanced around the hedges before entering the centerpiece of the maze. He moved by degrees, scanning the open space. The fountain bubbled as water cascaded out of the rose-shaped tubs as if an endless rainstorm had filled them to spilling over to the level below. Gray statuary and exotic flowering trees decorated the sanctuary's five-sided borders between the various entrances.

Wetheridge stood to the side of the hedges where the light cast from the full moon wouldn't touch him, and he could watch the main entrance without being seen. If Cora expected to meet him here, why would he hide?

Simon wondered, when Cora had shown Wetheridge no preference, why she would meet him now. Here. It twisted his heart to imagine what he hadn't recognized. Of course, she could have spoken with the man when Simon couldn't hear their conversation or at some time when he wasn't present.

The flash of a white dress through the leaves broke Simon from his thoughts. He strained to hear women's faint voices and heavy steps. They were giggling, followed by exaggerated hushing sounds as they rounded the corner right behind him. He jerked back and slipped into one of the dead ends where he hoped to be hidden in the shadows as they entered the back entrance to the hedgerow.

May and Lucy passed by without looking his direction, then paused at the opening Simon had looked through moments ago.

Who isn't *coming to the garden maze tonight?*

The women whispered back and forth as Simon ducked out of hiding and eased back out to the last corner, keeping quiet not only to maintain secrecy but to avoid scaring the wits out of the two women less than three strides in front of him. After they passed and stood near the entrance, he made a bit of noise and walked back to the opening to the central room of the hedge maze.

Wide-eyed, the women turned his way as he tramped forward. May swung a fist at him that he barely dodged while Lucy's hands flew up to cover a gasp.

"Shh!" May hissed in his direction. Then, with a little accusation in her voice, she asked, "Are you here to meet Cora?"

Lucy answered May before Simon could. "Everett said that Wetheridge went into the maze before Cora." She turned away from Simon. "He's there." Lucy pointed across the small enclosed lawn. "Everett assured me that Simon was following Wetheridge, too," she said to May, who turned to Simon and said, "Glad you finally made it." Then Lucy continued her train of thought. "And I want to know what he's about."

"She didn't tell you when she left—either of you?" Simon asked.

"There was a letter," Lucy started, but at that moment Cora entered the center of the hedge, looking around as if in expectation.

She continued to walk as if looking for someone, sideways, backward, and forwards swinging her head from side to side as she approached the fountain at the center.

Wetheridge skirted along the edge of the bushes, keeping to a shadow cast by the moonlight, walking nearer to the spot where Simon, Lucy, and May were concealed. Simon's heart raced, pounding in his chest. Why didn't he step from the shadows?

Cora must have heard a sound and twisted around, staring into the darkness when Wetheridge stepped out, apparently assuming they were alone. Even Simon could hear the man's voice.

"Surely you came to meet me here," Wetheridge said, his voice forceful. "As I did you." He stalked forward.

Cora backed away and skirted around the edge of the fountain, keeping it between them. She was now quite close to where Simon stood. "I did no such thing. I was merely out for a midnight stroll."

Simon watched as Wetheridge approached her with movements like a prowling cat.

"It seems your reputation will be in shatters," Wetheridge called toward her.

Simon tensed and made to move forward, but May pulled him back, shaking her head.

"I have no intention of telling anyone you barged in on my walk unwelcomed," Cora replied.

"Oh? But I shall," he answered, taking large steps to catch up with her.

Sure now that Cora had not arranged a tryst, Simon slid between Lucy and May and offered an elbow to each.

"We'll take care of this," May said, then pulled Lucy with her into the center, leaving Simon by the boundary wall.

Cora responded by joining her friends and twining her arm with Lucy's. "As I said, I was out for a stroll—with my friends. Good night."

"Perhaps I should stay and walk you back," Wetheridge suggested.

"No need," Lucy replied. "I trust you can find your way out." Then May flicked her fingers as if to shoo him along when he didn't move.

Wetheridge exited the center of the maze, but Simon had no idea whether he'd return to the house. The women exited through the front entrance while Simon retraced his steps through the green corridor to the opposite side of the yard in time to see Wetheridge re-enter the house.

Simon approached the women on the back lawn, and May said,

"Good evening, Your Grace." She turned to her friends and said, "Shall we rejoin the party?"

Simon bowed to the ladies, who returned curtsies. May and Lucy took Cora by the arms before he walked away. A million questions flooded his mind. What was she doing there? Why did she even come out? What letter were they talking about? What did Wetheridge want with her? That one was easy to answer. If he thought to ruin her and marry her, he might be surprised to know Simon had determined to give her an alternative choice, one he found vastly appealing.

He stopped and asked, "May I accompany you back to the house? I'll stay far enough away that I won't overhear your conversation."

May opened her mouth as if to object, but Cora interrupted. "Thank you."

Even if he were only five steps behind them, unless they were speaking in his direction or loudly, he wouldn't hear them well enough to understand anyway. Cora knew it, too. Would there be a time when he would be able to ask Cora about tonight? Did he have any right to question her choices at all? Perhaps he did if they counted each other friends.

The women strolled together arm in arm in front of him back to the veranda. They waited for him at the stairs, and he accompanied them inside. Wetheridge was conversing with Simon's mother near the door. As the small group entered, a surprised look fell on Wetheridge's face, as well as that of Simon's mother.

"Beautiful night for a walk is it not, Wetheridge?" Simon asked.

May and Lucy bobbed a curtsy, and Cora nodded to Simon's mother, then walked quickly behind Wetheridge to rejoin the party in the salon.

"Was something wrong, Wetheridge?" Simon asked. "I thought I saw you on the back lawn."

"Just getting some fresh air," he replied and hurried away.

"Mother, what have you and Wetheridge to discuss in private?" Simon asked.

"You know well his interest in your sister. I think it best to be amiable to the man who may be family one day."

She too left him. Simon was no closer to unraveling the mystery he'd witnessed in the maze. He strongly doubted the man's interest in his sister.

Before Simon rejoined the party, Everett approached him from the hallway. "What the devil is that man up to?" Everett asked.

Simon shook his head. "Perhaps he has decided to press his suit with Cora."

"Not likely she'll find that very welcome," Everett replied.

Simon hoped so. He would have believed that a day ago. Now, he was less certain. But he would be seeing her tomorrow since they would be having an outing of sorts.

***

The next day, Simon spied May and Cora standing at the kitchen door to the manor house in worn-looking dark skirts and white shirts as instructed when he drove a farm wagon to the garden gate. Lord Saalfeld sat beside him, his head swinging frequently both ways. The man was nervous but still willing to spend the day with two unmarried women without chaperones.

It was early in the morning and only servants were about—except for the two gentlemen dressed as commoners and the two ladies who would soon join them.

The ladies scurried to the wagon, black bonnets secured around their faces. Anyone looking on would imagine it was market day, and several servants were making an early start of it. Simon held the horses as Saalfeld jumped to the ground and assisted the ladies into the wagon.

"We're sitting in the back?" May asked as he pulled the ladies to the rear.

Simon held his breath. May had always seemed rigid about the expectations of her class. If she balked, Cora would not be spending the day with him.

"Today, I'm not an earl, and you're not a lady, my lady. When we're commoners, this is how it's done." Saalfeld's voice barely contained his excitement. "Step on the spoke of that wheel. Your other foot will step there, and then you'll swing your first leg over." He flashed her a rare smile—at least, one rarely seen by Simon. May seemed to bring out the best in his friend.

"Fine. Turn your back. I don't want you to see my ankles."

"We grew up next to each other. I've seen your ankles dangling from horses and trees more often than the queen wears jewels." Saalfeld laughed. "Have they grown their own appendages? That would be something to see."

"Yes, and I won't have you gossiping about it."

Cora moved past her friend. "Oh, for the love, May. See your ankles? Let's get going already." Cora stepped where Saalfeld had indicated and entered the wagon bed.

"Well, Cora. You've got some things to learn about this time—I mean place. Where's the mystique in just clambering up?" May lifted her hem and followed her in while Saalfeld stood to catch her if she took a misstep before he joined Simon.

Simon watched as Cora scooted to the front of the wagon bed where the women were to sit. He'd placed two cushions there to offer a bit of comfort on the wooden boards. Their seat would likely be much more comfortable than his. The narrow bench where he sat barely supported his derriere, effectively conducting the jar of every rut in the road straight up his spine.

"Will you tell us the big secret now?" Cora asked as the wagon began to move along the lane toward the road.

She was kneeling on her cushion and leaning toward him. Her face was barely behind his shoulder, and he could smell the lilac scent of her soap. At this moment, he wanted to say yes to anything she asked, but he would win her first. On with the plan. "No."

"Perhaps Your Grace would like us to guess your intentions." May sighed deeply. "Hmm. You're running a little short of money because of the outrageous sums you pay for simple box lunches and have made arrangements for us to supply some kind of labor to earn funds."

Cora continued the story. "Oh, yes. His Grace must have a terrible gambling problem as well. It seems he bets on shooting matches. The only way for him to repay the sums owed is to provide extra servants—us—for a lavish house party."

"And we are to wash the kitchen while the duke and earl muck out the horse stalls." May tapped Saalfeld on the shoulder. "You can muck out a stall, can you not?"

"Of course," he answered. "One stall to every five pans you wash."

Simon could hear the mock horror as Cora added, "Oh, May. What if we aren't a labor crew, but instead, we're secretly eloping? I mean, there are two of them and two of us."

"That's terribly inconvenient. Surely one of them would have mentioned that we needed to bring some personal items with us. At least a small valise. I'd need to bring a few dresses to choose from."

"I'd never choose this dress or hat to wear for my wedding. I'd need a little jewelry and some nicer shoes." Cora giggled. "And plenty of ribbons."

"And of course, if I were to elope, I'd need another carriage for my parents. I couldn't imagine them not there to witness my marriage."

"That makes it not an elopement," Saalfeld said.

"Sh. This is our story. You're already in hot water for having a gambling problem," May answered.

"That was Simon," Saalfeld countered.

May waved off the comment.

"And a lady's maid for us to look our best." Cora leaned over the wagon box again. "Shall we turn around and get a few more things?"

Lord Saalfeld answered, "You've found us out. There's no reason to continue now that it's no longer a secret. It's taken all the fun out of it, so we needn't complete our scheme."

Simon's heart hammered in his chest. This was truly what a couple must feel as they elope—sneaking out of town incognito before the house has arisen for the day. The thought had a certain appeal to him. However, today he had other plans.

"As entertaining as your guesses have been, you haven't hit upon the design of our day, ladies. In the Hessian bag, you'll find more props." Simon had gathered two well-used shawls and straw ladies' hats of similar age and disrepair. They would need them to blend into this crowd. "We're nearly there."

"Nearly where?" Cora asked, to Simon's pleasure. "There isn't a town in sight, just gently rolling hills—though I do love them."

"And sheep," May added.

Simon remained silent while only a few houses and a barn still blocked the clues to their outing. As soon as they rounded the next bend in the road, there would likely be a crowd beginning to gather.

And there was. Wagons, phaetons, and various carriages were parked along a circular dirt road. As expected, the polished conveyances parked near each other while the ones driven by those of lesser means congregated on the other side of the large loop. Simon drove to that side and pulled in alongside other farm wagons. Then he jumped from the driver's seat and lowered the tailgate.

Simon and Saalfeld sat on the edge and motioned for the ladies to join them.

Once settled, May said dully, "That's a flat course." When no one responded, she spoke again. "You brought us to a horse race. Why did we have to wear servants' clothes? We could be sitting over there." She motioned to the stylish carriages across the way before she continued. "And watch from the comfort of a buggy."

"That's all true," Simon replied. Then he leaned forward to look at the women's faces. He hoped that he'd made the right assumption that they would like this adventure. "But ladies of fashionable society are not allowed to leave their buggies and mingle with jockeys and horses. I thought you might enjoy the freedom of getting closer to the action of the race a bit more."

Cora slid from the wagon bed almost before he finished.

"You're right." She slipped her hand under his bicep and wrapped her fingers around his forearm. "In fact, I do want to see the horses up close. Will we be betting today or just spectating?"

"Now who has the gambling problem?" he teased Cora.

"I'll have you know I'm an outstanding judge of horseflesh."

"There's an opportunity to bet should we find a horse that seems a good investment." He was relieved that he would please Cora with this outing.

May jumped to the dirt as well. Cora smiled at her friend and winked when she said, "I propose we make a game of it. We'll place our bets and see who makes the better choices—the women or the men."

May quickly added, "The winning team will get to claim four privileges. . ." She cocked her head to the side and lifted her eyebrows at Saalfeld. ". . .within reason, of course, of the losing team."

Saalfeld laughed. "You might be surprised what I find reasonable if you would just ask."

"I doubt it," she answered, patting his arm. Then she turned to Cora. "That's two for each of us when we win."

Cora smiled up at Simon as he began leading her toward the horses. "I'll need to borrow some money to wager. I'm a little unprepared."

"I apologize for swooping you away this morning without your pin money." Simon wanted to be the one to supply that money. She would find him a more than generous husband—anything she wanted would be hers—if she would accept him. He turned his attention to the group and announced, "We each wager one pound on two out of the eight match races today. We'll tally the earnings, and the spoils will go to the winners. Agreed?"

With the wager fixed, Simon led the group to see the horses and jockeys.

"Is there a horse you prefer?" Simon asked from very close behind Cora's ear.

Cora took a deep breath, savoring the scent of the horses.

"Well, this one isn't tall enough," she said, walking on. "This one is, but it's rather short from the shoulder to hindquarters." She stopped at the next and examined it slowly. "This one is a possible winner. I won't decide yet until I've seen the rest."

Cora and Simon continued down the line of horses and then returned to the third one. "The front is powerful." The horse danced a bit at the commotion outside his stall. "He's anxious. He wants to run. I'll take this one. I doubt very highly that he's good for anything except racing."

After the men placed the bets, they returned to the women and led them to the fence. Both women squeezed in front of Simon and Saalfeld to watch the races. Simon encouraged Cora to stand on the bottom rung to get a better look, and he placed his hands on her waist to steady her. She angled back to lean against him and seemed happy that he stepped forward to facilitate it.

That earned him a sly smile and a giggle from Cora. They watched the races with great excitement and cheered their horses.

Simon knew the outcome of the women's bets as soon as he pocketed the payouts—six pounds, two half shillings, a thruppence, and a penny. Saalfeld's tally would be the deciding factor. Simon was torn between the advantages of winning or losing this bet. Of course he'd love to have special privileges, but he might equally enjoy having Cora ask something of him that only he could fulfill. Either way, this bet seemed like the best outcome of the day.

He emptied his pocket into the back of the wagon bed for the women to see and count their money. The women huddled together as Cora watched May count the coins. Saalfeld consulted Simon on their combined profit as well—two pounds, a shilling, and a grout.

When the men announced their total, May jumped to her feet in the wagon bed, followed by Cora, who shared a congratulatory hug. "We won. We nearly tripled them," May said.

"I'm already wondering what I'll demand for the boon of winning." The men stood on the dirt looking up at them. Cora continued, "We should be better sports and not brag, but we won. We won." She wrapped her arms around May once more.

Simon cleared his voice rather loudly and waited for the women to look his way. "Cora, I believe you borrowed two pounds from me to place the wagers."

Saalfeld laughed and added, "As did May." He thrust his palm toward the women. May grudgingly passed him two coins.

Cora likewise reached out to relinquish hers. "And where does that leave us?" Cora asked her partner.

But Simon answered first, his fingers tightening momentarily around hers. "We are horse to horse."

"Tied," May said.

"No one won?" Cora asked as she stepped back into the wagon.

May shook her head as she followed, but Simon couldn't let the opportunity slip away. "I believe we have four winners instead of none. I suggest that we split the windfall evenly with each of us taking one."

"Capital," Saalfeld agreed.

"Better than nothing," Cora said, settling beside May on the provided pillow to make the return trip to Everett's home. "I'll have to think on how I'll spend that favor, Mr. Duke."

Simon smiled and returned to the driver's seat. *So will I.*

When he returned to his room that night, he had a letter waiting for him, written in a familiar hand.

Dear Simon,

You are cordially invited to a private recital at eight in the evening day after tomorrow when we are back in Twickenham. I hope you will accept.

Yours,

Cora

P.S. I don't know the location for the event yet, so please check with Aunt Nellie about it an hour or two before. That adds to the mystery, doesn't it?

CHAPTER 14

Cora Rey

CORA SWAYED GENTLY WITH THE CARRIAGE, LOOKING OUT THE window at the countryside as they traveled back to Aunt Nellie's home. She didn't know why she had expected England to be flat, but instead, it rolled gently like waves across the soil, up and down, smoothly rising and sinking. So green—like Ohio, where she'd gone to college, and wooded like that too. The hills here were densely covered with trees and shrubs unless they had been cleared for farming. Those fields she liked the best, a thick green carpet surrounded by dry-stack rock walls, a boundary to keep the sheep in or out.

It was hard to imagine that, just a month ago, she'd arrived in England, then found herself tossed back to 1850 and playing the part of an heiress on an unprecedented, almost inconceivable vacation. But here she was, riding back to Twickenham Manor within days of returning to her own time. Thoughts of making a mistake consumed her. But which mistake?

Leaving. Shouldn't she just be grateful for the experience of a lifetime, for living a dream, and go back at the appointed time? After all, that's the way of vacations. You plan and save and go. They're amazing, whirlwind, walk-your-feet-off days that end all too soon.

Then with a long plane ride back home and a few posts to Facebook and Instagram, it's relegated to that part of the brain that stores wonderful memories. In that place, the colors of the sights you've seen fade, the scents of flowers and food dissipate, and the cherished faces of newly made friends blur.

Cora's body hummed nervously just under her skin. She was afraid to lose all of this and a part of herself along with those memories. Her mind reeled, and her emotions seemed out of control. Maybe the fear was hinting at the other mistake, though. Staying. What would she be giving up? This was the kind of decision you asked your parents to help you make, but she was alone for this one.

She decided that stay or go, she still planned to give Simon another gift of music. He had mentioned that he enjoyed the violin before his hearing loss, and she wanted him to hear it again. He should have received the invitation last night.

A week ago, the carriage had been alive with conversation as they traveled to Everett's house, but today, Lucy, her mother, and May also seemed to prefer the quiet of this journey back.

When they arrived, Aunt Nellie burst out through the door, her purple hem bouncing as she hurried to the carriage when they stopped. The footman hustled to reach the handle before she did and opened the door, then helped the women down.

"You've been gone so long. What a trip you've had, ladies. Your rooms are ready, and bath water will be taken up." Nellie gathered them around as a hen pulling chicks under her wing and led them up the steps. "Your comfy beds await you where you can rest, ladies. Come down for tea if you'd like, or I'll see you at dinner."

Aunt Nellie dropped off the women at the various rooms until only she and Cora were left in the long hallway.

"Are Reese and Kaitlin still here?" Cora asked. She wondered how their vacation had gone.

"Yes. They've had quite a time of it, too. So much has happened to you all, but those are their stories to tell." Nellie gave Cora a little hug at the door. "We need to talk, don't we? This is quite more than what you had planned, and ... "

The look on Aunt Nellie's face made Cora wonder if she knew more than she was letting on and what *that* was.

". . . And I have something to show you. It might explain a few things, or it might make it worse. I'll have to rethink that. Maybe I'll not show you quite yet. Anyhoo, until later."

"I could come now. I'm not really tired." Honestly, Cora welcomed the chance to be busy—anything to keep her mind off Simon. She had no desire to sit down or lie down. It would only give her mind more time to whirl with indecision.

"No, I've a couple of things to do first." Nellie patted Cora's hand and gave her a wan smile. "Come find me later—on the third floor."

"That's the fourth level, right?" Cora had noticed that in England, they called the first floor the one above the ground floor, but still she doubted she understood it.

Aunt Nellie nodded. "Yes, two floors above this one."

Cora reluctantly entered her room and asked the maid to help her unfasten her heavy traveling clothes, then dismissed her with instructions to wait an hour before sending the bath water. As soon as the door closed, Cora shrugged out of the dress and several layers of petticoats. The chemise was enough for a quick session of exercise.

She began stretching, lunging, and warming up. When worry crept in, she concentrated on her taut muscles or exhaling and pushed it from her mind.

The Krav Maga routine was an easy mental shift. She had always imagined an attacker and visualized the various ways to incapacitate or damage them. Her arms drove, and her legs leaned or kicked with power. She imagined someone behind or in front of her, or she was on the ground fighting someone above. The movement flowed—kick, hammer, elbow. She could feel the stress and indecision draining away. She pushed herself to increase the intensity. Cover, hook, clinch, knee—finding a comforting rhythm in the maneuvers. Advance, strike, retreat.

Her arms and legs burned, and sweat ran down her neck, back, and chest when she realized the bath water would soon be delivered and began her cooldown.

After the bath, she requested the lighter, yellow sprigged muslin dress and only one petticoat. The July weather had turned hot and muggy. The maid gave a puzzled look, and Cora added, "I'll forego the rest of the petticoats. The bell shape is just not that important to me."

After climbing the stairs and then following the sound of Aunt Nellie singing, Cora found her tucked in a far room, sitting on the floor. She stopped at the door before entering the room. The mural the women had found during their tour of Twickenham Manor covered the wall before her. Aunt Nellie, paintbrush in hand, dabbed at the mural, seeming to be finishing some shoes.

"What do you think? Too frilly?" she asked, her head tipping to the left.

Cora stood before the life-sized picture of herself, not having realized she'd approached the mural. The champagne-colored ball gown hung in three ever-widening tiers toward the floor. Each was bordered with a wide pink satin ribbon. Above that, small pink roses trailed along a twisting green vine. Her hand paused without touching the painting. It was as if the paint was dots of light clinging to the wall.

"It's dry," Nellie remarked. "The paint I use is magical but not wet like you'd expect."

Cora's finger followed one line of roses, feeling the thick paint, like frosting, that shaped the petals and buds as they bulged away from the wall. The neckline of the dress hung on the edge of her shoulders, and small puffy sleeves were trimmed with the same pink satin.

"It's perfect." She realized it was the same picture they had fallen through weeks ago, but seeing it freshly painted brought a dawning reality of the decision she had to make—and soon.

"Is it ready now?" Cora asked.

"The mural? No," Nellie answered. "It will be in two days—for the full moon. I've a little more magic to collect and apply, so it will work. That's the trick, you know—the magic. In a mural this size, it's been quite the chore." Aunt Nellie turned and pointed to the other side of the room. "Your new ball gown *is* ready, however."

Across the room, several dresses were hung. Cora recognized the blush of her dress immediately. Her head swung back and forth. It was the exact dress.

Aunt Nellie continued to chatter about the painting. "Oh, I could have done smaller paintings of each of you. I usually just do a portrait, but these dresses begged to be preserved. In the future, this will also be a reminder of your group's friendship. So I run out each morning and collect the magic from the grass before the sun burns it off." Aunt Nellie's voice trailed off as Cora removed her dress from the hanger.

Seed pearls edged the neckline and both sides of the satin ribbons. The dress's outer layer was a sheer organza with the vine embroidered in a twisting running stitch and the roses embroidered with thin ribbon. The under-fabric glittered as if it were shot through with pinpricks of light. She ran her hand over the fabric as if to brush it off, but it just winked and flashed as the skirt moved.

Aunt Nellie spoke up beside her. "I might have gotten a little carried away with your dress—a bit of magic overload is all. Not to worry—the sparkle will fade by Friday."

"Is this what you wanted to show me?" Cora asked.

"No. Well, I should say yes." Aunt Nellie clasped her hands neatly in front of her. "Yes. Definitely. This is it."

Cora doubted the truth of Nellie's claim, especially as the woman's eyes slid away from Cora's. She supposed she'd find out soon enough, whatever the big secret was. She decided to change the subject. "I'd like to use a small room tomorrow night."

"Of course. 'Tis time, isn't it?" Aunt Nellie steepled her fingers in front of her but didn't look to Cora to answer the question. "It will need to be private." She crossed her arms over her chest and raised one finger to tap lightly on her chin as she seemed to study the request. "I wouldn't want to see you get disturbed. Away from nosy guests. It could be locked. Preferably where you might not even be heard. Of course, I could make that happen anywhere."

If Cora hadn't made the initial request, Aunt Nellie's last statement would have seemed a little scary. But that was precisely the kind of room she needed.

"I have just the thing. Follow me down the stairs to the next level—just the right place."

Nellie led her to the other end of the sprawling mansion into a far corner. She opened doors on either side of the hallway. One was appointed as a sitting room and the other a library. "Both are lovely rooms. This one has a view of the River Thames, and this one looks out over the gardens. Both very romantic."

A cold trickle traveled down Cora's spine. She hadn't told Aunt Nellie what she wanted the room for, but the woman seemed to know anyway. A grassy lawn sprawled from the mansion, several acres in length. The river sparkled between the swaying trees at its banks. Two white boats bobbed in their moorings on the tide.

The room itself was beautiful, too. The walls were painted with a subtle mint green, but large white medallions surrounded with levels of carved moldings decorated most of the wall space. The medallions were bordered with twists of gold and ivy. The centers depicted fanciful scenes of faeries and humans in pastoral settings. Even the ceiling carried the theme. A small melodian organ sat against one wall, and richly upholstered chairs and couches clustered together, filling the center of the room.

"This one," Cora said.

"That's a wonderful choice." Nellie shut both doors and clasped her hands in front of her. "Will you need it tonight or tomorrow?"

"Both, if I may." Cora wanted to practice tonight before Simon joined her tomorrow.

"Oh, to be young!" Nellie giggled slightly with the words, then picked up one of Cora's hands to pat it. "Let's get it ready for you." She untied a waist purse and pulled it to open where it had been cinched shut. "Dip your hand in, please." Nellie pushed the bag in Cora's direction.

Cora did as requested and withdrew her hand again. A small gasp escaped her lips. Her hand glowed much the way the fabric on the dress had.

"Open the door."

As Cora's hand gripped the doorknob, the magical glow on her hands flowed like a ripple toward the shore, draining from her hand to surround the knob and soak inside it. She noticed that while the light transferred, she couldn't have removed her hand until it had all disappeared even if she wanted to. The latch disengaged with a popping sound and a gust of wind.

"Step inside, please." Nellie waved her inside the room. "We'll need to do this a few times." She pushed the purse toward Cora again. This time when Cora's hand was aglow with magic, Nellie said, "Now shut the door." As Cora complied, she added, "That way, you will be the only one to open or close this door until the magic is worn out. You need to do it on both sides once again, so you will be able to open and close it twice."

After completing the tasks again, Aunt Nellie pulled some magic dust from the bag and blew across her palm as she turned in a complete circle. "There. Soundproof, too. Now the room is yours and only yours until the magic has been used up."

She began walking back down the long hallway, mumbling a bit, "Oh, to be a fly on the wall. T'would be lovely to witness—hmm—

an easy bit of magic that. . .but no. I won't." She seemed to have decided when she stopped, her face turning toward Cora. "I won't. You'll have the privacy you want." They began walking again. "It's a lovely story. But it's your story."

Cora wondered what Aunt Nellie went on about. If she really knew what Cora planned, why was she determined to see it as romantic or even a story worth telling?

***

Two nights later, she left her room, closing the door quietly behind her. Thankfully, she and her college friends were quartered in the family suites. The newly arriving guests were housed in the farthest north wing of the manor. Most of the lights were out since they hadn't had an evening event and the guests had retired early. She was thankful for country hours tonight. She shouldn't cross paths with anyone she didn't know as she headed south.

Cora sneaked across the house half an hour before she had invited Simon to join her for the recital. She didn't want to risk them being seen together, ducking into a deserted hallway. If they were caught together, people might assume the worst. She thought how strange it was to have to sneak around just to meet with a friend.

Her heart told her that Simon had become more than a friend.

Cora twisted the knob, feeling a blast of wind, and slipped inside, leaving the door ajar behind her. Last night, she had prepared three pieces by Beethoven, Vivaldi, and Bruch. Simon might know the first two, but the third hadn't been composed quite yet.

Her heart raced with anticipation. She held the violin to her chin and moved her fingers as if she were playing but didn't raise the bow. It was a nervous habit from many years ago, something she'd do while she waited to perform, and it was still oddly comforting. She hoped Simon would be able to hear the music—that she wasn't setting him up for a disappointment. The last time had gone well, but the violin made a higher-pitched sound.

It seemed like hours before Simon arrived—black tailcoat,

burgundy vest, black tie, white shirt. *Oh, my!* She closed the door behind him and felt the spurt of breeze blow across her face.

"Thank you for coming." Cora cringed a little. She sounded so formal. Although her nerves were jittery, she didn't feel the paralyzing anxiety that had plagued her for years. She felt safe with him.

"You must know that I'm not likely to refuse you anything."

Simon's smile melted Cora's heart—definitely more than a friend. She reached for his hand and lightly held it as she moved with him to a couch and picked up her bow. Simon sat barely more than a foot beyond the reach of the scroll on top of the fingerboard. With a deep breath, she stood before him and began the Beethoven piece.

When she finished the piece, Simon applauded, appreciation evident on his face but not the surprise she'd seen with the piano experience.

This had gone differently in her mind. She'd hoped that because he was so much closer than he usually would have been during a performance, he would be able to enjoy it more. She wondered how much of the music he'd heard. Should she ask? Would he tell her? She thought he would. He seemed completely honest with her.

"Thanks." Cora gave a slight nod to her audience. "Are you willing to do a little experiment?"

Simon looked a bit skeptical but only briefly. "Yes. It went very well last time. What do you have in mind?"

"Just stand in front of me. Here." Cora pointed to a spot a little to her left. As he did, she realized immediately that their height difference would not let her new plan work—she couldn't reach the fingerboard around him and up that high. Even if she sat beside him, she wouldn't be able to play as she imagined. Then she spied the bench in front of the melodian. Were he to sit and she to kneel—it just might work.

"On second thought, could you pull that bench out into the room?" As he did, Cora ran her fingers over the white abalone keys sparkling with rainbows. One day soon, she'd have to come back to this room to play that little organ. She thrilled inwardly, anticipating adding a new instrument to her experience.

With the bench in the open space, Cora said, "Now have a seat on the end and straddle the corner, not like you would normally sit on this bench."

Simon complied and looked at her expectantly. "I'm going to kneel behind you, and—"

Simon stood abruptly.

She smiled nervously, wondering if she'd crossed some line of propriety. She laid her hand on his forearm. "It's okay. If you sit there, then I can place the violin under your jaw as I play it. It's an experiment, remember?" Simon sat back on the edge, but he didn't look comfortable—more like he was perching.

Cora knelt behind him with her feet hanging over the edge of the bench. She leaned forward and put her hand on the top of his shoulder while in his right ear, she said, "Please scoot back until you feel my knees."

Simon shook his head slowly as if telling himself that he shouldn't, but he slid back anyway. When he was in the right spot, Cora asked, "Please hold this," and passed him the bow. She settled the violin under his left jaw, then reclaimed the bow. "I'm going to play across you now."

Her left arm stretched across Simon's shoulders, and her hand took position on the fingerboard. Then she leaned against his back, rested her cheek behind his right ear, and held her bow above the strings. Simon stiffened a bit, but Cora played the first notes. His shoulders relaxed and he leaned a little into the instrument. It was working.

She continued to play, the music and the man filling her senses. She loved the smell that was uniquely Simon—something about the way his soap mixed with him was alluring. She closed her eyes and swayed with the music and felt Simon move in rhythm with her.

When she finished the second song, Simon's hand covered her

hand holding the bow, and brought it to his lips. He kissed her wrist and said, "Thank you." Then he took the bow and the violin from her and stood to place them on a chair near him.

"You're welcome, but I have another song."

When he turned back to her, Cora sat back against her ankles. His eyes were dark and intense. This was what a sparrow must feel like caught in the gaze of a cobra, completely mesmerized. He shrugged out of his tailcoat, laying it over the back of the chair, then took two steps and again sat on the bench, facing her and with one leg on each side. Cora, watching, felt frozen, not from fear but from powerful curiosity, longing. Simon's gaze and his smile—smoldering. She was aware of every movement he made, causing a string of firecrackers to ignite within her. She wanted to be held by him.

Cora swung her legs around to sit on the bench, and he pulled her into his embrace, her legs resting over his right leg as he cradled her to him. Her hands slid around to his back and she snuggled into his chest, again feeling his heart beating beneath her cheek. That was quickly becoming her favorite feeling. Admitting she was in much the same state as he was, she could hardly breathe around her own erratically beating heart.

There wasn't a century or a time to this. It simply felt right.

Simon's arms tightened around her. She thought she felt him kiss the top of her head. When she looked up, she was sure—he kissed her forehead. Cora stretched the slightest bit, her lips just a breath from his. She wanted to feel his mouth pressed to hers, but paused, waiting to see if Simon wanted it, too.

Slowly, Simon's face tilted toward her. At first he brushed his lips across hers, not a kiss but oh, the feel. The feather-light contact provoked a sigh from her. Back and forth his lips grazed hers as his fingers skimmed up her neck, traced her ear, then cupped her jaw before he whispered her name, "Cora." Then he pressed his mouth to hers.

Cora's hand reached to the back of his neck, and her fingers twined in his hair. Then she reached up to pull the pins from her own simple hairstyle and dropped them to the floor without releasing Simon's lips. The weight of her hair atop her head instantly fell away as her tresses lay across her shoulders and his arms.

A deep groan whispered in Simon, and his kisses became more fervent. This felt like the single most right experience of her life—to be here with him. Her mind staggered to claim any other coherent thought.

Moments later—Cora didn't know how many since time had stopped—Simon pulled Cora into a tight embrace. He buried his face in her shoulder and simply held her as he seemed to struggle to slow his breath.

She knew she couldn't leave Victorian England now. She had to see this through—to know what *this* was.

Simon smiled down at Cora as he leaned away from her. It seemed that neither of them had words beyond looking in each other's eyes. She knew their time together this evening was coming to an end. She pressed her hand to his cheek and kissed his other one.

"Thank you for coming to the concert tonight, Mr. Duke."

He kissed her lips once more, then leaned his forehead against hers. "The pleasure was mine. I'm your most ardent fan, Miss Cora." He stood and pulled her up with him. "Piano. Violin. Are there other instruments I might look forward to a performance from you in the future?"

"Yes, there are. I'll have to get you a schedule." So many more. Ideas spun with the excitement of reintroducing each one to him. Her heart leaped with happiness to share her music with him. Anxiety had fled.

One incredulous eyebrow quirked up with surprise. "I hope it is soon and often." He picked up his coat and shrugged into it.

They walked hand in hand to the door, and Cora twisted the knob. The rush of wind that had astounded her earlier was not the most amazing magic she had felt this evening. Her blood still simmered, and her head buzzed from the older magic she and

Simon had shared. Then he kissed her hand and slipped out the door.

Cora crossed the room back to the violin and packed it away. She sat on the sofa and reclined her head against the padding for a moment, the case in her lap. A plan began to form. She'd have to talk with Aunt Nellie in the morning about all the possibilities of time travel.

When she had dressed for bed, a note slipped under her door.

Dearest Lovely Cora,

I am quick becoming a music lover.

Always yours,

Simon

P.S. If I were of a mind to learn to play an instrument, it would certainly be the violin under your instruction.

Cora giggled and read the letter several times before sleep claimed her.

CHAPTER 15

Simon Tuttle

SIMON REGRETTED AGREEING TO MEET WITH EVERETT'S solicitor that morning. When they'd made the appointment, it seemed it would be convenient since Twickenham was closer to South London than his home in St. Albans, and they'd be there for the Full Moon Ball and a house party, anyway.

He'd much rather spend the day with Cora, but he hadn't seen her—or any women, for that matter. With the ball this evening, most of the women would sequester themselves in their rooms, doing whatever it was that took hours of primping before this evening.

He doubted very much that Cora would be so engaged. She was beautiful with little effort. He had proof. He'd seen her at her worst, drenched from her swim in a lake. Her blonde hair that had escaped the pins hung in natural curls around her face. Her eyes were bright with concern even as she soothed the man's frightened horse. Enchanting.

His mind often lapsed back to the recital the previous night. Unfortunately, that would not be the entertainment planned tonight. Still, dancing with her, feeling her in his arms, was enticing as well. He would choose his two dances carefully.

Simon took a breath. There was much to appreciate about Cora. He would love nothing more than to spend the rest of his life doing just that.

As he rose from breaking his fast, the footman approached with two letters on a silver salver, the first bearing Simon's formal address, The Most Noble Duke of Hertfordshire. He recognized the paper and the hand, guessing it would contain the monthly report he expected about one of his ventures. The second letter was neatly addressed simply to Hertfordshire. Who was familiar enough with him to address him as Hertfordshire but would also need to write to him? The scent of jasmine was faint but present. That was inclined to cause gossip—no doubt the footman had noticed as well. Simon fought the urge to wrinkle his nose at the offending letter and the unwelcomed attention it brought and walked to his room.

The letter was likely from a woman. But not Cora. He would have recognized her writing immediately. A smile quirked Simon's cheeks. Maybe Cora's only shortcoming was her penmanship. He had to admit that it had been steadily improving, but it still had occasional smudges and overly thick lines. Her governess must not have used a ruler to motivate her the way his teachers had. Additionally, Cora never would have sent a note through formal delivery instead of using Everett as they had been.

He separated the wafer seal from the paper and unfolded the letter, quickly scanning its contents. Lady Atkins was inviting him to a house party, "a small affair" as she put it. He would avoid any event that included both her name and the word "affair" at all costs. It bothered him that his mother and sisters thrust the woman into his company as often as they could. He wasn't going to encourage that by accepting this invitation.

He opened the second letter and sat at the small desk in the corner of his room. He'd established a school near his home in Hertfordshire for children who were shunned by society and abandoned by their families. The school was private, remote, and protected from society's knowledge and judgment. He funded it completely on a property that he acquired as part of the ducal estate, but the old church had been left to ruins decades before. Housing wings and workrooms were being added, and the existing walls were being shored up.

He felt a particular kinship to the students, as all were deaf. It had taken some time to make it habitable, and then for his employees to comb the orphanages in nearby counties and have the children transported to his school, but for the past half year, there had been fourteen students learning trades they could employ to support themselves in the future.

The headmaster's report updated him on repairs made and other expenses. All seemed in order. He wondered what Cora would think of the little school.

Simon thought she might be surprised. He was sure she would be pleased. In fact, he thought she might even share ideas for its functioning since she had experience with a school such as this. That was it. He'd invite her to his home.

Admitting it might be just an excuse to spend more time with her, he decided to move ahead with the plan. He'd organize a small stag hunt with Everett, Saalfeld, and himself, and the women who interested each of them. Lord and Lady Cottrell would also be invited, as would Lord and Lady Radnor. Three days of hunting and a week of socializing. He pulled out a sheet of paper and penned instructions to his housekeeper. She would be able to start making the necessary arrangements ahead of his return next week. He penned a personal note of invitation to his proposed guests and sealed each one.

After he delivered them to the butler to arrange delivery, he left with Everett to go to the solicitor's office. Any other day, the journey of more than two hours into the heart of London, the time spent in the meeting, then back out again wouldn't seem a burden. He'd right enjoy the ride and the company. Not today. They should have arranged for the man to come to them.

The meeting went as planned. They were narrowing down their choices of investments to steel, railroads, or shipping interests. Simon considered the potential of each market and listed the advantages and risks of each venture. Since becoming Hertfordshire, the weight of caring for so many people pressed heavily on him—especially the responsibility he felt toward his sisters. This investment included funds from the estate and money he had set aside from before he became duke. That would secure his sisters' independence—not in an extravagant way, but it would allow them choice.

Aunt Nellie's house was only half an hour away when Everett abruptly broke into Simon's thoughts and changed the subject.

"I'm going to do it. I'm going to talk with Lucy's father."

Simon heard the resolve and the apology in his friend's voice. "I wish you the best. She's a fine woman. She might even deserve better."

Everett's smile flashed widely. "Oh, she does. That's why I need to ask before she figures that out."

"Her father might refuse your suit simply because you've waited much too long. His butler is quite the bruiser."

"You're full of optimism, you jackanapes. If I wasn't nervous before, now I have to consider if he'll throw me from the house before I can offer for her."

Simon laughed but cleared his throat and added, "You've saved me, you know. I wouldn't have been able to enter society without your help."

"I'm not getting married right away. I'll still be around to help."

Everett's voice betrayed his lack of enthusiasm to wait, and Simon answered, "Less, I hope. And you needn't keep Lucy waiting

—I'll be fine. Get married and refill that children's wing with rowdy boys and girls."

Everett laughed deeply. "Likely, you'll be married yourself soon enough."

They rode the remainder of the journey in silence—each consumed by their thoughts of the future. Simon knew getting married wasn't a challenge for him, should he desire it. There had been plenty of mothers volunteering their daughters for the position. But when he thought of a hypothetical wife, Cora's face filled his imagination, leaving no room for other choices.

Marrying for love—it frightened him. It wasn't what his family did. They had married for connections or money or prestige, even just to comply with an arrangement made when they were babies. His own parents were tolerant, if not always respectful, of each other.

He wanted to give and receive the better part of life. Respect, yes. Tolerance when needed. But more than that—awe, humor, intelligent discussion, passion, and if heaven were willing to so bless their union, the shared love of their children—all that marriage and family could have to offer. His heart burned for it, and he saw its possibility in Cora's eyes. He'd certainly never thought he'd love his wife, and yet, here she was. He would love her with every walk through a garden, dance at a ball, or quiet evening by a winter's fire. He would love her with gentle words and soft touches. He would love Cora with all his heart.

If she would let him.

CHAPTER 16

Cora Rey

A month ago, Cora didn't think there was anything more important than attending a ball in Victorian England. But tonight, she just wanted it over. The excitement of her friends to return home didn't touch her. The orchestra played. The people danced, and a few possible matches were made.

During the midnight supper, Cora spoke quickly to May as soon as the men went to retrieve their plates. "You travel between here and there frequently. How does it work?"

"Remember that night we met at Nellie's ball a month ago, just after you arrived? I wasn't there for the midnight supper because I left to the future."

Cora could feel her eyebrows lower as she tried to understand what May was saying.

"I had a summer term to complete for an August graduation."

"That doesn't make sense." Cora shook her head and tried to imagine how that worked.

"Yes, it does if time is a fuzzball. I met you at the ball." May checked around the room to see if the men were returning yet, then leaned closer to Cora. "Just before midnight, I left for three months. Then I came back the same day of the ball. It was shortly after you met my mother."

Cora's fingertips pressed on her temples as she considered what she'd heard.

May continued. "You have to let go of the timeline concept. I'm an RN now. That was my last term. I've never left this century for more than a few hours, but I've spent years in the other one, too."

"Maybe if I try to think of it as a loop. You left on a three-month loop, then came back to the point you left." May bobbed her head, and Cora continued. "Congratulations. That's some major work. You're probably exhausted living two lives, but you have a promising future in whichever time you live in."

"I don't feel like I'm living two lives—just mine. This is only different for you. It's normal for me. The two centuries don't have to sync. When I'm gone for three months, I age that much even though I return the same night in the past. The people who know me here think I'm twenty-two, but if I add in the four years my bachelor's degree took, I'm really twenty-six." May's gaze left Cora's, and Cora knew she was watching Saalfeld.

May's voice took on a yearning quality. "I've lived this way for a long time. Like you, each full moon, I have another decision to make. Do I stay or do I go? Where will I make my life?" May reached for Cora's hands folded in her lap and gave them a gentle squeeze. "I imagine you're starting to think on that decision yourself."

"How did you decide?"

"I haven't." There was sorrow in May's eyes, and Cora noticed her blinking rapidly. "It seems my head is there, and my heart is here. Sometimes it feels like I'm being pulled apart."

The longing in her gaze toward Saalfeld was apparent. She hadn't decided—that must be why May held him a little farther away from her heart than Cora thought she really wanted to. It was like a wound that opened as the moon waxed stronger.

May sat up straighter. "It's a full moon tonight." She didn't elaborate.

She knows I'm having to make the same decision she's had to make for the past few years. Like the tide, the magic pulls on you until you make the decision to stay or go.

"I'm leaving here during a ball, and I'll arrive there during a ball. Such a happy coincidence of the universe." Cora could tell that her voice sounded more strained than happy. Maybe May wouldn't notice.

May shook her head. "Nellie has a ball on every full moon. They're her way of saying 'bon voyage' to anyone coming or going. The woman loves her job."

"Are you going?" Cora asked.

"Not tonight. I'm officially on summer vacation. At some point, I think I'll take a graduation trip but not until I'm rested and can really enjoy it."

The men returned, and their table filled with polite dinner conversation.

After the apple tart was served, May said something to the group about needing Cora to help her with her hem, and they left the supper together but parted company in the foyer after a quick hug. Cora had no desire to say any parting words. She supposed that was because she'd made the decision to stay—for now.

"I'll see you here or there." May turned toward the ladies' retiring room.

From the staircase, Cora saw her friends excusing themselves from their parties. She lifted her skirts and took the stairs two at a time. She needed a moment to talk with Aunt Nellie before the others arrived.

She burst into the room and heard Nellie yip with surprise from beside the door.

"Have you decided, then?" she asked as she looked to be nearly bouncing out of her slippers with excitement.

Cora didn't have time to consider why Nellie asked that or what more she might know but instead said, "Yes. I'm staying for now, but I don't want the others to know."

Aunt Nellie's face lit up, and she clapped her hands together. "That's easy. Just don't fall back." Just then the door opened, and her friends entered.

Cora looked at the group and at Nellie. She would have to ask if she would be able to take Simon to the future. The possibilities flooded her mind. She wouldn't leave him behind. He could have the best that modern medicine had to offer—he might get his hearing back, if that was something he wanted to pursue.

"We've just a moment to get this done," Nellie said, glancing at an hourglass on the table, the top precariously low on sand. "Stand before your portrait please." She shooed them into place near the wall. "We don't have any stowaways, do we?" She snickered at those words.

Cora felt a twist of worry in her stomach. Was she making the right choice? Her heart answered yes, a thousand times yes.

"Not to worry now. I haven't blown anything up in three days." Aunt Nellie chuckled. "I also haven't tried to send anything to another time that hadn't first traveled here on its own. I haven't mastered that yet."

"We were arm in arm when we fell through the portrait the first time. Do we need to do that this time?" Cyrus asked.

"No, this time you have a bookmark of sorts to get you back to the same time and place together." Nellie nervously looked at the hourglass. "Hurry now. Closer to the wall." She pulled her waist purse open and gathered a handful of glowing dust, and then fisted her other hand into the pouch to get more. "Now, stand on one foot and place the other on the wall. When the light flashes, you'll fall to the future." She had a little sentimental look to her when she added, "I suppose I'll see you there."

Cora shifted, but she didn't place her foot on the wall. Her long dress concealed her ruse.

Aunt Nellie cupped her hands together and squished them as if she was making a snowball. Only a few grains of magic escaped her grasp and trickled toward the carpet, their light blinking out as they fell. The ball in her hands glowed, intensifying with each compression of her palms. Soon Nellie's hands began to glow as well, then her arms, then her entire body. "Here you go!" she shouted. Holding the tiny pulsing inferno in one hand, she clapped it solidly with the other. Lightning radiated from the collision, and blazing light flooded the room.

When she pushed her hands toward the group, a burst of magic blew past Cora, and her friends seemed to melt into the mural like flaming molecules at light speed.

They were gone. Aunt Nellie brushed her hands together, residual dust falling away.

"Will they know I'm not there?" Cora asked.

"Not if your plan continues to the end, but that remains to be determined by your choices. Myself in the future will take care of what they need to know if anything at all." Nellie smiled and hooked Cora by the elbow. "Now, let's return to the dance and that handsome man of yours. Shall we?"

They paused by a few painting supplies still on a table. Cora noticed a faint glow from a bowl.

"Oh, dear. I have a little magic left over." Nellie pinched some dust between her finger and thumb and began sprinkling it on the table in the shape of a square. "You might need a wee bit later." When Nellie waved her hand over the shape, a small purse lay on the tabletop. She scooped it up and dumped the magic dust from the bowl into it. "For privacy, you know." She winked at Cora and gave her the purse. Then Nellie dumped the rest of the dust into her own pocket.

"I do look forward to seeing Kaitlyn, Reese, Cyrus, and Jem," Aunt Nellie said.

Cora's thoughts twisted, knowing that although they'd just seen them, her friends were a couple of centuries away by now and already being greeted by the modern Aunt Nellie, who will not have seen them in over a century since the time today when she sent them back. Crazy.

Nellie's excited chatter continued as they descended. "This is the night, you know? Such a big decision. The kind that changes lives—yours and his. That seems like a lot of pressure. Oh, but don't let that worry you. In fact, forget I ever said that. You'll do what you must. And so will he. It will all turn out tip-top in the end."

"Do you think you'll ever be able to send someone like your experiment?" Cora asked.

"Perhaps," Nellie answered.

When they entered the ballroom, Simon was standing close to the door. Cora could see several mothers and daughters conveniently nearby in case he glanced in their direction, allowing them to approach or to speak to him. But he didn't move until he saw her, then he extended his arms to both Cora and Nellie. After a few steps, Nellie muttered what must have been an excuse to leave, and Simon and Cora continued their walk across the room.

"What if I were to claim a third dance?" he asked without stopping. "I didn't plan tonight well. I should have saved one for after supper. I regret my greed at spending both my dances with you before. I blame the orchestra. Who would have guessed there would be two waltzes?"

Cora's heart flipped. It was an excellent argument and reasonable, too. She smiled, remembering his arms around her and her hand in his but still shook her head slightly. "Your mother might have apoplexy. I'd hate to cause her harm."

"Perhaps a stroll in the garden, then?" he offered. "Or would you rather stay and dance?"

Her fingers put slight pressure on his forearm, and she smiled up at him. "I haven't a desire to dance with anyone else." Cora thought it a very pointed answer, but it was true. "If your dances are spent, then mine are, too."

Simon's eyes looked at her softly. It was like he was finally at peace with his place in her life. His smile was warm as he led her through the French doors to the veranda and down the steps to the back lawn. Lamps dotted the entire field and illuminated dozens of benches set about for guests to use to escape the crush of the ballroom or the heat the crowding caused. There were hordes of people socializing there, too.

"Maybe we could sit and talk." Cora pointed to a remote bench being vacated by a couple. When they arrived, Simon gave her a moment to settle her skirt before he sat beside her. As she looked back toward the house, Cora saw Nellie on the veranda blowing dust toward them. The tiny particles glided around them on the windless night, and the crowds moved away to the other side of the lawn.

He didn't say a word, but Simon took her hand in his, and Cora leaned toward him. The moon shone like molten silver behind thin clouds, a sterling medallion high in the night sky. Simon leaned across Cora and tugged one small swath of hair from behind her ear, easing it out of the pins that held it, and twisted it around his finger before he let it fall over her left shoulder.

His finger grazed her neck, trailing wonderful chills down her spine and sparking in her stomach. "It's called a love-lock, though I don't know why." He began winding the tendril on his finder again. "You've worn one before. I liked it on you. Very much." He twisted the length of it. "It teased me all through dinner that night. I wanted to curl it around my finger."

She held very still, almost afraid to breathe, as Simon's finger twirled its way out of her hair again, leaving a perfect ringlet.

"Did you receive my invitation?" Simon asked, his face very close to hers.

"Yes," Cora answered without offering any other information. She was fairly certain that Nellie had ensured their privacy moments ago. Were she to kiss him, no one would be the wiser.

"And are you coming?" he asked.

"I sent you a reply. You'll have to read it yourself to know. If I say now, I'll spoil your anticipation for the letter." She kissed his cheek and stood. "Shall we stroll?"

He stood beside her, and they walked along the rose path.

CHAPTER 17

Simon Tuttle

BEFORE REMOVING HIS COAT OR LOOSENING HIS NECK CLOTH, Simon found and opened the letter. Cora had been right—his anticipation was intense to hear her reply.

Dearest Simon,

Yes.

Sincerely,

Cora

Simon barked out a laugh. This was the answer she coyly withheld from him as they sat on the garden bench? Suddenly, he considered other questions he might ask that would warrant such a simple answer and greatly please him to receive. Would you care to dance? Will you come with me? Would you stay longer? Can I do something for you? May I kiss you? Would you be my duchess, my wife? May I hold you? The list seemed inexhaustible.

He hoped that in the future he would receive many such

answers from Cora. Then he read and reread her answer. Five words—each one seemed significant to him. "Dearest"—he hoped she chose that word carefully and meant it keenly. "Simon." She didn't use "Duke" or "Mister" or any other title that obscured who he really was. He wanted her to see *him* and the simple use of his name told him that she did. Finally, "sincerely." He wondered which synonym could be substituted here and retain her emotional intent. Genuinely. Profoundly. Wholeheartedly.

After savoring the message, he continued reading the postscript to the letter.

P.S. As you know, I'm a good shot. Is the hunt competitive? It's okay if it's not. I just want to have my game face on if I need it. Are there rules I ought to know about hunting parties?

My father thought it was important for me to learn to shoot and began taking me with him after my ninth birthday. My first hunting trip was for rabbit. We bagged a couple and took them home. He was a firm believer in two things: if you shoot it, you clean it, and if you shoot it, you eat it. That's something I respect. I did both and felt such pride in my accomplishment that I volunteered to attend hunts with him whenever he asked.

What will we be hunting? Whatever it is, we'll be eating it. Now that you know my two rules, how do you feel about having me come along?

My father and I spent many hunting seasons together over the years. I've bagged and eaten deer, antelope, elk, bear (very mild flavor), bison (not unlike well-aged beef but with an even richer flavor), and various fowl. I have only ever refused to hunt pheasant. They're too beautiful to shoot. So I hope that isn't what you've invited me for, or I will have to stay in the house and sew a pillow or something equally dull.

Simon read the letter several times. The delight never faded. Before going to bed, he stacked it with the others she'd sent.

The next morning, though strictly speaking it was past midday, Simon ambled past the door to the family dining room for the third time in an hour to see if Cora had come down for breakfast yet. Apparently, his sisters and Lady Atkins had entered since the last time he'd checked. There was no way he would enter now and risk getting invited to sit near them. He had a much more inviting plan for a breakfast companion. He ducked back around the doorway.

Simon knew Cora was up, so he'd just wait for her to appear. He'd walked past her assigned bedchamber before he'd come downstairs an hour and a half ago and heard battle sounds. He'd smiled, imagining her exercising inside like he'd witnessed a month ago. She was small but fierce.

He would soon have to leave Aunt Nellie's house to check on some business interests on his way to returning to his home. That meant only one more day of Cora's company before several days without. He'd make the most of it—riding, taking walks, games or cards possibly—whatever she'd like.

"Good morning, Your Grace."

Simon spun on his heels to find Cora scooting behind him to enter the breakfast room. "No, you don't. There will be no "Your Grace" or "Duke" or anything except Simon between us." He offered his arm, and they entered together. He didn't even tick his eyes toward the other women but led Cora directly to the sideboard laden with everything a guest might want.

Simon enjoyed watching her fill her plate—ham, tomatoes, baked beans, mushrooms, eggs with crumbled black pudding. She sat at the corner of the table as far away from the other women as possible. Predictable and preferable.

He carried his own plate, balancing the extra scones, and laid it at the head of the table across the corner from Cora, putting her on his right. As he did, two scones tipped on the edge but didn't fall.

"Oh, Simon, do come sit with *us* this morning," his sister Georgia said overly loudly even for Simon's hearing.

It annoyed him that his sister would so blatantly ignore Cora's presence. He hoped that in her exuberance to pair him with Lady Atkins, her manners slipped unintentionally. He nodded toward the ladies and managed the smallest smile. "Good morning. I'm afraid now that my plate is set, I dare not pick it up again. Since

Miss Rey is likewise already sitting, we'll stay. Enjoy your breakfast."

As Cora began cutting a piece of ham, he noticed that each of the other women had but toast and tea set before them. There were so many little things he loved about this woman. Before he and Cora finished, he asked, "Would you care to go riding today?"

"Darn. I'll have to say no. Aunt Nellie has arranged an outing for the children, and I'm helping attend them. We're going to the river, so they can play in the water—really to have a picnic and fishing, but we all know how that's going to turn out."

"Perhaps next week, then." Simon tried not to show it, but he felt robbed of her company. He had received a message that he needed to leave earlier than he'd originally planned, so he could take a small detour to assess a bridge that had been damaged in recent rainstorms. At the latest, he needed to leave before evening. He was grateful that she had accepted his invitation to his home, and they were not parting company for a long period, merely a few days.

"Why don't you come with us?" Cora's touch to his shoulder turned his attention immediately to her. "Not really a ducal thing to do, so you'll have to leave your persona behind and just be yourself for a few hours."

Was she challenging him? He was never more himself than when he was with her. Cora's smile said she knew exactly what she was doing—that her request was just the thing she knew he'd rather do.

"Thank you. I accept."

"Wear something that can get muddy. We're meeting at the pavilion in an hour."

When the time had passed, the children ran ahead with Nellie and a maid as Simon and Cora followed the group. By the time they got to the banks of the pond, Aunt Nellie had tossed in a number of lines and had children settled in for fishing. Simon directed Cora to a simple wooden bridge overlooking the stream that fed the pond and pulled her down to sit with him on the edge.

They sat silently, Cora watching the children and Simon watching her. She was sitting so close that her arm gently brushed against him as her feet swung beneath the deck of the bridge.

The afternoon sun shone without clouds obscuring the sky—a rare thing that. They sat companionably for a few minutes before he asked, "You said that your mother was deaf. What was that like?" Simon worried that his condition would worsen with age, as hearing often did. How would he communicate with friends and family? Would he just be left alone and outcast? Perhaps he was hoping that her experience would give him hope.

"I don't know. Being Deaf was normal for my mom, and I didn't know anything else. I could hear my dad, and I could see my mom."

"How did she get your attention when you were in trouble?"

"I never got in trouble."

Simon laughed.

"Well, she signed my name, or she waved her arms or stamped her feet to get my attention."

"Could she speak?" Simon's question seemed to startle Cora.

"No. But many who are deaf can. I guess you wouldn't know the possibilities not having grown up around it. We used sign when it was just our family around. It was my mother's language—it was her voice. Her hands moved in a way that conveyed the words that *anyone* could sign, but in a way that was uniquely her. If I could have seen only her hands signing, I would have been able to pick her out from the way they moved."

Simon noted the partial smile on Cora's lips at the memory.

"What did your name look like?" he asked, then immediately wondered if he shouldn't have. "Is it too personal?"

"It's personal but not private—it's my name. A name sign is given to you by someone who is Deaf. It's highly personalized and carries meaning beyond labeling you. The name my mother gave me was—" Cora went silent and raised her right fingers to her slightly puckered lips, then moved then to touch above her heart.

"That means Cora. She told me I was like a kiss to her heart." Cora made the movements again. "I miss her every day."

"Did you have a name for her?" Simon asked. He wanted to reach for her hand but didn't want to hamper her ability to sign the word to him.

Cora nodded slowly, then raised her hand, placing her thumb near her mouth. Then she dropped her hand to touch her chest with her middle finger. "Technically, this means Mother," she said as she touched her face again, her palm open. "And this means heart," she said as her fingers swung down to touch over her heart. "But together, they're my mother's name from me. I guess I associated heart with her because of her reason for my name." Her eyes misted over and she added, "My dad told me that as a toddler, I would just sign Mother for her. Then one day when I was four, I added 'heart' to it and never stopped or changed again."

She looked into his eyes, and he felt the intensity of her gaze. "It felt good to sign her name just now. We share the sign for "heart" in our names. It's like we have the same middle name." Her eyes had unshed tears in them. "It's been a long time since I had anyone to talk to about her. With my friends, I use words. They seemed watered down in a way, without the meaning embedded in the movements. There's comfort to feel her name in my hands and on my face and chest." Simon noted a tear escaping the corner of her eye. "It's more real to me." She nodded, confirming that truth to herself.

Simon momentarily covered her hand that rested on her lap with his own. Not a word was spoken, but their smiles matched each other's before they began watching the fishing scene again.

"Would you show me other things you could say to your mother?" He didn't shift his eyes away from the children nearest them, afraid she would sense his vulnerability. After a long pause, when he looked at her, she smiled hugely at him. For some reason, his request seemed to please her.

"What would you like to know how to say?"

"I don't know. I just find it fascinating that your mother spoke that way with you."

"And my father. She spoke with both of us. It's just the way it's done where I'm from. Since my father and I could hear, we spoke the words and signed them as well, so we were all included when we were in public, but in private we just signed. There were few secrets in our home."

"Everything? You could sign everything?" He'd thought there might be a bank of important words that they had shared. It opened his mind to consider full conversations. What would it be like to drop the language barriers that held people back?

While he lived in Scotland, he'd learned about a school in Edinburgh that taught children to talk with their hands. Before he left, he'd toured the private facility but didn't gain anything substantial that could help. He noticed that some children spelled out words with their hands or they lip read as he did.

He missed so much of what went on around him, and yet he felt extremely blessed to have retained some hearing. Many hadn't as a result of wounds, illness, and injuries in addition to those who were born without hearing. The people in the community who were deaf were left on the margins of society, especially those of lesser means. He imagined the good that could come of this language Cora knew.

Cora nodded in reply to his question. "Anything you can say, you can sign." Her hands moved up and down in front of her, and she said, "Children."

Then she pantomimed what looked to Simon like her holding a fishing pole, and he guessed, "Fishing."

"Yes," she said as she nodded her fist in front of her.

"I see what you mean by the movements also having extra meaning," he said.

Then her open hand fanned upward twice on her chest. "Happy."

Simon opened his palm as she had done and repeated the gesture. "Me too."

A wave of water, too much to have been an accident, flung across the front of them both. Two boys near them had waded into a knee-deep pool and were scooping their hands across the top of the water, firing the waves in every direction in their glee. Simon slipped from the bridge and joined in the fun.

Although he could move a great deal more water with each scoop, there were many more children all intent on dousing him as their only target. The cool water was refreshing on what was turning into a hot day, and the battle continued for several minutes.

After the children ran out of the stream in retreat, Simon looked for Cora. She sat near the shore with the children's strings of fish at her feet. "Are you quite done, Your Grace?" she called.

"I suppose since the enemy has disengaged."

Aunt Nellie wrapped the children in blankets and began passing out sandwiches. Simon, huddled in a blanket as well, sat next to Cora to eat a bite, too. Curiosity niggled at him until he asked, "How did your parents meet? Their difference seems like something that could keep them apart."

"It might have only my father didn't know it. They were in a math class in college." Simon realized that his eyebrows had risen at the idea of a woman in a college class with a man, but Cora continued. "He saw a beautiful though quiet and very studious woman. He said he knew at once he had to meet her, so he wrote a note and asked the students between them to pass it to her."

Cora stopped as if that was all there was to their story, but Simon nudged her for more. "And ... ?"

"And she read it. Then she wrote a reply saying that he could continue to send her notes in class, and she would let him know if she was interested in meeting him face-to-face. My father wrote more notes to my mother than he did about the math lectures for the next two weeks, and she agreed to meet with him after class. He caught up to her just outside the classroom door, and she handed him another note. It said simply, 'I'm Deaf. I can read your lips and read your notes, but unless you can sign, we might not be able to get to know each other.' My father took that as a personal challenge. He dropped a class, added a sign language class, and continued to write notes to my mother as they began to court."

Perhaps Cora hadn't made the connection that Simon had—that their courtship was enhanced by writing to each other as well—but it made him feel a kinship to Cora's parents.

"And if they hadn't any paper, they would write messages on each other's hands," Cora said.

Simon held his hand, palm up in front of Cora. "How did that work?" he asked, unable to keep the mischief from his voice.

Cora's answering smile told him that she was willing to play along with his request for a demonstration. Her small hand cradled his as one slender finger moved across his open hand. A tickling sensation followed her fingertip, and reverberated through Simon's arm and chest. Although her head bent slightly to watch as she wrote, occasionally she glanced up, and the sight took Simon's breath away. He wanted to fold her in his arms and stare into her eyes. His body ached with the restraint he felt at continuing to hold himself away from her. The only way he could think to sate the desire was to kiss her. He looked into her eyes again and down to the smile on her lips. He stopped himself from leaning toward her. Not here—the children. What he wouldn't give to be alone with her right then.

That's when he noticed that her finger had stopped moving, and she asked, "What did I write?"

"I haven't the faintest idea," he answered honestly. His mind had been utterly otherwise engaged. "You'd best try again."

She softly chuckled and said, "And you'd best concentrate."

"I was. Just not on the letters."

Aunt Nellie called out that they were heading back to the house. Simon extended his arm to Cora and escorted her back to Twickenham Manor.

CHAPTER 18

Cora Rey

ALTHOUGH A FEW HOUSEGUESTS STILL REMAINED AT Twickenham Manor, the party had ended for Cora five days ago when Simon left. The guests who would continue on to Simon's home for the hunting party remained, as well as Wetheridge, unfortunately. Cora noticed that he seemed to be wherever she was, standing only a few feet away. He was quick to offer his arm as an escort. For the past few days, he had been polite, sedate, attentive, and reserved—entirely annoying.

In a lapse of judgment that only lasted two seconds, Cora wished Simon's sisters were still there to keep him occupied, but then Lady Atkins would be also. Wetheridge was the lesser of two evils—maybe. Lady Atkins would never seek out her company—so no worries there.

Cora was hiding in the gardens, having evaded him after breakfast. She might have to take a tray in her room for her meals for the next two days to avoid him completely. She was tired of being polite. *No, I don't wish to take a ride with you. No, I don't want to walk with you in the gardens. No, you cannot be of assistance to me today on a shopping errand. No, no, no.* Sheesh.

On the bright side, Cora had spent many hours in the little music room on the second floor where she and Simon had held their latest concert. It was a little bit of a workout for her foot to pump the bellows, but the tiny organ was a rare treat to play. The melodeon's sound was somewhere between a harmonica and a bagpipe. Cora found it especially suited to country tunes. Her memory played a song in her mind, and she imagined the music around her, swaying to the beat as she walked.

Something dark moved to her right. Cora sucked in a quick breath as a man stepped out from a side trail between two bushes. To her relief, it was Everett.

"Sorry to startle you," he said.

"I thought you were someone else." Cora sat on a nearby garden bench and let out a sigh.

"Wetheridge was conscripted by Aunt Nellie to drive into Mayfair and pick up some tea cakes at Gunter's for breakfast tomorrow. You're safe at least until supper." The easy smile Everett always seemed to have melted into a serious expression. "Actually, there is something I wanted to talk with you about."

Their last "serious conversation" sprang to Cora's memory. He had warned her not to break Simon's heart. "You don't need to worry. I'm not playing with Simon's heart. I've given up the marriage game completely. I truly enjoy his company. You're a great friend to worry for him, but you needn't as far as I'm concerned."

Everett's smile returned. "Well, that's not what I wanted to talk with you about, but it's nice to know. Rather personal, really. You didn't need to defend your feelings to me."

"Oh." Cora could feel her cheeks warm. She smirked in Everett's direction. As if he never involved himself in personal matters. But instead of pursuing it, she changed the subject and asked, "What is it, then?"

Beginning to pace away from her, then suddenly turning back and pacing some more, Everett stopped and blurted, "I'm going to propose to Lucy." Then the pacing resumed, his hands clasped tightly behind his back.

"Congratulations?" Cora wondered what the matter was. They seemed an ideal couple to her. She sat facing him with her arms folded in her lap until he came to a stop before her.

"I don't know how. I mean, I know the words, but I want this to be special. It has to be right. Lucy has waited so long, and I want her to be sure of my. . .attachment to her." Everett's eyes slid toward Cora and quickly away.

"You love her." Why was that so hard to admit? They used the euphemism "attached," but it could mean any number of things.

"Yes."

"Make sure you say that part. Those three little words."

Everett's head jerked a nod. "Right. Capital. What else?"

He looked at her with need and desperation. The man was falling apart.

Cora rose from the bench. "Sit down and take a breath." She thought it went without saying but perhaps not. "There's the part about 'Will you marry me?'"

"All right. This is good. I say, 'I love you. Will you marry me?' That's it, then." He stood, and Cora knew he was going to leave.

"Wait. The best part comes between those two sentences." Cora sat and pulled him back down beside her. "Why are you marrying her? Of all the women you know, why her?"

The stress fell away from Everett's shoulders. "Lucy is beautiful and kind. The sort of woman who is equally comfortable with a crowd or just the two of us." He looked out toward the hedge, but Cora was sure he was seeing Lucy in his mind instead. "You may not know that she has a quiet sense of humor. Just a quick comment. Sometimes I'm not sure I hear it, but her lips quirk a bit, and I know I did. And she's accepting. She treats people with fairness and respect. She's a better person than I could have ever hoped to live my life with."

Cora was truly happy for her dear friend—for both of them. Her eyes were a little cloudy, and emotion lodged in her throat at the sincere admiration in Everett's confession.

He stiffened and pinned Cora with a look. "What if she says no?" The look of desperation crept back onto his face.

"Everything you just told me goes between the first two sentences. You've got this. Talk to her father. Talk to her. Flowers don't hurt. Tell me the good news when you're done."

Everett stood and tugged at his sleeves. "I will." With a nod, he walked off.

CHAPTER 19

Simon Tuttle

SIMON GAZED OUT THE WINDOW TOWARD THE RUINS OF THE OLD Roman wall without seeing it but knowing that Cora's carriage appearing around that corner would be his first sighting of her arrival. In fact, he'd sat at his desk staring out the window toward the front drive for most of the day, waiting for a carriage that would bring her to Leavensfield Court. Anticipation thrummed through his veins. It had been a week and a day since he'd held her at the ball, seven days since they'd sat together on the bridge, a day since he'd written a letter to her, and not even a minute since he'd last thought of her.

He worried if he'd made a mistake, arranging the hunt in haste. He would have hunted whether or not he had guests. They would simply make it more enjoyable. This house party wasn't designed as a social event. The guests were a small list, and attention hadn't been given for equal numbers. He had arranged meals and the hunts but left the remaining time for the guests to entertain themselves.

Before noon, the red-and-black box of Aunt Nellie's carriage waddled around the wall and continued up his road behind four horses. He stood in the foyer to greet his guests. Seconds ticked by like minutes. How long could it *take* for the short drive? Just as he decided to return to the window to check on their progress, the door opened.

Simon stood frozen in place as he watched Cora cross the threshold. She wasn't just coming to *his* home. It was as if she were coming *home*. His chest filled with air that seemed to glow with light, pushing warmth throughout his body. At that moment, Simon didn't care where she was born. He didn't care what society thought his responsibility toward marriage might be. He didn't consider his family's opinion on the matter, either. No. All he knew was that she was here at his request. Profound appreciation and desire filled him.

Cora smiled at him from across the foyer, her eyes twinkling as stray curly blonde locks that had escaped her traveling hat floated around her face. He was lost.

Behind him, his mother cleared her throat. "Invite our guests into the green salon, please." Simon opened his mouth to make an introduction, but his mother waved him off and then continued with her gaze fixed on Cora. "You needn't bother with an introduction. We've met, and I doubt her manners have improved." Then her attention swung to her son. "She's American, after all."

With an exaggerated sniff, his mother briskly turned to the salon, and Simon faced Cora to apologize. He'd deal with his mother later.

To his surprise, Cora had a growing smirk on her lips. "I'm trying not to smile, but the most I'm accomplishing is not to laugh. Apparently, our last meeting was memorable for your mother."

Before he could ask about it, more guests entered the house. He greeted each and directed them to the salon. While Simon spoke with Everett's mother, May took Cora by the arm, and off they went.

The group gathering in the salon was generally lively though it had been a two-day trip from Twickenham to St. Albans, sleeping over in Edgware. After a spot of tea, Simon's mother announced they would be shown to their rooms to freshen themselves for an early dinner. Of course she started in order of precedence, leaving Cora to be settled last. For once, Simon appreciated his mother's strict formality.

"I arranged for you to be assigned to the rose room," Simon whispered. "It overlooks the formal gardens above the roses. On the wall is a landscape painting of one of my favorite places on the estate. I'm interested in hearing your interpretation of the picture. Perhaps your insight on whether or not I should have it reframed as well."

He didn't notice Cora taking any extra meaning from his statement when she said, "I would like to compare the painting to the location that inspired it. If we have time for such an outing, that is."

"I'd be pleased to escort you." He leaned closer and whispered, "There is a letter behind it for you."

At that, her eyes brightened, and she graced him with a coquettish grin.

Too soon, his mother sent Cora off with a servant. Before he could leave the room, his mother stepped in front of him. "Have you the inclination to embarrass yourself and this family? You must disentangle yourself before we are an on-dit in every drawing room in London."

"I'm not entangled nor engaged, Mother."

"Of course not, given the guest list. And the one person trying to get her claws into you is unfit to be your duchess." When Simon opened his mouth to retort to her accusation, she shushed him, saying, "I have it on good authority, so you'd best not try to deny the time you have spent with that American."

Simon considered the coze his mother had seemed to have

with Lady Radnor during tea. Neither woman was generous toward him, and he expected that Lady Radnor threw the shadiest light on every situation that came to her memory concerning Simon and Cora. He was happy for Everett that Lucy was nothing like her mother.

"I hardly need to remind you that I'm a man and not a boy. Your advice on my personal life is unwelcome."

She shook her head slowly, and for a moment, Simon hoped that she finally understood his position as head of the family. When her chin rose, he saw the familiar, dismissive pity in her eyes. "You were never raised to be a duke, and you're making a muddle of it. It's evident you need guidance." She turned and walked to the door.

"I won't tolerate your judgment or opinion about the company I keep." Simon kept his tongue about the other matter she raised. He often wondered if he was unfit to be duke. The back of his mind whispered, "yes." It was no matter since he was and he had to make the best of it. Still, the blow from his mother ached.

"You're too kind by half to that little misfit. If you don't know how to free yourself, I'll put my mind to it."

"I won't hear of it, Mother."

"No, you probably won't." With those words hanging in the room, she left.

Simon wondered what she meant by them. He imagined that she was condescending toward him due to his lack of hearing. But it could also be that she had never involved herself much in his life, and besides some pointed advice, he doubted she would act differently now. Still, he would be glad when his sisters returned home and took her attention away from him.

He committed to renovating the dowager house on the other side of the estate earlier than previously planned. The new roof could begin immediately with decorating following on its heels. She could be settled there when she returned from London's Little Season in two months' time. He set himself to writing letters to tradesmen until it was time to change.

When the group gathered for dinner, Simon noted the seating arrangement had Cora too far from him for conversation, and a large bouquet centerpiece obscured his vision of her as well. It wasn't until after the meal that he would get to speak with her. He called for the soup to be served, then found himself hurrying through that offering and each that followed. This might be the fastest dinner the house had experienced in its six-hundred-year history.

When the ladies separated from the men, and the servants appeared with port to be served, he announced, "We won't linger this evening, gentlemen. No doubt the women found the traveling fatiguing and will seek their beds early." The eyes of a few men were round with surprise, but Everett's looked as if he was laughing behind them.

He might feel the same as Simon, answering in agreement, "Let's join the ladies."

The women appeared to have barely settled as they walked into the drawing room. Simon particularly appreciated his mother's apparent surprise.

Simon's eyes quickly found Cora standing at the far end of the room as he stated, "We missed your company, ladies."

The group dispersed, settling into small conversations, and Simon considered the best way to gain Cora's company. He greeted each grouping around the room, though briefly. He hoped the conversations didn't seem as hurried as he knew they were. Each time he moved from a group, Everett stepped into his place. With his obligation satisfied, Simon joined Cora and May, who quickly excused herself.

"I haven't had a moment to myself yet to retrieve your letter, so I'm very curious about it. You mentioned that it reveals a special location." Cora said. "Is it a place we could visit?"

Simon nodded at the question.

Cora asked, "Will you satisfy that curiosity tomorrow?"

"Of which location do you speak?" Simon's mother spoke

over his right shoulder. He turned to find her taking a final step to join them.

"Nothing of interest," he answered. Was her plan for the coming days to interrupt his every conversation with Cora?

"As I expected. You've a room of guests *you* invited—as a surprise to me. Since you didn't engage me to be the hostess or even tell me you were having a party, see to them yourself. You don't have the privilege of secluding yourself in a corner."

Although Simon doubted that his mother's concern was for the other guests, he extended his arm to Cora and escorted her to a group.

Within the hour, more than a few of the ladies yawned behind their fans. Everett approached Simon. "I'd like to make use of your office for a meeting with Lord Radnor if you won't be using it." Everett's expression seemed confident, but a wavering edge to his words revealed some apprehension. "I asked him for a meeting, but I have to let him know the place."

"Of course. Does Lucy know?"

"I told her I'd be meeting with him. I made clear my affection for her, but I didn't ask the question. Not yet."

Nervous energy snaked through Simon's muscles even though it wasn't his happiness being determined. He clapped Everett on the back. "Good luck."

The next morning at the appointed time, Simon led Cora out the door on their adventure to find the mystery location.

The driveway scooted alongside the kitchen garden and then farther out to the formal gardens. Cora nudged him and pointed toward the small pavilion with white Roman columns where Everett and Lucy stood within each other's arms. Simon decided that she must have said yes.

"I suppose they're engaged now. Should we be hearing an announcement soon?" Cora smiled up at Simon. "How long are typical engagements?"

"Two weeks if they register civilly, three weeks if they have banns read, or only days if Everett purchases a special license."

"That wouldn't surprise me. And Lucy would probably welcome it."

"Indeed." Simon imagined he would feel much the same.

It was only a two-mile walk to Nanny Kate's cottage, but the road was slippery and full of puddles from the rain last night. Simon and Cora would have been a muddy mess by the time they arrived. Instead, they sat atop the curricle, well out of the way of the muck flicking to the road behind them. The large wheels sloshed and sucked in the mud, and the horses' feet did the same.

As Simon approached the field overlooking the small cottages belonging to the tenants, he began taking measure of each building, checking the thatch of the roofs, the slant of any walls, the condition of the rock fences, even which homes had smoke in the stack and which didn't. He made a mental list of repairs he thought might be needed soon as well as tenants he needed to check on. He'd have to get back here soon with his estate manager.

"Stop!" Cora rose to her feet, holding to Simon's shoulder to steady herself as he pulled the horses to a stop. "This is it." Her face was bright at her discovery. "The picture in my room." She pointed along the horizon. "The small hill, the stand of trees just there, and the river. There are more homes, but this is the place, isn't it?"

"It is."

"I can see why you wanted a hunting party to come out here," Cora said, pointing to the trees and fields on her right. "There are red birds everywhere. Are they on the list for hunting?"

"Yes." Simon turned to see where she pointed. "Those are red grouse. The hunting season for them starts August first, so we'll hunt rabbits now and then grouse. If we don't, the estate will be overrun, and I'll have to give the fields over to them entirely."

Cora looked at him with wonder in her expression. "There are so many."

"Yes, we've fed them well this year on the remnants of the harvest. The tenants have had a good crop. If we want that next year, many of these birds have to go."

Cora sat back down, and Simon called to the horse to move on.

She was quiet. A little furrow formed between her brows. Simon wondered what she was considering but waited to see if she would speak up. He could see his destination down the road, and excitement was building for him to make this important introduction to Cora.

Simon pulled the curricle to the side of the road in front of the small home, jumped from his seat, and tethered his horse to a tree that would allow it to graze on the grass nearby. Then he turned to Cora to help her from her seat.

The high-seated curricle made for an uneasy descent for women and the full skirts they wore, but Cora gathered them into one hand, then placed her boot on the topmost mounting step.

"Catch me," she called as she sprang from the step.

Simon's hands circled her waist, and he slowed her jump. In the end, she was face-to-face with him as she slid down his length to the ground.

"That's quite a step." Her words sounded deliciously breathy.

If they were somewhere more private, he might take advantage of her being so near. He thought the look in her eye said that she might as well.

Simon stepped back and offered his arm to Cora. "There's someone I'd like you to meet." They walked up the path. The cottage door opened, and a gangly youth came out.

"Thomas, is that you?" Simon asked.

The young man's head dipped. "Aye. Mum is putting on some tea and asked me to see you in."

Simon extended his hand. "You know, the last time I saw you, you were no higher than this." It hovered around his waist. "You were wet up to your knees, and you had a hat full of fish."

"Yes, Your Grace. Poaching, I was." Thomas pulled his hat from his head and wrung it in his hands.

"It seemed like a good time to give you leave to go fishing on the estate."

"My mum still keeps that letter."

"Miss Rey, may I introduce you to Tom Cooper. Tom, this is Miss Rey."

"Pleased to meet you, miss." He led them back to the house. "This way, Your Grace."

Together, they entered the cool shadow of the modest home.

"Is that my Simon?" The familiar voice called from the kitchen as if echoing from his past. *My Simon.* The words enlarged his heart. The woman standing inside the kitchen was his support, his solid footing in a family and home where he was at the margin. With Nannie Kate, he was loved and protected and doted upon. Here in this cottage, more than in Leavensfield Court, Nanny Kate was the family he always came home to.

When Simon had been sent off to school, her services were no longer needed as a nanny. She married and quickly had two children. The oldest was a daughter, who would be about seventeen now, and the second was young man who had greeted them. Simon was happy that she'd had the opportunity to have children. She was a doting mother to him as well as her own.

She was older now than his memories had preserved her. Gray hair had completely overcome the brown. Her eyes had little lines that deepened when she smiled but were as bright as he remembered.

They sat together in her kitchen—the two women he loved the most, sharing oatcakes and a kettle of tea. He knew that this woman's good opinion of Cora was more important to him than that of his own mother. From the easy conversation and frequent laughs, there was acceptance on both sides.

"My daughter, Kirsten, is getting married," she said. "Oh, it won't be a fancy affair, but we're happy just the same. He's been the apprentice of the blacksmith."

"When is the wedding?" Simon asked.

"In a few days," she remarked, refilling Cora's cup.

Simon reached out and patted the older woman's hand that rested on the table near him. "I'd like to provide a dinner if you'll allow me," he said.

He noticed the older woman's eyes becoming cloudy, and her other hand settled the kettle, then rested on top of his with a gentle squeeze. "You'd do that for us? Would you?"

"And more. I'll see a small amount settled on her husband as well. I only need to know how many people will attend, and I'll have my staff begin preparations."

"You're a good one, you are, Simon." She lifted her apron and swiped the cloth across her eyes.

The visit concluded, and they were back in his curricle and underway home. They'd been silent for a few moments when Cora said, "This is your favorite place on the estate because of Nanny Kate, isn't it?"

Simon nodded and answered, "You can't choose your family, but she did choose me." He reached back to his earliest memories and continued. "Nanny Kate was there. She anchored me to my past and even now gives me strength—confidence that somehow I'll be able to do this."

"She probably knew you better than many others and knew your character."

Her words and smile encouraged him to go on. "My father had dismissed me as irrelevant, possibly as soon as I was born. My mother didn't seem to care about nurturing until years later when my sisters arrived. And my brothers seemed to be aware of the family's indifference, only noticing me to mock me. But Nanny Kate was my rock."

"I'm so glad you had her." Cora hugged his left arm.

Simon was too. "She taught and counseled me, and if I needed help, she would try to find a way. She could coax a smile or laugh from me even on the saddest days. When death altered my family and my future, specifically, Nanny Kate was the only one who put her arms around me with tenderness and understanding."

"Thank you for introducing us. It's an honor."

Their carriage topped the small rise and sloshed back through the mud toward Leavensfield. In the drive, Simon recognized his sisters, Lady Atkins, and Wetheridge arriving. He'd chosen this week for the hunting party because his family had plans to be busy in London with whatever affair Lady Atkins had planned. Not only had his mother's plans changed, but apparently his sisters' had too. And they brought Wetheridge along. Simon didn't believe in coincidences.

CHAPTER 20

Cora Rey

The organization of the hunt was fascinating to Cora. A good number of the surrounding gentry also joined the hunting party. The gamekeeper, dressed in a brilliant red coat and black velvet hat, directed the beaters, shooters, and hounds with the precision of an army commander. What Cora wouldn't give to wear jeans that day. The men had the luxury of pants tucked into their Hessians while the ladies' mud-covered skirts swung heavily around their boots.

They hunted close to paths and roads to ease the women's movement—knee-high grass and way too much skirt proved noisy to navigate, frightening away the game. The beaters, driving the rabbits before them, appeared in the field soon after the shooters were set up in a long stretch of a line. Then they were sent off to another field as the shooters began. Finally, the pickers and hounds retrieved the fallen quarry.

At the end of the day, Simon reported that they had bagged more than three hundred rabbits. The hunters celebrated and congratulated each other.

Cora was sick. There was no way that the rabbits' lives would not be wasted. It hadn't been apparent to her how much had been taken since the shooters moved on to the next field before the pickers and hounds had all the game recovered. She resolved that today was her first and last experience with Victorian-era hunting.

The guests chattered around her, but Cora withdrew. How could Simon knowingly put her in this position? She felt betrayed. The hunting party re-gathered at the carriages for the ride home. As he did when they had come to the fields that morning, Simon sat across from her. Different from that morning, she ignored him —pointedly. She wanted to chew him out but would hold her tongue until other people weren't around to give them an audience.

When she glanced past him, she saw concern. She wondered if he wanted to say something as badly as she did. It had better start with "Please forgive me ... "

Simon lingered as the women were handed out, then extended his arm to Cora as they walked toward the house. He veered off to a flowerbed with an iron bench.

"Are you upset with me?" His voice was low, and his eyes darted around to see if anyone else idled in the area.

There was no one. She took a deep breath and blew it out between her pursed lips to calm her voice. Every bump and turn in the carriage had annoyed her, adding to her already agitated mood. "Of course I'm upset with you," she hissed. "More than three hundred rabbits for a group that's less than thirty? We'd each have to eat ten rabbits. You knew my rules for hunting. I wish you'd warned me—I wouldn't have come."

"Why would you expect to eat ten rabbits?"

Cora stood and threw her hands in the air. "Exactly! I wouldn't." She stomped toward the front entrance, then back toward him as he rose from the bench. "And neither will anyone else at the house party." Barely restraining herself from poking her finger into his chest to punctuate each word, she added, "That is my point." Instead, she walked away without looking back.

She kept to her room for teatime and for dinner, requesting that a tray be delivered with only rabbit. So many things seemed right about living in this century—slower pace, appreciation for culture, music, and history, and Simon, who made all of those things more important. But many things didn't fit—women's fashions that were generally ruffle-covered torture devices, education, civil rights, hunting practices. Perhaps the longer she lived here, the less intrigued she would be by the experience. That's all it was supposed to be—an experience, not a commitment.

The sky was tinted dark when May came to her room. "We missed you at dinner."

"I had a lot to think about."

"Anything important?" May flung herself into the green striped chair by the hearth and popped one leg over the overstuffed armrest. Cora thought that if May weren't wearing miles of silk, she would look just like a college roommate. Cora supposed that in May's other century, she probably had roommates, too.

"Just unraveling the mysteries of the universe."

"Oh, just that. Well, don't give it too much time. Fuzzballs don't unravel."

"I thought *time* was the fuzzball," Cora quipped in return.

"The universe *is* time." May turned toward the window. "We look at those stars. Their light has been traveling for a million years, and yet we see it now at this time. We're looking very far into the past. Both times exist together in the universe. Anyway ... " May stood to leave, but fished her hand down her cleavage, withdrawing a letter. "Simon thought I could get this to you."

"Thank you."

"I felt a bit like an English spy carrying secret documents for the war effort." She handed it to Cora. "Will you go with us tomorrow? We're hunting red grouse. It's the opening day."

"I don't think so." She was fairly certain the answer was no, but she didn't care to say so yet.

When May left, she slid her finger under the wafer and opened the letter. The salutation made her gasp.

My Love,

I am terribly sorry.

Simon

P.S. I should have explained the hunt to you. I had no idea it was so different in England than you would have experienced in America. Our family's estate is large and has many people dependent on it for their lives and income. Perhaps it is not so at your home. Nevertheless, the rabbits taken today will benefit many beyond the stones of Leavensfield. Some were dressed and packed in the icehouse to be used later. The rest were delivered to the homes round about to be eaten by dozens of families, many in great need. The hunt seasons feed more than the souls in my home or even my employ. It is a rare time of plenty for those who might live very modestly otherwise. Even a few lucky hounds will feast, too. Some rabbits were dressed out for dinner this evening, a rabbit fricassee, a rich, tender meat resting in a creamy mushroom sauce—my favorite meal. I asked Cook to save you some in the larder in case you felt well enough to eat later. If you decide not to come down before the clock strikes eleven, I shall have no choice but to eat it myself in honor of one of your own hunting rules. I think I shall be at the door to the kitchen garden precisely at ten fifty-five, should you wonder.

Cora looked at the clock—only ten minutes from now. There wasn't time to call for any help to dress, and it probably wasn't advisable to let anyone know that she was running off to meet with him, anyway. She dug through the wardrobe, finding the gown she'd worn when she'd been transported back in time. Although it resembled an authentic nineteenth-century gown but more Regency than Victorian, it had a zipper—she could dress herself.

After putting on her shoes, she caught her reflection in the mirror and tugged the pins out and then ran a brush through her hair. She pulled the sides up and pinned at least that much in place, then eased open her door and checked to see if anyone was in the hallway. Clear. She left and closed the door, but instead of turning to go down the formal staircase, she turned the other direction and headed for the servants' stairs.

She hurried down two flights, her slippers tapping out a staccato beat as she ran, only startling a maid and a footman in curiously tight quarters and meeting no others. Was she in time? If not, she had no idea where to look for a larder or even precisely what one was. Cora wondered if she could just wander around and discover where Simon was. *That* wouldn't look suspicious or anything.

When she entered the large workroom adjacent to the kitchen, Simon stood next to the doorjamb, holding several plates, the top one heaped with food. In his other hand, he held a large bowl covered with a small plate.

"You're late, so I retrieved the rabbit anyway."

"You have a few plates there."

"I was expecting company." With a tip of Simon's head, Cora followed him to the wooden table that served as workspace during meal prep where he motioned her to sit. She did, and he set plates and silver out for them to use, then served her a quarter of rabbit.

From the very first bite, Cora appreciated Simon's praise for the dish. In fact, he might have understated its merits. The fast food of her century paled against the hearty, savory foods in this. Even restaurant dishes lacked the complexity and depth of these.

With the last mushroom and the last bit of sauce eaten, he removed the plate from the top of the bowl. "Dessert?" he asked, tipping the bowl slightly to show the contents.

Cora had no idea what was in the little crocks at the bottom, but anything under the fluffy whipped cream would be fine with her. She looked to Simon to fill in the answer.

"Almond pot de crème," he said, carefully lifting a shallow bowl and holding it in front of her.

"Oh. Custard. It smells wonderful."

Simon dramatically covered Cora's mouth with his hand and

glanced around the kitchen with a look of fear on his face. "My French cook would deny us the pleasure of these little pots of wonderful if he heard you call it 'custard.' Not a very French term, you see."

Cora widened her eyes and nodded emphatically, picking up her spoon. Simon placed a small pot in front of each of them. As with everything she'd tasted here, the dessert wasn't as sweet as its modern counterpart, but maybe her tastes had changed. The almonds and cream were the featured flavors instead of sugar. She much preferred the clean taste.

When they were finished, Simon disappeared briefly into the kitchen with their dishes and returned. "You missed Everett's announcement at dinner this evening."

Cora felt the rush of excitement. "He and Lucy are engaged?"

"Yes. They plan to marry in a month. Her mother has some shopping to do and won't allow it earlier."

"I'll bet he was disappointed." Simon nodded, and Cora added, "But maybe not more than Lucy."

"I believe you're right." He took a drink of wine. With some uncertainty in his voice, he asked, "Will you hunt with us tomorrow?"

Cora did the same as she stalled for time. She'd made assumptions and blamed Simon for her conclusions. "Yes. I'm sorry I didn't understand. I should have asked. I judged you poorly."

"I could forgive you—for that last spoonful of crème." Simon pointed his spoon toward her bowl, but she quickly scooped up the dessert with her own spoon. A mixture of surprise and disappointment crossed his face followed by a deep laugh.

It felt good to laugh beside him. Very good. "That's a fair deal. I'll take it." She lifted her spoon to his lips.

His hand covered hers, and he smoothly turned the spoon back toward her, saying, "I couldn't extort that last bite from you. But I'll accept your apology."

Cora knew Simon was deeply principled even when he was

playful. He was a good man. The spoon dropped into her crock only a second before her lips met his. She swung her legs over his lap, and he deepened their kiss. Her head swam with excitement, a sort of dizzy pleasure. Did he feel the same?

After several spine-tingling moments, Cora felt him take a deep breath and lean away.

"Having you in my home has touched me deeply. I look forward to seeing you each morning, spending as much of the day with you as I can contrive, then ending the day with you again. Only one thing is lacking to make me the most happy man ... "

Simon gently moved her legs and then slid to the floor on one knee.

He's not ... he wouldn't ... Part of her ached to hear words of love and commitment to a lifetime spent together. Another part still clung to her life—her real life.

He reached for her hand.

He's going to do this. Now. That's what this is. "Stop! You can't." *I don't know if I'm staying or not.* He had no idea who she was really. And, how was she supposed to tell him? He couldn't propose. "You'll ruin everything."

Cora jumped from the bench and ran. At the kitchen door, she turned and said, "We won't talk of this tomorrow. We'll have breakfast and go hunting. That's all." She didn't even pause as she turned the corners while running up the servants' stairs. She panted before the door to the rose room. Why the big panic? But she knew—she was being chased by her own indecision, her own doubts. Why didn't she just hear him out and explain that she wasn't ready to consider the question?

Her hand rested on the doorknob, but she didn't turn it. His face had turned up toward hers with such love in his gaze, gentleness in his smile. The tenderness in the mere touch of his fingers on hers still flooded her senses. The simple answer might have been that she was afraid of breaking his heart. That she had to run far from it. However, the fear bubbling up from the truth was far more threatening in that moment—she ran from her own intense desire to say yes.

Her whole body felt weak. She would go to bed, but she knew sleep wouldn't come. She had to decide what to do. She turned the latch and pushed on the door to her room. A single candle's light guttered from the breeze it made as it opened.

Lady Atkins sat on Cora's bed, her arms across her chest. She unfolded and stood. "I've been waiting for you."

Cora tensed and kept silent. She could take her. She didn't trust Lady Atkins and stayed wary of her.

"I've been wanting to have a little chat with you for quite some time now."

"Maybe you should have extended an invitation instead of entering my room unwelcomed." Cora could feel her muscles ready.

"Oh, dear. We're starting off on the wrong foot."

Cora noted the smirk on the woman's face. Hardly repentant. "I'd say. You can leave now." Cora stepped away from the doorway.

As Lady Atkins walked past, she said, "Simon might sneak off to the kitchens with you at midnight, but he'll only dally with you before casting you aside. Men like him don't marry women like you." She pulled the doorknob behind her, then stopped. "I have an agreement with his family. He's only playing with you. It's pathetic, really." Then she stepped into the hall and slammed the door.

What a viper. Cora knew the man Lady Atkins claimed to know well enough to marry, and that man would never propose to Cora if he had a previous agreement. His honor meant too much to him.

At breakfast the next morning, Cora noticed Simon appeared to have gotten as little sleep as she did. He was somewhat quiet but often glanced her way. She knew because she was doing the same. May and Everett had puzzled looks as their attention was often on the couple, too.

Before heading to the fields, Simon announced, "Much of today's bag will provide a feast for the marriage celebration for a daughter of one of the estate's retainers this evening. We will provide an evening of cards here, but if any would like to attend the wedding party, you are welcome."

The hunt went much as the previous one had. Cora was pleased that today's sport would provide the happy start for Nanny Kate's daughter's new life. As they walked home, Cora asked Simon, "How many do you think will attend the wedding?"

"None."

Her attention twisted to his face. "None?"

"Well, not more than a couple. It's beneath them to attend the wedding of a laborer. Everett would want to attend just to dance with Lucy, but her parents will forbid it. Lady May might attend, and Saalfeld will follow her, as he would anywhere. That's it. And us." He looked at Cora with an incredulous glance.

Did he doubt she'd want to go? "Then the four of us will have to have enough enjoyment for the rest." Cora wondered if Lady Atkins would attend just to be near Simon but decided that the woman would consider it slumming and wouldn't go. Good.

The next day and just as Simon had predicted, the only other couple to attend with them was May and Saalfeld. It suited Cora very well. Unlike formal events, it was perfectly acceptable to dance numerous times without censure. And so, both couples did.

Each time Simon took Cora into his arms, her body ached to stay there. As they passed by each other when the steps didn't require them to hold, Simon winked flirtatiously and incidentally touched her, causing goose flesh to erupt from the spot. And for the hundred times he smiled at her with real enjoyment, she melted. Crap—she was in love.

When they returned to their carriage to go home, Simon leaned over to Cora. "Have you considered the question I didn't get to ask?"

She shook her head, then slowly made eye contact. "I don't know my own mind yet. When I do, you'll be the first to know."

"Then I'll wait ... and hope."

She reminded herself that this was why she'd stayed past when her roommates returned. She hadn't known her own mind. She still didn't. Hearing him say that he still had hope, gave her a little, too.

Simon handed Cora down when they arrived at Leavensfield. "Are you interested in an outing tomorrow?"

"Of course. What do you have planned?" The couple walked extra slowly toward the house.

"A surprise."

She loved the twinkle in his gaze as he said that. "For me or for everyone at the house party?"

He leaned very close to her ear and blew across her neck before saying, "Only for you."

"Yes. I'm very interested in your outing. What time will we go?"

"Before breakfast, so others won't join us." They ascended the steps, and the butler opened the door wide.

"I'll skip my workout and meet you in the parlor."

"Meet me in the stables instead. We'll be riding."

At the appointed time the next morning, Cora, leaving through the kitchen door, met Simon, who must have exited through the front door, on the path to the stables. "Is our ride today to one of your favorite places on the estate as well?"

"It is, and I'm predicting it will become one of yours."

Cora appreciated the excitement in his voice and the gleam in his gaze. He truly enjoyed surprising her. She in turn liked that he wanted to. "I'm intrigued," she said. "Will you give me a hint about the place?"

Simon thought for a moment, but they arrived at the stables before he answered. Two horses were saddled and waiting.

Cora reached out with one hand to greet Simon's horse, Hrimfaxi. "We met the other night, big fella," she cooed close to his face.

"May I present Seti?"

Cora moved to greet that horse and let him have the scent of her. "Another name from mythology. I'm sensing a trend, Simon."

"It was a particular fascination for a while."

They both swung into their saddles, and Simon led them northward on an ordinary though not well-worn road. "About that hint?" Cora reminded him.

Simon nodded. "It was abandoned decades ago, but it is quite populated. It is a place of poverty, but everyone has sufficient for their needs. This place is founded on a shared past to change the future."

"A riddle?" She faced him to see a growing smile. "I have absolutely no idea."

"You'll have to wait and see. The road is fine today. Shall we speed up our journey a bit?"

Cora nudged her horse into a lope at the same time as Simon. The ride was enjoyable as they alternated between canter, walk, trot, and back again. The scenery became increasingly remote with few houses and fewer people wandering about.

After a couple of hours, Simon guided them to a stable. "We'll leave the horses here. Our destination is just over that hill."

Cora held the hem of her dress off the dirt while she accepted Simon's extended arm. Then they took off on foot. Near the rise, Cora could see the jagged crenellation on top of a great square tower. With each step they took, the building revealed itself slowly over the rise of the hill. The walls were made of the same gray stone as the tower and looked to be of ancient design. When they reached the top of the hill, Cora could see the entire building. Though not huge, it had a presence and likely a history. The slats on the roof were grown over in places with green moss as were the flagstone walkways.

"What's the name of the building?"

"It's Clarencestead Abbey. The central tower is a remnant of the Roman strongholds in the area. Centuries later, the lower-level rooms and walls were added, and it became a cloister for nuns.

Finally, it was *liberated* from religious duties by King Henry VIII when he dissolved the monasteries in England. It became private property and was joined to the dukedom."

"I'm sure there's more to the fascinating history."

"There is, but that's not why we're here." The arched doorway at the front, centered at the bottom of the tower, opened as they approached.

Cora's curiosity was piqued, but before she could ask more, an older couple met them.

"We got your letter," the man said.

Nearly over the top of his words, the woman said, "We've been waiting since early for you to arrive." Then she turned to Cora. "Welcome. Welcome."

"Cora, may I present Mr. and Mrs. Miller, the caretakers of the Clarencestead Abbey School." Greetings were exchanged. Then the woman's arm rounded Cora's shoulders and pulled her alongside as they stepped into the cool interior. There was an earthy smell to the building, not like mud and not offensive, just clean earth. It was welcoming.

"A school?" Cora asked. "Is it yours?" She threw a quick glance at Simon as the woman walked Cora down a short hallway with Simon following behind.

"Of a sort," Simon replied.

As they neared an open door, Cora recognized random sounds. Her heartbeat raced with excitement. In this century, a school for children who were typically developing would have been quiet enough to hear a pin drop. She knew these children didn't know their sounds were loud. Flashes of her own childhood and early education warmed her through. She knew the children must be deaf.

"This school is the only school like it in ... "

Cora was no longer listening to the adults in the hallway. She whirled toward Simon with a spontaneous hug, then bustled through the door, realizing too late that she might be interrupting a lesson. A couple of children saw her and pointed, causing others to look her way. She waved and with a large smile said hello and signed, "My name is Cora." Most of the children waved back.

"The children have just finished their morning chores and will have a bite to eat before lessons begin. Would you like to join them?" Mrs. Miller asked.

Cora nodded as she walked into the group, settling into a chair at a large wooden table. A servant entered, carrying a tray of cookies—"biscuits" Simon would call them.

The children sat at the tables as the servants began making the rounds, depositing a cookie for each child and filling little mugs with a ladle of milk. That's when Cora noticed something she hadn't expected to see. None of the children signed for the treat nor for thanking the servants.

"How do they communicate?" she asked Simon and the Millers, who were just joining her. Her heart constricted, suspecting they were being raised oral. In this time, that was the best they could do, hoping they assimilated into a world of voices.

Mrs. Miller answered, "We are teaching them to write, but it is slow going."

"All of the children are learning to read lips," Simon added.

Cora knew that meant they would get every few words and guess at the rest. "I'm also a teacher. May I?" She motioned toward the servant.

Simon answered, "Of course," with a puzzled look on his face.

"Do the servants hear and speak?" Cora asked.

"Yes," Mrs. Miller answered.

Cora approached the servant. "Withhold the cookie for a moment, please." The woman looked toward the Millers, who nodded to her. Cora placed her hand flat like a plate, then with a cupped hand, touched her fingertips to her palm, turning, and touching the palm again. "Biscuit," she said. Then she knelt beside a girl in a yellow dress, and with her lips at the child's eye level, repeated the sign and said, "Biscuit."

Next, Cora placed the child's hand on top of hers and signed for "cookie" on the child's palm. Her heart was so full it seemed to climb into her throat, making it feel thick. Finally, she removed her hands and encouraged the child to sign "cookie" at the same time as she did. The child's hesitant motions were rewarded with a cookie.

Cora smiled at the child and felt her eyes must be alight with happiness. Then she repeated the process with the next child, but by the time she got to the third, the child was enthusiastically signing before she could teach him. The rest of the children began signing for the little treat though some needed more support than others. The happiness she felt was near to bursting in her chest. With tears in her eyes, she stood beside Simon. She watched as the servant circulated the room again, waiting for the children to sign before setting down their second biscuit.

Tears brimmed in her eyes. Her hand touched her chest as her pulse raced. She had given them a word. As a teacher, she had taught many signs to children, but never before had she given a child their very first word. Her breath stuttered through her nose as she struggled to regain her composure.

Her voice was barely a sigh when she finally said, "This is an amazing place." She noticed Simon's and the Millers' eyes were welling also.

"What else could you teach them, miss?" Mr. Miller asked.

Simon answered, "Anything is possible. They could learn to say anything."

They stayed until the tables were cleaned, and the lessons began. With little slates and beans as counters, they worked simple math problems, the older students helping the younger.

Again at the abbey's entrance, Cora asked, "May I come again?"

"Whenever you wish," Simon answered, then bid adieu to the caretakers. When they had gotten on their way, he asked, "If you were to say what the children were doing in their lessons, how would it look?"

Cora said and signed "math" and "addition." Simon's hands repeated the motions. For the rest of the walk, Cora signed as she and Simon spoke. It felt liberating. It felt joyful. It felt like home. This was her first language of love, and she cherished the feeling.

Once back at Leavensfield, they entered through the front door together, then went to change from their riding clothes.

Refreshed but famished, Cora stepped into the green salon in time for afternoon tea. Although Simon's mother offered Cora a cup and saucer, she did so with narrowed eyes and pursed lips. Apparently, she had noticed their absence today. Simon entered a few moments later.

Lady Georgia Tuttle clapped her hands with excitement. "Simon, we've decided to add a musicale to the entertainments. You approve, don't you?" asked the elder of Simon's sisters.

Oh, heavens! Please, Simon, say no.

"Say, yes. It will be great fun." Lady Virginia Tuttle was nearly bouncing in her chair, awaiting his approval.

"I would love to participate," Lady Atkins added.

The dowager set her tea aside to await the answer. "What do you say, Simon? We haven't had a musicale for a couple of years. It would be a lovely evening."

Does no one in his family consider how much Simon might hate that kind of event?

"As you wish, Mother." Simon answered.

Cora caught a sly glance between Virginia and Georgia before they raised their teacups to cover their lips. A moment later, Georgia settled her cup on the table and stood. "I was hoping you would allow it. I've made a game of choosing instruments." She picked up a silver bowl from the hearth. "I've placed the names of several instruments in the bowl. Whichever you choose, you play. We will each have three days to practice, and then we'll perform for the houseguests." She placed the bowl within the reach of each lady in attendance. May declined to play, claiming it would likely ruin the evening.

After each pulled out a slip of paper, Georgia announced she would play the violin, Virginia the piano, and Lady Atkins the piano also. Simon's mother refused to play an instrument but offered to sing if another guest would accompany her. When the bowl came to Cora, several papers were folded at the bottom. She wondered which other instruments were in the music room at Simon's house. Three days wasn't nearly enough time if she drew an instrument she didn't know—especially with the standards she ruthlessly held herself to. Still, everyone drawing a slip had taken that chance—she wouldn't cower from it either.

She chose a paper and unfolded it. "Harp," she read aloud. Simon's mother raised her eyebrows and stared at his sisters, who dropped their heads as if to cover their smiles. Simon looked likewise surprised.

"Well, three days," Virginia repeated, hurrying to put the bowl away on the hearth. "I'll have the other women choose when I see them later today."

"I'm looking forward to the performances," Lady Atkins added. "When may I use your music room, Simon? I'll need a little practice to brush up a new piece I've learned."

"I'll post a schedule after the other women have chosen," Georgia said.

When the family gathered for dinner that night, Georgia announced that the schedule was posted. Simon's mother said that Lucy and her mother would play a duet with a violin and viola, and another guest would play the flute. Cora was relieved she hadn't pulled that slip of paper, but the woman didn't seem nervous at all.

Cora spent as much time as she could at the school. It was convenient that her practice time was scheduled around the same time the gentlemen joined the ladies in the parlor after dinner. Yes, how convenient. Not. Still, she enjoyed the uninterrupted time during the day to go to the school. She loved how quickly the students were picking up the signs, and she carried their happiness back with her to Leavensfield.

One evening, before she entered the family dining room, she heard her name and stopped before entering. Out of sight, she heard Simon's mother and Lady Atkins discussing her. The nerve! She debated between entering and disrupting them and waiting to hear what they were saying. Eavesdropping won.

Simon's mother was speaking. "That Cora person is an unwelcome guest in my home, while you are like family to me. She should leave, not you."

Lady Atkins answered, "Your son seems to think she is welcome."

"She's a novelty. An American. They have no culture, no history, no refinement." The dowager harrumphed. "His fascination with her will wane like a child's when his toy becomes old."

"I have no intention of waiting for her to become old."

"Don't worry. She's only after his money or his title."

That's rich. She's speaking to the one person that would be true of and doesn't even realize it.

His mother continued. "There can never be an honorable relationship between them. He can't marry her. He won't be willing to be a social outcast. He understands his duty to the title. We'll give it a little nudge, and he'll abandon her."

What? Neither woman seemed to know Simon at all. Her appetite was gone, especially if it meant sharing a room with these women. She spun on her heels. Maybe a second session of a workout would do her some good. Several steps away, she stopped again. No. She'd rather enjoy a breakfast where their conversation was stifled by her presence. She turned back, but the two women exited the breakfast room before she got there and walked her way.

Kill them with kindness. But when the women were within a few steps, both of them turned their faces to the wall and refused to meet her gaze as they walked by. "Good morning," she said brightly, anyway.

After a quick breakfast, she left Leavensfield, intending to stay away most of the day. She almost wished she'd gone to London with Lucy and May to shop for Lucy's wedding, but she had wanted to be near Simon whenever possible. Since he spent so much time with matters of the estate, she often went to the children's school without him. In the evenings after dinner, she practiced in the music room or did kickboxing, then took walks outside before retiring.

That night, she heard Simon's mother speaking to Wetheridge. "If you marry the girl, your problems as well as mine will be solved. Take her across the border and marry her. Soon."

Should she tell Simon? He'd been worried about his sister's interest in Wetheridge, and it seemed that now his mother was involved, too. He would want to protect his sister though Cora believed his sister would welcome it, and with her mother's blessing, there might not be much Simon could do to stop it. Really, what would she say? "I heard your mother say this, but I don't know who it was about, but it might be your sister." That was worse than gossip.

The third day, she spent more time at the school. The children greeted her enthusiastically, embracing each sign she showed them. Teaching was its own reward, and, this was unlike any teaching experience she'd had. These children needed her desperately. They had no language. Well, not exactly—they were learning to read lips as a way to take part in someone else's language. Signing could give them their own.

***

Simon was going to be back the next day. She'd missed him so much. She wanted him to see the children's progress as well. As she joined the guests in the salon before dinner, Simon's mother stood in the middle of the room, but began walking in her direction.

Within a step, she whispered, "Oh, are you still here? Take your place at the end of the line." Then she faced the center of the room and spoke to the other guests. "Dinner is being served." The guests ordered themselves by precedence and filed out. The numbers were uneven, and Cora was unescorted, as was Lucy since Everett wasn't expected back until the next day.

Cora extended her arm to her friend, and they accompanied each other through the doorway. Wetheridge met them in the hall, having joined the group late. "As luck would have it, it's my pleasure to attend to two beautiful women for supper." He bowed and led them behind the group.

It was a kind gesture. Cora hadn't expected Wetheridge to be chivalrous but was pleasantly surprised.

CHAPTER 21

Simon Tuttle

Simon had barely returned home when his mother followed him up the stairs to his room.

"You have to do something, Simon. I will not have your name disparaged and your sisters' opportunities frittered away because you have an unfortunate attraction to a woman who's little better than a servant."

Simon came to a stop. His mother barely halted in time not to collide with him. "You will not speak of my attraction as if it is any of your concern." He took a deep breath to hold his temper, and without looking her way, informed her, "I'm having the dowager house refurbished. You'll move in as soon as it's completed."

"I'll happily move there if you leave off with that American. They are little more than the byproduct, the waste of England cast off decades ago. Lady Atkins is—"

Simon whirled to face her, his voice stern. "You'll move

whether you're happy or not. Stay out of what's my business alone." Though she didn't say more, he wondered if their conversation had convinced his mother to stop meddling. He hoped so—but he doubted it. The workmen he met with on his recent trip assured him they would have repairs completed within a month. Right now, that felt like a month too long.

He bathed the dust and horse smell of his travels from his body and dressed with precision. Tonight after dinner was the musicale. His mind pulled up the cherished memories of Cora's private concerts. Unfortunately, tonight would be unlike either of those. It was doubtful that he would hear even half the notes played by any of the musicians.

He did look forward to seeing Cora and watching as she played. He loved the passion that rang through her notes, the excitement in her eyes, and the satisfaction in the slight smile that tugged at her lips. Did she know that when she was deep into the enjoyment of the music, her eyes closed, and her breathing deepened? It was as if she became music.

Simon entered the salon. No one else had arrived. He looked toward the clock on the mantel—he was very early. His mother and sisters wouldn't be here for at least ten minutes, assuring that they would be in place a quarter of an hour before their guests began to arrive.

Sitting on the mantel was the silver bowl that had carried the papers for the instrument selection. It had been quite a surprise to him when Cora's paper had been a harp. Neither of his sisters, his mother, nor Lady Atkins played that instrument. He had been surprised that they would include it and risk humiliation if they had to prepare a song. As far as he knew, the instrument hadn't been played since his father's sister had played it when Simon was a child.

He walked over and picked up the bowl, curious what instruments hadn't been selected. He unfolded one after another, dropping each to the side. When the bowl was empty, eight papers sprinkled across the tabletop—they all said "harp."

Simon's mother entered the room and gave barely a glance at him. He was determined that she would answer for the trick being played out.

Georgia and Virginia came in immediately. They greeted their mother first, then Simon. Their eyes dropped to the table, the papers, and then back up to him. To Simon, it looked as if they would flee the room. "Stop." The girls stopped but didn't face him. "I don't need to know why you did it. It's obvious you have planned an embarrassment for Miss Rey."

"What are you talking about?" his mother asked, sounding annoyed and finally looking his way.

"She doesn't know," Virginia said. "It's just a game. We didn't think you would take such offense."

Simon pinned the girls with a stare. He knew his mouth was sealed tightly against the harsh words he wanted to say. After a slow walk toward them and a long silence, he said, "I'll inform Miss Rey that she isn't obligated to attend the musicale this evening. If she chooses not to attend, I will not, either."

Protest flared in his mother's eyes, but Miss Atkins arrived at that moment. Her eyes too went to the bowl and papers on the table. "Have I come at a bad time?" Her voice was shrill and her hands clasped in front of her tightly. Red crept up her neck and cheeks.

Simon realized that she also had drawn out a paper in his presence and had lied about its contents. She had been privy to the fraud as well. How could his family think this woman would ever be a good match for him? They didn't. They only thought Lady Atkins was a good match for *them* without considering him at all.

The doors opened again, and Lord and Lady Cottrell, Lady May Cottrell, and Cora entered. When Simon took a step toward the group, his mother rose suddenly and put her hand on his arm to retain him. He sidestepped and continued to the new arrivals. After greeting each one, he said, "Miss Rey, I would like your opinion about something." He swept his hand toward the windows at the far end of the room.

"Of course."

As they walked across the room, it seemed as if the whole room was silent so as to listen to their conversation. Or maybe it wasn't, and he just couldn't hear the conversations behind him. When they stopped at the last window, Simon asked, "Are you set on participating in the musicale tonight?"

"Yes, but that's an unusual question. Why do you ask?"

Simon glanced over his shoulder to see his mother, sisters, and Lady Atkins all looking their way. "The drawing for instruments was false. All the slips of paper said "harp," and my sisters and Lady Atkins lied after choosing."

Cora's expression hardly changed, but she nodded. "They were hoping for my failure." She smiled, and her eyes seemed to Simon to light from within. "Well, they're in for quite a surprise." She put her hand on Simon's arm. "Lucky for me, it's one of the instruments I play."

"Piano, violin, harp—how many instruments *do* you play?" Simon asked as he placed his hand over hers in the crook of his elbow.

"Quite a few." Cora's smile broadened, and she winked. "But not as many as my father did."

"You aren't going to tell me, are you?"

"No. My plan is to show you." She leaned closer and whispered, "One by one."

Simon liked that plan very much.

"I'm sorry the musicale will be less than enjoyable for you. However, don't worry about me. It just became infinitely more interesting."

Simon liked the mischievous look on Cora's face and turned to lead her back, but she tugged gently on his arm, and they stopped. "I'll arrange a private concert for you with the harp if you'd care to check your calendar for the next few days."

"It would be my pleasure." He walked her back, and the noise of the room became more apparent to him. The room had filled, and all the guests were accounted for as they exited to dinner.

CHAPTER 22

Cora Rey

CORA WAS GRATEFUL THAT DINNER QUICKLY FOLLOWED THE conversation she'd had with Simon about his sisters' scam. It was just another part of this evening she'd rather not spend too much time thinking about. When Simon offered to dismiss her from the evening's entertainment, she nearly jumped at it but not for the reason he thought. Yes, his sisters' trick was despicable, but she wanted to avoid performing—period. Instinct pushed her to quit, but determination not to let the fear of it rule her life kept her lips closed.

To keep the stage fright at bay while preparing her piece this past week, Cora had tried to fool herself during practices, repeating that she was playing for herself or at other times for her father. She pretended she was in her father's study and tried not to think about being in front of an audience. She imagined his dark mahogany desk and bookcases. She even fabricated modern reasons for the sounds she was hearing—it was *her* horses she could hear; the crunching gravel was a *car* moving slowly down the lane; the rain was a welcome storm at her usually dry home in Texas.

At dinner, Cora could hardly eat, though Wetheridge prompted her at each succeeding course. She made an effort—a bit of fish, a little soup, a cooked beet. The less she ate, the less she would throw up later, if it came to that. She was determined that it would not.

More guests arrived after dinner, including Aunt Nellie, and soon the musicale began. The anxiety of waiting for each musician in turn increased the distress of the wait. When she was growing up and had performed, she could wait back stage, watching as the other participants left the green room in the order of their performance. Usually, she only saw and heard one or two performers before her. If she found herself feeling the stress of needing to perform perfectly, she would remind herself that this was for her own enjoyment. If others enjoyed it, that was a bonus. That thought had seemed to free her momentarily. She was hopeful that she would conquer this tonight.

Cora tried just to be part of the audience. She found herself taking deep breaths and exhaling slowly. It helped. She kept up a mental dialogue as each person performed. She commented on their dresses and hair. She thought about how she'd met them. She even distracted herself by thinking about the history of the music they played. Her nerves still felt tangled but farther below the surface now. During the performance before hers, she concentrated on gaining pleasure from the musician.

When the applause faded away, Cora straightened her shoulders and walked carefully to the harp. She'd positioned the chair earlier, so it was one less thing to worry about. She settled on the seat, then pulled the soundbox toward her right shoulder—the balance shifted until it was nearly weightless. It seemed like an old friend slanting toward her for an embrace. The harp had always calmed her, assured her. It was a constant when she felt her life was falling apart during her father's decline. She pulled up a fleeting thought to examine it—playing the harp had become something different for her because of that experience. It became part of life and love and family. It felt that way whenever playing for Simon, too.

Her heart burned. Performing was no longer a critical judgment of herself. It was a gift she could give to each audience. Her knees braced lightly against the soundbox. Her right wrist leaned against the soundboard, and she raised her left elbow, positioning her fingers for the first notes.

Cora closed her eyes. She imagined Simon sitting beside her. He might use a stick as they had with the piano, this time pressing it to the harp's soundboard near her right arm. She imagined his chest against her back and the warmth of his leg running the length of hers. She could almost feel his slow, deep breaths calming her and smell the familiar scent of his soap. Tonight, she would imagine that she played a tribute to her father with Simon as the only audience.

She had considered playing classical pieces but eventually settled on a Metallica song that was as old as she was. It had been one of her dad's favorites, and the song she had played for him when he took his final breath.

The lyrics rang through her mind with the notes, and her heart felt constricted and ready to burst at the same time. Her father had lived with passion—truly nothing else mattered. Now and again, she tapped on the soundboard with her shoe or with her ring for emphasis during the refrain of the haunting melody—not typical for this time period, but this was more a song for her father than it was for this audience. The final notes repeated like rain softly falling, tinkling from the highest strings. Poignant. Ethereal.

As they faded, her awareness of her audience returned. Cora noted that both May and Lady Cottrell had tears in their eyes as did Aunt Nellie. She nodded toward them, acknowledging the shared experience. She returned the harp to its upright position.

James, May's brother, clapped enthusiastically—probably a Metallica fan.

The music clung to her. She felt healed and whole. Simon, though he probably couldn't hear all the notes, looked on with love as his ardent applause joined with the others. She curtsied to the audience. Her gaze caught Simon's sisters and Lady Adkins before taking her seat. Varying expressions of disbelief and anger crossed their faces.

Next, Lucy and her mother played a duet, then Simon's mother followed as the last performer of the evening. She stood near the piano, her bearing confident and regal, as her accompanist began walking up the center aisle where she'd been sitting at the back of the room—the very back, by the door.

Cora recognized the look on the young woman's face—terror. The girl stopped walking midway up the room and began shaking her head. She wasn't going to make it. She put her hand to her stomach and then to her mouth and ran from the room.

Cora hoped she would reach a private spot before completely losing her dinner. She would find her later to talk.

Conversations murmured around the room, and Cora knew it was best if the show went on. With barely a thought, she stood and walked to the piano. She seated herself and settled the pages of the arrangement to her liking, then looked at the dowager duchess for a cue to begin.

Simon's mother paused and stared at Cora, uncertainty marring her usual arrogance. Cora answered with one silent swift nod, then hit the beginning notes of the introduction. The woman's voice was strong and moving as she sang "Da Tempeste." It was meant to be sung with power and was. Her trilling high notes would have made Handel proud—pitch perfect.

When it ended, the audience thanked their hostess with zealous applause. Cora was surprised when Simon's mother waved the crowd to acknowledge Cora as well. She hoped there had been a sort of truce brokered between them.

The guests and performers made their way to the refreshments and gathered in small groups for conversation.

Cora retrieved a glass of punch and heard Simon's younger sister. "She saved the evening. It could have been an embarrassing end to the musicale otherwise."

Simon's mother replied, "She played the song passably well."

The nerve! Cora butted in though she knew she shouldn't. Looking directly into the dowager's eyes, she said, "I've heard it said that Americans have no culture or refinement. Of course, that person was grotesquely misinformed." Before she turned to leave, she added, "You're welcome. And that was better than passable."

As Cora turned away, her limbs shook with a little adrenaline left over from the tongue-lashing she'd just dealt. It was mixed with satisfaction as well. Lady Cottrell engaged Cora immediately in conversation, and Simon's family moved away.

For the two days following the musicale, Cora visited the school as often as she could for as long as she could. Simon accompanied her on the ride there and spent a few minutes before he went on estate business that would last until evening.

As she prepared to leave the school the second day, she noticed children signing about someone new. She didn't recognize the sign and thought it must be a name. She had a suspicion, but questioned the students, signing "Who?" followed by the sign she'd seen—the letter C raised near their cheeks, followed by their pointer finger spiraling downward.

The shy, black-haired girl pointed to Cora.

"And who is this?" Cora signed "muscles".

The girls signed, "Duke."

She didn't recognize the other sign, either, but it looked enough like swooning that she got the gist. The girls had made up nicknames for her and Simon and decided they were in love. Apparently, it was obvious to even children.

The next day was the final event of the hunting party—the hunt ball. Cora wore a midnight blue ball gown. The brocade border along the bottom half of the silk skirt weighted the fabric enough so that when she walked or turned, the whole dress shimmered like ripples on water in the moonlight. She'd instructed the maid to pull her hair into masses of curls that began on the crown of her head and continued down the back, pinned with roses nestled in between. At the nape of her neck, the curls knotted in an elaborate bun, and a few loose tendrils of curls cascaded down her back to her waist.

Fashion was a plus in favor of this century. She dressed like a princess often. Even better—Simon looked the part of a prince. He never wore bright colors, preferring not to stand out, but how could he not at six feet tall with broad shoulders, a gorgeous face, and a smoldering smile. Cora felt heat flush through her. Oh, his smile. Really, there was no way he could hide.

And he was hers. Or at least, she was mostly sure he was. She was proud of the man he was. In her heart, she knew nothing was lacking. Of every choice available to him, a powerful man in his time and country, he chose her. Her stomach sparkled in anticipation of seeing him and feeling his hand at her waist.

The depth of their relationship stunned her and made her question it. How could she marry a man she'd only met seven weeks ago? She thought of Simon—how could she not?

In twenty-first-century dating, schedules often conflicted, and she might go out with a man only three or four times in a month. At that same rate, it was as if she'd been dating Simon for nearly a year. In her own time, she would interact with the man in contrived situations—movies, dinners, ball games. She wouldn't see his life, his work, and his family as she had Simon's. She also knew Simon by the people he loved the most and the work he chose.

She saw him at the door and joined the queue of guests to greet their host and hostess. When her turn came, and she and Aunt Nellie stepped forward, Simon's mother leaned down to straighten her hem as if it had been caught in her shoe. Cora heard the woman behind her gasp. Simon's expression was thunderous. His mother seemed to take an inordinate amount of time making the adjustment. A few feet away, Lady Atkins was laughing at the situation. Embarrassment warmed Cora's cheeks as she stepped past the dowager.

Simon bowed. "I hope I am not too late to ask you for the first set, Miss Rey."

Cora smiled and agreed.

At that moment, his mother hissed in Simon's direction, "Lady Atkins mentioned that she would dance the first set with you."

"I'm sure you misunderstood something, Mother. I haven't talked with your friend about the ball this evening. Perhaps she was speaking of someone else." Then Simon readdressed Cora. "It is my honor. Thank you." He bowed deeply this time, then lifted her fingers for a kiss.

When the room was comfortably crowded, and the orchestra was playing prelude music, Simon stepped in front of Cora and extended his hand. He led her around the perimeter of the dance area and stopped nearest the orchestra, waiting for the dance floor to fill before nodding to the conductor.

Wetheridge and Lady Atkins also paired. The couple kept up a constant conversation with Wetheridge frequently looking at Simon and Cora. Cora wondered what could be so compelling but realized that both of them had shown rather pointed interest in her and Simon.

Before the end of the song, Simon said, "I must apologize. My mother's rude behavior toward you was inexcusable."

"You don't need to apologize. *She* should, but she won't. And anyway, I'm not going to wilt over it."

When the song was finished, Simon walked her back to the side to stand with the Cottrell family. Before the midnight supper, they danced again and then he walked her into the dinner.

Simon leaned close and asked, "If I should request another dance, would you accept?"

Cora's fork was poised halfway to her mouth. She wondered if this was Victorian code for, "If I asked you to marry me, would you accept?" She'd considered that very question heavily for the past few weeks. "Yes. I would like nothing more."

Simon pulled his napkin from his lap and dropped it on the table. "Would you care to take a walk in the garden while we wait for the orchestra to begin?"

Obviously their plates were still full, and they'd hardly eaten. Cora giggled to see how seize-the-moment he was being. It made her giddy to tell him yes again. "I'll meet you by the roses in a few minutes." They left the table and went different directions—Simon to the garden, and Cora to the stairs.

She wanted to go to her bedroom to pick up the little pouch Aunt Nellie had given her. She was certain this would be a wonderful time to have uninterrupted privacy courtesy of the faerie dust.

After retrieving it, she walked back down the hallway. Lady Atkins stepped in front of her. "Her Grace asked me to find you. It seems she wishes to have a private conversation with you."

Cora was sure that was the very last thing she would consider doing right now. She gritted her teeth and began to move around the woman without a reply.

"I believe she wants to deliver an apology."

With a pang, Cora knew that if she were to marry Simon, she would want to get along with his family. She hesitated, measuring how important that might be. Her stomach twisted. She could spare a few minutes to start her future off on a better footing. She followed Lady Atkins to an exterior door that led to the orangery.

A nearly full moon and the glass roof lit the building enough to see the path and plants lining it clearly though shadows were thick beyond them. The moist, loamy air seemed an unlikely place for a reconciliation, but the dowager must want to protect her pride and not be seen giving an apology. Cora followed a few steps behind down the center path and sat on a rock bench that Lady Atkins motioned to.

"I'll give you privacy."

As Lady Atkins walked away, a quilt fell over Cora, and arms locked tightly around her, pinning her arms to her side. Though she'd trained for years, imagining a similar situation, she was unprepared for the fear that iced her veins and muscles. She screamed and kicked. The weight of the person held her to the bench when she tried to slip forward. More arms secured the quilt around her feet, and then she felt a rope twist around the blanket.

Cora jerked and tried to wiggle away. Self-defense training had stressed that you should do everything possible to keep from being taken to a second location. When she was pulled to stand, she buckled her knees and fell to the ground where she began to roll. A strong kick hit her stomach.

"Don't damage my wife."

Cora recognized Wetheridge's voice. His wife?

Cora heard Lady Atkins' voice. "I told you to drug her first."

Wetheridge answered, "With what? It's not like I plan to poison people and carry it around with me should an opportunity arise."

"Good thing I do. You'll want this when you stop for the night. Unless you plan to keep her in your carriage all the way to Scotland."

Shocked, Cora realized that Simon's mother had been arranging Cora's abduction, not her own daughter's elopement.

Some brute picked Cora up and flung her over his shoulder, walking fast. Wetheridge wasn't large enough to do that. Who else was helping? Cora didn't give up. She continued to yell. She flexed and straightened her stomach like doing sit-ups and tried to roll from the man's shoulder until hands pressed her head and held it down, pushing her face into the man's back. She could barely cock her jaw to the side to breathe through her mouth.

Would there be anyone close enough to see them leave or hear her screaming? The orangery was near ... Cora scanned the property in her mind. It was near nothing. It sat just off the far end of the house near the main road with an orchard separating it from the formal gardens. The barn was even farther. No one would suspect a thing until tomorrow—except for Simon. He was waiting for her. She would just disappear until it was too late.

A measure of fear was allayed by the knowledge that since

Wetheridge thought she would be his wife, he wouldn't allow her to be harmed. There was also relief in knowing that she wasn't a prisoner to this time or to a marriage she didn't want. If Wetheridge thought she'd go quietly, he would be surprised by the humiliation she was planning to hand him.

CHAPTER 23

Simon Tuttle

SIMON ENTERED THE HOUSE WHEN THE MUSIC SIGNALED THE END of the supper and the resumption of dancing. Where was Cora? He'd been waiting beside the wishing pond for a quarter of an hour. Worry tried to nudge into his thoughts, but he pushed it out with memories of watching her fight. She could take care of herself. And what was there at a ball to bring out her fight? He chastised himself for being ridiculous.

He scanned the room for her blue dress, but it was nowhere to be seen. May and Saalfeld stood with Lord and Lady Cottrell. Lucy and Everett only had eyes for each other. Had Cora changed her mind and gone back to her room to avoid him and the proposal she surely knew was coming? Simon left the ballroom and took the stairs to the family wing and continued down the hall to the rose bedroom.

There was no light shining beneath the door, but that didn't mean the room was empty. He twisted the knob and pushed on the door. It was unlocked. "Cora, are you in there?"

He didn't hear a sound in return, but that might only mean he couldn't hear it.

He looked both ways and pushed the door open to step inside, closing it firmly behind him. The room was dark. Only a little moonlight shone through the open curtains. She wasn't there. Her traveling trunk sat on the floor. He opened the lid and saw that it was still full. She hadn't left for good. Simon felt like a thief going through her things.

The door opened suddenly, and shadows danced along the walls and floor from the candlelight entering the room.

Simon's mother shrieked. "What are you doing in here?"

"And you?" Simon countered. His mother stood rigidly still, her eyes shifting as if making up some fib. "Obviously, we are both looking for Cora," he said. "Why?"

His mother sagged and sat at the edge of the bed and set the candle aside. "I ... " She swallowed deeply.

She didn't make eye contact with Simon, and his nerves heightened. "What aren't you saying?"

"She ... Lady Atkins, that is, has done a terrible thing." The dowager's head shook, and her hands trembled as she lifted them to cover her mouth.

Simon couldn't bear the wait. He lifted his mother to her feet. "Mother, tell me what you know. Where is Cora?"

"Lady Atkins induced Wetheridge to take her to Scotland. They're going to be married."

Simon knew there was much more to this. "They will not!" his voice boomed, and his mother startled. Cora would not have willingly gone with Wetheridge.

"They can't be that far ahead of me." Simon was quickly leaving the room.

"You can't leave. We have guests."

"The only one I care about right now is no longer here. Get a wrap. You're coming with me." Simon pulled on her arm, and they left the room. "Where is Lady Atkins? Does she know which road they were to take?" Would Wetheridge take her to Gretna Green or to Coldstream or some other little border town? The road to Coldstream was a direct shot. Still, he could have taken an east or west road. Gretna Green was farther south, though off to the west, but the total journey would be a little shorter. Considering the roads and possibilities, Simon almost missed hearing his mother's feeble answer as they reached her door.

"I didn't ask."

Aunt Nellie approached the couple. "I got some news from Lady Atkins, unwilling though she was, and will go with you. Their carriage took the road on the west side of your estate."

"Coldstream." A vicious thought tumbled through Simon's head, and he entertained it momentarily. If Wetheridge married Cora, she would immediately become a widow.

"It appears," Nellie replied. "Lady Atkins is locked in the kitchen pantry until we return."

"If you're going, I could stay and—" the dowager began.

Simon cut off whatever his mother was going to say. "You're coming, and you're going to beg forgiveness for your part before she returns. Get a shawl or don't, but we are all leaving now."

Aunt Nellie said, "I've requested your horse and a carriage on your behalf." Then she turned to Simon's mother. "Lord and Lady Cottrell will take care of your daughters and guests. Shall we be off?"

When the carriage arrived, Simon handed his mother in.

Aunt Nellie swatted the dowager on the seat and crowded close behind her on the steps without waiting for Simon's help. "Get in there, Your Grace, or we'll miss the best part."

A groom arrived, leading Zephyr, the horse Simon purchased a few months ago. "He's barely broke, but dangerously fast."

Simon jumped into the saddle and kicked the horse to a run.

***

The dowager duchess huffed an exaggerated breath. "I don't

know why we're bothering to follow. Simon will reach them long before we arrive."

Nellie pulled a small pouch from her pocket and dumped some glistening dust into her palm. "Is the latch secure, Your Grace?" she asked, pointing to the door they'd entered. When the woman turned her attention to check it, Nellie blew the dust toward the front of the vehicle. It disappeared as it passed through the carriage walls to the horses, as she intended. "I'm sure we'll get along rather quickly."

CHAPTER 24

Cora Rey

THE BAROUCHE STOPPED, AND CORA HEARD THE DOOR OPEN. They would have to untie her to take her into a building. Surely she could free herself or get help from someone here.

"Go get us a room," Wetheridge commanded someone, and then she was lifted to sit. Immediately the quilt became wet around her face and was being pressed to her mouth and nose with a cloying sweet smell. It reminded her of old detective movies where a damp rag of chloroform was held to someone's face until they were unconscious. She swung her head from side to side but couldn't escape the smell. She held her breath until she gasped.

Her head swam, and her muscles felt weak. She sagged against the seat. Although she had some awareness of being unwrapped, she couldn't move her own legs or arms very well. She wanted to panic, but her current state sapped her will to think.

She was lifted to her feet—they felt heavy and numb. Her knees wobbled under the weight of standing.

"Please forgive me," Wetheridge said as a very large, very hairy man grabbed her arm as they entered the public house. She thought the sun should soon be rising, but the horizon wasn't turning gray yet.

A man in an apron approached. Cora could feel her eyes cross and wander left and then right. Her eyelids blinked slowly, and her voice was a muffled moan instead of the words she tried to say.

"I'm sorry to say that my wife is roaring drunk. I'll take her to our room immediately. Please have a box of food prepared for our man to bring up to us. We haven't need of anything else from you tonight. We'll leave in a couple of hours," Wetheridge said.

As they walked up the stairs with Cora suspended between them, it seemed as if it were in slow motion, each step jerking her from one side to the other. However, she felt tingling in her toes and lower legs. She hoped the effects of the drug were starting to wear off. As soon as it did, Cora had already determined a plan of attack.

The men set her at the edge of the bed, and Wetheridge picked up her feet, setting them on the mattress, then stuffed a pillow under her head. "I'm sorry for this rough bit of courting. I'd really hoped to win you honestly, but well, you had ideas to the contrary."

Cora pushed her tongue around behind her teeth, feeling the rough edges. She thought her arms were stronger than moments ago, too. She was thankful Wetheridge didn't know what he was doing when it came to drugging someone.

"I'm really not a bad sort. Just desperate. I believe you'll come to accept me. Maybe even like me. I had thought to marry you and solve the problems of my estate, but then when you wouldn't have me, I thought Lady Atkins could step in."

Cora could tighten her arm and leg muscles, feeling the rope around her ankles. She could clench her glutes, but her stomach muscles were still very sluggish.

Wetheridge arranged Cora's dress to cover her legs. "She wants what you apparently had, though, so this is her solution. We all get what we want, I suppose. Well, except you." Then with harshness in his voice, he added, "And His Grace."

He smoothed Cora's hair away from her face. "I'm truly sorry. We aren't starting off in the best way."

It took all her willpower not to slap his hand away. He needed to believe she was immobile until she could act with full force. She rolled her eyes aimlessly and made some moaning sounds as if she were trying to speak to keep up the ruse.

The hairy man showed up again much later and set a box of food on a small table. He and Wetheridge sat down to eat. Cora tested her muscles every now and again, contracting and flexing what she could without drawing attention to herself to increase blood flow and hopefully speed her recovery.

The men ate at their leisure, talking about Wetheridge's estate.

Her head was feeling clearer, and her body, stronger.

"When will you transfer that piece of land in Blackwater?" the gruff man asked.

"As soon as we return to Lifton, and Cora is safely on my estate."

Not going to happen.

The man's chair scraped across the floor. "I'll get a couple of hours of sleep."

As soon as the door closed behind the man, Cora hissed, "Privy." She held her eyelids as if she were sleepy. "I need the privy." She smacked her lips together. "And water." This wasn't only a ploy. Her whole body craved a drink, and she needed the restroom.

A sawhorse-like contraption sat in the corner of the room with a bedpan affixed. She thought one of the improvements Simon's house would get when she became his duchess was a flushing toilet or two. May's house had them. Though they were primitive, it was much preferred to this.

Cora laughed at herself. Possibly the most stressful event in her life was about to happen, and she was thinking about toilets.

Wetheridge untied the rope that had tied one of her ankles to the bed, and Cora stretched before she sat up. Slowly she placed her feet on the floor and stood, being sure to wobble. Wetheridge backed away and pointed at what passed for a necessary in this century.

"May I have privacy?" she whispered.

"We'll soon be husband and wife, and your dress will cover you sufficiently."

Pig. "You have a rope tied to my leg. I can't run. At least turn your back." Cora continued to walk toward the bedpan.

Wetheridge bowed and faced away from her.

She grabbed the bedpan from the privy and swung it with all her might, hitting him in the head above his right ear. Her hope was that it was hard enough to drop him, but he only stumbled to the side and turned toward her. She was ready. The rope was slack, and she jumped into a kick to his gut. He bent over, and she hammered downward on his head. He rolled away from her and stood up, but Cora threw a right hook into his temple. Wetheridge crumpled to the floor.

She had to work quickly before Wetheridge's henchman returned. She dragged Wetheridge to the bed, pulling him up on the mattress. She used the rope from her leg to tie him to the headboard. She pulled his trousers off and tore his shirt from his back, leaving him in his drawers, so he wouldn't follow her if he escaped.

Men were shouting out on the stairs. She didn't think it possible, but adrenaline kicked up another notch. It sounded like bodies slamming against the walls. She readied herself for a fight and opened the door to see Simon pull the big man past him. The man fell down the stairs and crumpled at the bottom without moving, his leg obviously broken among other injuries.

Simon bled from his nose and a cut near his eye. He stumbled up the final steps to Cora. She used Wetheridge's shirt to wipe the blood away. Simon's lips landed on hers, and his fingers tangled in her hair. Cora reciprocated, pushing all the concern and relief she felt into that kiss.

"Excuse me." Cora heard Aunt Nellie behind Simon. "Pardon me," she repeated, squeezing past the onlookers who had gathered. "I wanted to drop by for this bit." Aunt Nellie pressed her toe against the door, and it creaked back open. She peeked around the doorjamb and began to laugh. "Oh, yes. I'm so glad I did." Nellie looked around. "You really knocked him out. And there's the bedpan." She laughed again. "I thought it was just a story, you know." Mirth still filled her eyes, but she stopped laughing to say, "Officially, I'm here to be your chaperone. The story goes, I got tired at the ball and decided to start home. You, of course, offered to accompany me, Cora." She patted Cora's arm. "You're such a sweet girl. Thank you." The woman winked at her. "The constable is on his way." Then Nellie peeked into the room and laughed out loud again.

Simon's lips rested on Cora's ear. "Marry me. I was crazy with worry, imagining what harm could come to you."

"I have to tell you a truth before you ask me."

"I've already asked. I want to marry you as soon as possible, no matter what you have to tell me."

The constable arrived, and Simon related what he knew. It appeared to surprise the officer that Cora wanted to make a statement as well.

Simon removed his coat and pulled it high around Cora's shoulders, covering the back of her head. "I'm ready to leave if you are."

"I am."

"I'll settle with the constable. Nellie, would you take Cora to my carriage?"

"Of course," Aunt Nellie said.

As soon as Simon disappeared back into the room with the constable, Aunt Nellie said to Cora, "He's saving your reputation, dear, but I can do better." She pulled a small satchel from her pocket. "Allow me." She pinched some dust and blew it into Cora's face. "There. No one will even see you leave. It will wear off in a minute. Let's hurry."

Nellie pushed through the small crowd, and Cora followed in her wake as they moved to the door. Nellie again blew a little dust into the room. "No one will remember seeing you enter tonight, now." They moved outside and toward the carriage standing in the lane.

"We'll wait on the other side." Nellie grabbed her hand and led her around the back.

A few moments later, Simon arrived, and they all climbed into the carriage to join Simon's mother.

The group was silent for the duration of the ride back to Leavensfield. When the carriage stopped, Simon pegged his mother with a look. "You have much to say, Mother. I'll wait just outside until that's completed."

Nellie smiled up at Simon, then sweetly turned her attention to the women. The dowager duchess stared at Nellie in silence.

"Oh, I'll wait inside the house, I suppose. Toodle-oo." Then she leaned over and whispered to Cora, "You can fill me in later." Nellie left the carriage, shutting the door behind her, then opened it immediately. "I know—I'll see to Lady Atkins. That will be fun!" Cora gave the woman a startled expression. "No need to worry. I'm good at this. And you're welcome." Then she left.

The two women sat silently, Cora half-wondering if Nellie would pop back in.

When the women decided they were truly alone, their attention returned to each other. The duchess started, "I'm sorry this happened to you, Miss Rey."

Cora continued to wait. When it looked like the woman was readying to leave, she said, "That's not good enough. Sit down and try again." Cora stretched her leg out to block the bottom of the door. "You suggested he take me."

Simon's mother shifted back against the squabs, her mouth a tight line. "I didn't know he was abducting you. I thought he meant to appeal to you and gain your agreement. Then yes, I wanted him to take you to Scotland with haste to remove you from Simon's life."

Cora was surprised that the woman actually told her. She thought she'd have to confront her with what she'd overheard.

The duchess continued. "I mean to save my son's future and that of my grandchildren. Americans know little of the demands of a title and care even less than that. If peers don't respect a man, he will be cut off from society as will his future generations."

Cora recognized passion in the woman's voice and perhaps sincerity as well.

"Not only him, but his sisters, too. What match could they hope to make with a brother who is not trusted? It's a very high price for one family to pay so that you could marry him."

"I appreciate your candor." Cora removed her foot from across the threshold, and Simon's mother left.

Simon was at the door. Cora's heart fluttered, and a pit grew in her stomach. She couldn't ignore his mother's plea, but she also wanted to follow her heart. Simon had to know the truth before she could make a decision that would change the course of their lives and possibly history.

When he stretched his hand toward her, she said, "I believe we had a meeting planned hours ago. Where shall I meet you?"

"Oh, no. I don't plan on letting you off my arm until we reach the wishing pond."

CHAPTER 25

Simon Tuttle

SIMON MOTIONED TO A BENCH ALONG THE SIDE OF THE POND least visible to the house. It was sheltered on one side by a tall hedge. The other three sides were awash with the steel gray of morning. When he sat beside Cora, he swiveled to the side and put his hand to her cheek, guiding her face toward his. Their lips met, and he felt her lean into him as her hands reached around his neck, pulling him closer. A low moan escaped from him, and Cora's lips pressed firmer to his.

Every wish in his heart linked to her. When she broke the kiss, Simon pecked her lips, then leaned barely away. "Marry me. Let me love you every day."

Cora looked down and was silent. When she finally lifted her eyes to his, he saw unshed tears and a sad smile. His heart nearly stopped. Was she trying to find a way to reject his offer? He knew he wouldn't give up. He'd continue to court her for as long as it took.

"I have a big truth to tell you. This seems like a good time." Cora swiped a tear from her cheek. "You don't know me." She stood, walking two steps away. When Simon made to stand, she pushed her hand toward him, and he stopped.

He said, "I know you though it's true that there's so much more to learn." He knew there would be new revelations every day as there had been just hours ago. He had noticed her composure at the inn, her careful selection of words she told the constable, her detailed accounting of the events, and her satisfaction when the constable remarked on the skillful way Wetheridge was trussed up to the bed. Though he'd thought to save her, pride filled him that she could save herself. His mind returned to Cora's words. "I'm asking you to let me discover new things about you for the rest of our lives."

She walked back and sat beside him again. "I mean, I'm not from here. Or even from the America you know."

Simon felt his eyebrows pull together.

"I'm from a different time—a time in the future."

Simon could see the resolve on her face, her eyes intently staring into his, almost daring him to believe. He couldn't. He must have misunderstood or heard her wrong. "I'm sorry. What did you say?"

Cora leaned closer and repeated. "I was born more than a hundred years in the future."

Now it was Simon's turn to move. His chest thudded, and his legs felt wooden. What was her purpose in telling this story? Was she a fraud? He couldn't believe it of her, yet, she must wish him to think so. Why?

"I grew up in Texas during the turn of the twenty-first century. We have carriages with something like the steam engines trains have instead of horses. We can talk to each other over wires, much like the telegraph, but we hear voices instead of static signals. Wait—you don't have that yet, do you?" Cora didn't wait for Simon to reply, but said, "Women are educated—well, everyone is. They vote, own property, and live independently without stigma. And medicine—the advances are incredible—completely wiping out some diseases, giving people back their sight or hearing." She stood before him, her posture defeated. "I've hidden a very important part of me from you."

"Please stop." Simon scooted as far away as the bench allowed and slumped with his hands on his knees. His heart was truly broken. "I hadn't known that you were so strongly repulsed by my suit that you would make this fiction to scare me off—as if I were lucky to be rid of you." He stood and bowed. "It's been a long night and no doubt you will wish to rest. May I walk you to the house?"

"I'm telling you the truth." She boldly met his eyes.

Simon schooled his face and said nothing.

She fought back tears, obviously determined not to fall apart in front of him. "I'll find my own way back." Her voice broke slightly.

"Good day." Before he left, he turned back. "My offer stands," he said with cold dignity. He would retain his honor even in this.

Once inside, he called his family to his office. His mother and sisters, with rigid backs and stoic expressions, sat on the leather sofa and chairs.

He stood from behind his desk and walked to the rug directly in front of the women. "Mother, Georgia, Virginia, I am in earnest for you to understand my position. At no time will I consult you on the event of my marriage."

His mother began to sputter, "Surely—"

His voice raised. "At no time. You are dismissed."

He kept to his office, writing letters, reviewing ledgers, planning improvements to the estate—anything to keep him away from Cora and everyone else. His chest felt hollow. After Simon readied for dinner that evening, his butler delivered a small black box. "The young lady asked that I put this into your hand only along with this letter of directions for its use."

Simon took the items and shut his door. He sat on his bed, then broke the seal on the letter and began reading.

Dearest Simon,

I must regain your confidence. It means my happiness for you to believe me.

The opening words stung him. He wanted to drop the page and chase the sorrow he felt from his chest, but he was curious about Cora's message and read on.

This device is from my time. Please press your finger to the circle at the bottom to turn on the light. You'll see some small pictures. Press the one that looks like sheet music. When the picture changes, press the triangle. Hold the small grid of holes to your right ear.

Simon did as the letter directed and startled at the music emanating from the box. He held it close to his ear and listened, then threw it onto his bed. What was it? He reached for it again and hesitated. He picked it up. When he touched the bars that had replaced the triangle, the music stopped. He pressed the original circle, and the small pictures reappeared. Questions filled his mind as he turned it over again and again, listening and examining, pressing over the pictures and watching to see the results. He slipped it into his coat, and turned the black box over and over in his pocket. This changed everything.

He sat in the salon before dinner, waiting for Cora to come. Which she did—early. He pulled the box from his coat pocket and held it out to Cora.

"What did you think of it, Mr. Duke?" she asked with a familiar tease to her voice.

He shook his head regretfully, not taking his eyes off hers. "I'm sorry."

"Don't be. I'm not crazy, at least relative to my confession. I'm not a witch, but many things in my time would seem magical to you." She looked up at him with dreamy eyes and took a step closer. "And I'm not trying to dodge a proposal from a handsome, kind-hearted man who is more amazing than any dream I've ever had."

Simon lifted her hand to his lips. He kissed the back, then slowly removed the glove and kissed her wrist. "Will you?" he asked. The half-second before she answered was an eternity.

She jumped into his arms. "Yes!" Her open smile sent his pulse racing.

He swept her, weightless, from the floor. The touch of her lips was a delirious sensation. This kiss was full of promises and a future together. Raising his head from hers, he gazed into her eyes. Then he kissed her neck and whispered into her ear, "I can't wait until you're my Mrs. Duke."

They stood together in the salon as the other family members arrived. Simon announced their engagement before walking in to dinner with Cora on his arm, first through the door.

CHAPTER 26

Cora Rey

Aunt Nellie winked at Cora as she left during the midnight dinner at the monthly Twickenham Manor Full Moon Ball while the ley lines were active. The house staff was never sure if someone would pop in, but tonight, Cora would fall into the faerie magic and go back to her century. She squeezed Simon's hand under the table, and they stood together, following Nellie to the top floor of the manor house.

Simon stood in the doorway, staring at the mural at the end of the room. "So, not just you?" he asked. "All of the Americans who visited."

Cora looked at the faces of her college roommates and felt sorrow tightening her throat. She would miss them. But that's the way of graduations—everyone moves on to their rest-of-their-lives. "We all came together, but they went back without me. I still had some very important business." She reached for his hand with both of hers and pulled him along as she walked backward into the room. "Are you going to be okay watching this? I admit it was a little disconcerting for me to see my friends disappear."

Simon didn't answer right away, and Cora noticed his eyes fixed to the mural.

"Maybe, Simon, you'll be the first to travel without the ley lines." Aunt Nellie smiled. "I'm experimenting with that." Her face took on a worried look. "But not now. There would be horrible results." She began muttering. "I've not blown up a mammal." She shivered, then replied to Simon again. "No, not now."

Cora watched emotions play across Simon's face—fear, surprise, questioning, wonder. He pulled Cora into his arms. She leaned into him and hugged him tightly. It would be hard to let go, to miss this while she was away, but she had to say good bye to her other life, to people she knew, and to her parents. And when she came back, she would have his comfort and closeness for the rest of her life.

Simon whispered in her ear, "You'll come back?" His arms pulled her even closer to him.

Cora's head leaned back, and she saw concern in his deep blue eyes. "I'll come back with my dowry on the next full moon—our wedding day. You'll have time to read the banns and move your mother to the cottage." Oh, she was going to miss those eyes. She laid her cheek against his chest.

"You'll need a minute." Aunt Nellie cleared her throat. "I'll just —put some more magic on the mural. Over there. You can never have too much, really." She waved her hand over her shoulder as she walked away. "Take your time. I have plenty of time, quite literally."

Cora and Simon moved to stand by the window at the far end of the room. They stood silently together, enjoying the closeness. Cora knew she had something to ask but had never found the right time. It would make no difference to her, but she needed Simon to know that he also had a choice.

"The day I told you about me and my time, there was something I didn't tell you about." She took a breath and plunged in. "Doctors can do much more than you would imagine. They could likely return your hearing or at the least improve it." She looked into his face and saw curiosity and maybe a little worry around the eyes. "I choose to be here, but if you want to go with me instead, we could go back together when Nellie figures that out."

"You needn't worry. When you confessed that you were from the future, you mentioned medical advances. I've wondered about that—many times. If it was possible, what would I do? I was tempted by the idea." Simon's knuckles softly grazed Cora's cheek, sending a delicious chill down her spine. "I've learned much from the change that losing my hearing wrought in my life, and I may yet learn from it." His arm circled her shoulders and pulled her closer. "The school. Who would have done it if not someone who came to understand the needs of the children? If I left, who would carry on? And who would care for my family? No, I would not change myself."

The last thing Cora wanted was for Simon to think she thought something was wrong with him. There wasn't. "In every way, you're perfect and perfect for me. I just wanted you to know."

"I'm asking so much of you. Your world has incredible things I can't even dream of here. Can you give all that up?" he asked.

"It's pretty amazing here, too." Her hands pushed up on his chest and behind his neck. "Don't think I've made this decision lightly." She stretched on her toes, slowly sliding up in the circle of his arms. "I think I'm going to love it here." She kissed his jaw and felt it clench beneath her lips.

From the other side of the room, Aunt Nellie's voice giggled as she said, "And now I'd better go get paint or faerie dust or some such. Or just leave. Well, open the door when you're ready."

Cora was grateful to have a few more moments with Simon. She felt excited and anxious and nervous all at once. She studied his face, memorized each angle and curve. Though not quite dimples, his grin created two little creases that framed his smile. Her fingers skimmed over his cheeks, jaw, and chin. Then her thumb brushed his lips before she kissed him. The fingers on her right hand slid up his neck and into his sandy hair.

Simon swooped her legs from beneath her and carried her to a sofa, but his lips were on hers as they moved. The strength in his arms flamed her desire. He carried her as if she were weightless. Then just as quickly, she was sitting on his lap, kissing him and being kissed in return. It could have been minutes or hours. His chest rose and fell with deep, slow breaths. Her heart thrilled to know that when she returned, she would lie beside him and wake each morning to his love.

He whispered her name as his lips caressed her neck. Her head tilted back, and Simon nibbled at the soft skin where her neck met her shoulder, coaxing a giggle from her.

"Do you have to leave?" he asked. "We'll have more money than we could ever spend. You don't need to go for your dowry."

Yes, her heart told her she had to go this time, but one day, she would gladly say no. Her chest burned at both answers. "Yes, I have to go. I have friends to see and goodbyes to say. I'd like to bring my dowry anyway. It's a gift from my father."

Simon didn't say more but cuddled her to his chest as they sat silently. After a long moment, he asked, "Is it time?"

Cora's hand cupped his jaw, and her head tilted until her temple resting against his. "Yes." They stood, and Simon went to open the door and returned.

He lifted her wrist to his lips and kissed it gently. "I find it hard not to touch you." He held his lips to her skin for several seconds before saying, "I wrote you a letter." Then he pulled out a folded page. When Cora reached for it, he said, "I could give it to you now, but where's the fun in that?" He walked to the window and lifted the sill, revealing a pocket between the stone exterior and the plastered lapboard wall. "It will be waiting for you here."

Aunt Nellie came in holding a pouch Cora recognized. "I suppose you're ready to get after it."

Cora nodded and took a step. Simon pulled her back, caging her within his arms tightly against his solid chest. His mouth fell on hers, and Cora gave back every feeling he infused in the kiss—a kiss of promises and love and a lifetime of passion.

When they separated, Nellie walked with Cora to the wall. She backed up to it and raised one foot against it.

"Are you ready?" Nellie said, holding the little purse open and dipping out an amount of dust into her palm. Then she drew what looked like a clock in the dust.

"Does it hurt?" Simon asked.

At the same time Nellie said, "No," Cora answered, "A little." Cora looked at Nellie sideways. Cora had fibbed a bit. Yes, it hurt, but she didn't want Simon to know the extent.

Aunt Nellie's hands lifted in front of her, then packed a magical ball tightly in her palms. The glow from the coalescing dust intensified. Cora heard a little gasp from Simon and noticed that Nellie's whole body was glowing. *It won't be long now.*

"Here you go!" Nellie shouted, holding the magic like a pulsing star. Then she clapped her hands together. Light submerged Cora in a complete whiteout, and the bits of magic fired through her. The feeling of being sandblasted subsided as quickly as it had begun. It took a moment for her eyes to adjust after the lightning faded. Her friends were tumbled on the rug around her. Her head spun but seemed to be slowing, centering.

Cora was lying on her back, looking at the modern chandelier that hung from the medallion in the center of the room above. "It worked," she whispered to herself, then louder to the group. "It worked." Although she'd been sent back two months after her friends, she'd arrived at the same time.

"You doubted me?" the modern Nellie said, lifting her hands to her heart as if she were aghast.

Cora stood, then stumbled to the window casing and leaned against it. The whirling in her head grew, and she blinked her eyes hard, mentally pushing back a wave of nausea. She sank to her knees.

"Take a moment to breathe. Your letter is safely there. It won't do to knock yourself out cold before you can read it."

Cora would have sworn that Nellie looked identical or even a little younger than the version of herself she'd just left. "You look exactly the same," she said while pushing to a stand.

"Pish-posh. I don't. This is a new dress." Nellie gave Cora a quick hug, her cheek pressing to Cora's. "It feels like ages since I saw you—the other you, anyway. You have lots to do now, don't you? We'll chat later."

Cora could see everyone there—Reese, Kaitlin, Cyrus, and Jem. And she'd arrived at the same time as they had.

Aunt Nellie turned to the rest of the group. "Welcome back. I've been expecting you." She lifted her arm and looked at the watch on her wrist. "For the last forty-three minutes or so. That's the way of the magic. It can drop you right back where you started —for the most part." Then she mumbled, "When all goes well." She walked around, greeting her returning guests.

A tray of tea sat on a table. "May I offer you some refreshment?" she asked the group.

"Is it your special spiked version?" Cora asked.

Nellie smiled. "Yes, it is special, and it is spiked but not to help you accept your circumstances this time. Only to give you energy."

The group accepted. Then a few minutes later, several other faeries entered to escort everyone to their rooms. Cora hung back for a moment. When everyone was gone, she retrieved the letter from the wall before being accompanied to her room.

"Ring the bell, miss, if you need anything." The fae woman pointed to the silk rope behind the canopy drapes.

"Thank you, Miller. I'm glad you're still here."

"As you say, miss."

Cora walked to the mini-fridge and pulled out a bottle of water, downing it in seconds. Apparently, thirst was a side effect of traveling by molecule. Then Cora sat on the edge of her bed and opened Simon's letter.

My Dearest Love,

The salutation pierced Cora. The three words created longing and comfort for her. Simon might still be in the room with the mural or on the grounds of Twickenham Manor. She had been in his arms less than ten minutes ago, but the ache of separation brought tears to her eyes. She blotted them with a tissue and continued to read.

I am filled with both hope and sorrow. Although I've waited a lifetime for you, I find it hard to cheerfully wait another month. Know this. Not a moment will pass without memories of you swamping my mind. You will never be truly gone to me. You, your essence will stay with me. I admire how fierce you can be yet gentle, especially with children. I respect you for your acceptance, your understanding, your sense of right. I adore you for your unselfish gift of music. You are my world, my life. I will cherish you for all time. Even now, my heart is in the future, and I long to hold you soon.

Faithfully yours,
Simon
P.S. I love you.

CHAPTER 27

Cora Rey

When the girls gathered for breakfast, Cora sat quietly, not knowing what to say. There would be time for that later. For now, she listened to them tell about their Victorian vacations.

With the food eaten and the adventures told, they decided to take a last walk around the gardens before packing for their return flight. They stood on the dock, looking out over the Thames toward Swan Island.

"It's not the same." Reese remarked. "It's different and more comfortable. It was so incredible, but I'm glad to be in my own time."

Traffic was light on the road behind them, but it still drew Cora's attention and seemed out of place. Or she was. "I'm going back."

Her friends turned to face her, each with varying degrees of surprise in their expressions. "There's something you don't know. I didn't come back when you all did."

"Last night. We all came back last night," Kaitlyn said.

"Time is a fuzzball, and I jumped on a different strand. They both landed here, together." Cora smiled at how she could actually believe that now, but she did. In her mind, she saw two loops of time, both starting at the same place, but her friends on the smaller one and hers larger—both starting and stopping at the same point.

"I stayed a couple of months longer, then returned at the same time as you." Soon, she'd board the train again. The same warning would sound at each stop on their way toward the airport. "Mind the gap. Mind the gap. Mind the gap." But this time the gap Cora felt was the one that separated her from Simon. "I had to know where to be. I'm going back on the next full moon to marry Simon. I'd like it if you would be my bridesmaids."

"Oh, you're going to be our own Jane Austen. Of course, I'll come." Kaitlyn hugged her.

"She never married," Reese said. She joined the hug.

"Elizabeth Bennett, then," Kaitlyn said as they began walking back to Twickenham Manor.

"She's fictional," Reese added.

"Stop it," Kaitlyn demanded. "You're ruining the happily-ever-afterness of the moment.

Reece shrugged.

***

It took two weeks to get herself ready to return to England. She had to figure out what to do with the money from the sale of her parents' home and the life insurance money from her father. Cora sold everything she owned and emptied her bank accounts. The best way she thought to take her "dowry" with her was to buy diamonds—lots of them—to be delivered under security to Nellie's house. Then she and her bridesmaids would each carry a sack of them in their purses.

A week before the full moon, she returned to Waco, Texas. She walked through the town and the college, indulging in memories. She stopped to have barbecue and a Dr. Pepper before she left town. She'd be back, but she didn't know when.

She made a short drive across town. This was the last goodbye she'd have to make before her wedding. She entered the sanctuary through the iron gates into the calming green of the Oakwood Cemetery. She was never truly alone here. People came to feel close to family members long departed, and others just to walk or sit in the peaceful acreage or admire the statues. The hot summer day cooled in the shadows of the towering oaks on both sides of the drive as she walked. Birds' songs muffled the hum of the city behind her.

Headstones and stately monuments dotted the grass. She wondered what she'd say to her parents if they were beside her. She'd made this walk dozens of times with her father to visit her mother's site. Now, they were all here—together.

She sat on the grass, looking at the monument inscribed with their names. She remembered a poem she'd heard once about a dash between the years.

It touched her how final a decision to marry was. Just as her parents weren't parted, even in death, lying here together, so would she be with Simon. Her chest clenched at the thought that today, in this time, he was dead. Sorrow filled her with the prospect of never living his dash with him, not knowing what he accomplished and who he became if she couldn't return. It was her place to be there and hold him. Even then, someday, one of them would have the loss of the other.

Cora had watched that with her own parents. She knew it from losing them both. Living gave memories and emotions that sustained you over the years after loss. Cora couldn't imagine herself without making those kinds of memories with Simon. That had convinced her to seize the time with him now—each day a gift to be treasured up, like her father had told her.

Her father would have loved the opportunity to be pulled into the past and crawl through history with his own experiences. He would support her for that reason and for the love she'd found. He and her mother had had feet in two cultures and had found love and happiness together. She and Simon would do the same.

She sat at her parents' feet, her hands pouring out her heart, telling them all about the children and the school, having a chance to give them words and language and community. She told them of the man who loved her as they had loved each other, of her dreams for a family, of her hope for happiness. She told them of the other time, of her own future in the past, of how she would miss them, of how deeply she loved the man.

When her words were still, and her hands were settled in her lap, and her eyes were dry but sore, she knew without a doubt she could leave the cemetery and Waco and her time.

CHAPTER 28

Simon Tuttle

Simon could only cling to the words Cora had said when she left a month ago. The full moon and Aunt Nellie's party was tonight. He hadn't seen Cora, and as far as he knew, no one else had either. Whenever he questioned Nellie, she spouted off a platitude. "All in good time." Then she giggled. Or, "Time will tell." And, "Time is on your side." Apparently, Nellie found it hysterical, but Simon didn't share the humor.

He stared at the life-sized mural. Although his family enjoyed the morning's festivities at Nellie's monthly party, Simon had waited alone in the room for several hours already. Cora's part of the mural was a shadow of the woman he longed to hold. The wedding was in an hour. Nellie had assured him the time was right and all would go as planned.

There was a tea service waiting in the middle of the room. Now and again, Nellie walked through the room and zapped it with a streak of lighting from her finger. "Just keeping it warm," she'd say. Finally, she looked at Simon, really looked at him. "You'll need a little something for yourself when this is over." She pointed to the teapot again. Magic sparks whizzed toward the pot. "Poor duke," she clucked, patting him on the shoulder. "It's almost over."

Although Simon knew she meant it to be reassuring, it wasn't quite. Longing and fear ran through his veins. Would she be safe? Would she come back? The questions filling his mind cast him adrift. Maybe his longing created the change, but he thought Cora's painting glowed with life. Her face more radiant, her smile brighter, her eyes sparkling. It brought him to his feet in anticipation.

The room swirled with magical wind. It didn't move his hair or clothes but blew into and through him as it twisted around the room, pelting him with rain that wasn't wet. The glow of the paint grew in intensity. Heat swelled. Simon stood and approached the mural. The radiance seemed to push against him, forcing him to step back. With a crack of lightning, Cora tumbled through the painting into a heap of white-colored confection onto the floor. Other colorful dresses toppled beside her, each of the women looking dazed. Two men returned with them, already dressed for the ball and the wedding at midnight. Everyone from the mural was lying on the floor at his feet.

Simon ran to Cora and fell to his knees, his arms wrapping her securely though she swayed. Cora's hand rested on his cheek. He drew a deep breath, closed his eyes, and savored the warmth.

With firm pressure, she guided his right ear to her lips. "I love you, and now, I'm home."

All the air in the room seemed to be sucked out, leaving him breathless. His lips pressed against her temple. His world tipped and righted itself. "I love you," he whispered. "Now and forever."

SIMON AND CORA HAVE THEIR HAPPILY EVER AFTER. IF YOU

enjoyed their story, please leave a review for P.S. I Love You on Amazon.

The next story we wrote for the Twickenham Time Travel Romance Series, Mistletoe Mayhem, starts right where this one ends. Turn the page to read a sneak peek and to go to Simon and Cora's wedding.

MISTLETOE MAYHEM

Twickenham, England
October 1850

Lady May Cottrell waited in the drawing room, staring out the window. The clouds had hung heavily in the sky earlier that morning, but blue sky was pushing them aside for a lovely afternoon. She was driving out with Henry today. She could hardly wait and had been sitting there for the past half hour, hoping he'd come earlier than he'd arranged.

Between the weeks she spent in this century and the months she'd spent in the twenty-first century finishing her college degree, she had sorely missed Henry. Although he'd been a best friend to her for many years, the past several years he'd also lodged into her heart. She fought the attraction, knowing that the life of a time traveler was hard to explain. For her, it was even harder to figure out where she truly belonged. And so far, she hadn't. But she was determined to put that dilemma out of her mind and enjoy Henry's company today.

When his black curricle entered their drive, she jumped from the couch. He hadn't even made it to the walk when May bounded down the steps, her coat flying behind her. "I'm so glad you asked me to ride out with you today. I'm ready for a diversion." She grabbed his hand, and he hurried to keep up with her as they went back to his waiting horse.

As he handed her into the open carriage, she asked, "What do you have planned for us?"

"I thought we'd follow the River Crane south from here." He settled himself beside her and shook the reins for his horse to pull. "Then we'd stop in an orchard and have a picnic."

"And would that orchard be a specific one?" she asked. All the while she looked at his profile and admired his rugged good looks. His black hair curled below his hat. She knew it was soft and thick. Long dense eyelashes that any woman would envy framed his striking brown eyes.

"It would. Do you know it?" Each word made the dimple in his cheek deepen momentarily.

"Of course, I do." It had been a favorite spot of theirs growing up as it was situated at the farthest point from the house on the estate. May scooted closer to Henry on the seat. "I haven't been there in years."

The horse ambled down the road in the fresh autumn air. The Cottrells' estate was very nearly the countryside, with London to the east and sparse settlements to the west, including the tenant homes attached to their land. May had mostly grown up in Victorian England, but spent a significant amount of time in modern England and modern Virginia as well. But *this* was almost perfect—the beautiful countryside and Henry.

When they arrived at the orchard, Henry helped her down, then retrieved the basket and blanket. They snacked on the simple meal and chatted.

"Shall we take a walk?" she asked as Henry slid the basket onto the curricle's boot. He extended his arm to her, and they walked beneath the boughs. May tugged on his arm and led him to the far end of the orchard. She leaned against a tree and smiled at him.

Her pulse raced. She'd never shown this to anyone, but since they were here—a sort of confession from when she was a schoolgirl.

Henry stood beside her, both leaning against the tree. Their fingers intertwined. "Shall I pick you an apple?"

May shook her head. "Look here," she said, pointing to the back side of the trunk. Instead of leaning around to look, Henry walked behind her and peered over her shoulder. His arms wrapped around her, and she leaned back onto his chest.

The tree had compensated for the wounds she'd caused by carving their initials into its bark by creating raised ridges further defining and outlining the initials.

"Is that for us?" he whispered though her hair.

Her breath caught. She could only nod.

His strong hands rested on her hips and turned her slowly to face him. The back of his knuckles grazed over her cheek as he gazed into her eyes. She was captured by what she saw. His eyes searched hers, and his lips parted. Desire filled the silence between them.

Oh, she loved Henry.

He took a step closer, and she raised her hands to his shoulders, then around his neck. His lips brushed hers slowly, tenderly. Tingles erupted through her chest. She pulled him close and gave herself into his kisses. She closed her eyes and filled her other senses with him—his touch, his smell. His voice was low and barely controlled as it rumbled in her ear when he said her name. She could feel his struggle for breath much the same as her own.

He broke the kiss. His hand caressed her cheek. "I'd better get you back." Before they reached his carriage, he bent over and picked a few wild flowers, handing them to her after she was seated.

Everything about Henry drew her in. She wanted to forget part of herself at least for some of the time. But her dilemma was ever present. *Who are you really, May? Where do you—all of you—belong?* The questions pushed and pulled her from one time to another, like she was two halves and never whole in either century. The confusion felt like tiny cracks crisscrossing her heart.

May was surprised when Henry entered her home with her.

"I have a meeting with your father," he said, answering her questioning look.

Her mouth dropped into a perfect O, but she didn't say a word as he took a seat in the parlor.

Mistletoe Mayhem begins right where P.S. I Love You ends. Two couples. One love potion. And a whole lot of mayhem. Aunt Nellie is going to have some explaining to do!

Download Mistletoe Mayhem

ALSO BY JO NOELLE

Twickenham Time Travel Romance

P.S. I Love You

Mistletoe Mayhem

Love Match

Bucket List Billionaire Romance

Immediately Wanted: Fiancée

Suddenly Required: Bride

Peak City Romance

Secondhand Hearts

Falling for You

Love and Other Crazy Plans

Cowboys and Angels

Lucky in Love

Waiting on Waylon

Kisses With KC

Suffrage and Suitors

Learning to Love

Truly His Type

Home for the Holiday

Invitation From Isla

Match for the Mayor

Romantic comedy

Newbie

All By My Selfie

One Last Summer

Young Adult Romance

Lexi's Pathetic Fictional Love Life

Amnesty

Years & an Ocean

See all of Jo Noelle's books on Amazon.com

ABOUT THE AUTHOR

Jo Noelle is a Colorado native but lived in several other mountain states--Idaho, Utah, and California. She has two adult children and three small kids.

She teaches teachers and students about reading and writing, grows freakishly large tomatoes, enjoys cooking (especially desserts), builds furniture, sews beautiful dresses, and likes to go hiking in the nearby mountains.

Oh, and by the way, she's two people--Canda and Deanna, a mother/daughter writing team.

We write dessert romance—satisfyingly sweet, so you'll come back for more.

Join Jo's Readers Group and hear all the great news about new releases and sales.

Visit Jo's website

Connect with Jo Noelle online:

Facebook

Amazon Author Page

Follow Jo Noelle on Bookbub

We are always striving to improve our books. If you see an error, we would appreciate knowing about it. Please email Jo@JoNoelle.com